Copyright Notice

© Michael Jones 2023
All rights reserved.

No part of this publication may be reproduced, distributed, or transmitted in any form or by any means, including photocopying, recording, or other electronic or mechanical methods, without the prior written permission of the publisher, except in the case of brief quotations embodied in critical reviews and certain other noncommercial uses permitted by copyright law.

This book is a work of fiction. Names, characters, places, and incidents are either products of the author's imagination or are used fictitiously. Any resemblance to actual persons, living or dead, events, or locales is entirely coincidental.

Unauthorized copying, reproduction, or distribution of this work is prohibited and may result in civil and criminal penalties, including fines and imprisonment.

Your support of the author's rights and intellectual property is sincerely appreciated. Thank you for respecting the hard work and creativity that went into producing this book.

Contents

Chapter 1: The Fractured Mind

The night air, thick with the promise of undisclosed perils, enveloped the city, its electric tension a silent herald of the hidden dangers that prowled in the dark. Alexander Bennett, adrenaline coursing through his veins, wove his way through the shadowy maze of ancient alleyways that snake through the older quarters of the city. Each step was a calculated risk, a desperate effort to elude the unseen predator whose gunfire—a discordant symphony of danger—reverberated off the cobblestones, a relentless pursuit marked by the scent of impending death. Despite the fear that clawed at his sanity, Alex moved with an almost ethereal grace, each step a testament to a will that refused to succumb, his every sense sharpened to the imminent threat of oblivion.

In that moment of peril, bullets hailed from the hidden assailant's weapon, each shot punctuating the still night with its lethal intent. The walls around Alex erupted in a hail of splintering mortar and brick, shards flying like lethal rain, grazing his skin with their biting sting. This deadly barrage was a chilling testament to the assailant's skill, a stark reminder of how precariously close death stalked at his heels. Alex's senses were overwhelmed by the destruction, the air thick with the scent of gunpowder and fear. As he attempted to evade his unseen foe, a bullet found its mark—a cold impact followed by a searing, burning sensation that stole the breath from his lungs and sent him crashing to the ground, the world tilting into darkness.

Abruptly, the grip of the nightmare loosened, yielding to the stark, unforgiving light of reality. Alex's eyes flew open, a sharp intake of breath punctuating his abrupt return to consciousness, his body slick with the cold sweat of terror. Disoriented, he battled to orient himself within the familiar yet suddenly alien confines of his apartment, his heart a drumbeat of residual fear from the chase that had seemed so real moments before. Instinctively, his hand flew to his side, grasping at the area where the bullet had struck in his dream. To his relief and confusion, his fingers found unbroken skin—only the lingering phantom pain of a memory too vivid to be merely a figment of his imagination.

Lifting himself from the couch, Alex moved with a sluggishness that betrayed his lingering disorientation. His feet shuffled across the cluttered floor, each step a conscious effort to reclaim some semblance of normalcy in the wake of his tumultuous dream. He made his way to the kitchen, where the sink overflowed with dishes from days past, a testament to his current state of neglect. With a resigned sigh, he began the mundane task of sifting through the ceramic and metal remnants of meals forgotten, searching for a vessel less tainted than the rest. His fingers, still trembling slightly from the adrenaline of his nightmares, finally closed around the least offensive of the dirty glasses. He rinsed it quickly under the tap, more out of habit than any real expectation of cleanliness.

Turning the faucet, Alex filled the glass with water, the cool liquid a stark contrast to the stifling heat that permeated his apartment. He gulped down the water greedily, the refreshment it offered only highlighting the oppressive warmth even more. In a moment of desperation for relief, he tipped the glass and let the remaining water cascade over his head, the droplets trailing down his face and neck, a brief respite from the sweltering air that hung around him like a thick blanket. As water dripped onto the floor, untouched by the effort to clean it up, Alex closed his eyes, savoring the fleeting coolness.

In that brief interlude of calm, his mind wandered to a past summer's day, not unlike this one, where the heat seemed to press down with an unbearable weight. He remembered the laughter of children cutting through the heavy air—a sound so rare in the tense atmosphere of the building. The neighbor's daughter and son, usually so shy and withdrawn, had ventured to his door, their faces alight with the innocent joy of youth. Their mother, a shadow in the background, watched with eyes that seldom met his, a palpable fear veiling her gaze. Alex had offered to buy them ice cream, a small gesture of kindness in the sweltering heat. When their father had returned, he was surprisingly amiable, thanking Alex warmly for his generosity, a stark contrast to the simmering hostility that usually characterized their interactions.

But this memory, pleasant as it was, fractured under the weight of a darker recollection. Not long after that day, he had seen the young boy again, his arm encased in a stark white cast, eyes dimmed by pain. And the mother—her face bore a bruise, stark against her pale skin, a visual echo of the silent cries that sometimes pierced through the thin walls of the apartment building. These images, so at odds with the warmth of that summer day, painted a picture of a hidden turmoil within the family upstairs.

Shaking the water from his hair, Alex was pulled back from his reverie by the present reality of his solitary apartment. The brief journey into memory left him with a bittersweet taste, a mix of nostalgia and a keen awareness of the chasm that lay between the world outside his door and the one within.

As clarity gradually imposed itself upon his senses, Alex took stock of the chaotic landscape of his apartment. Amidst the disorder lay books brimming with esoteric lore, maps annotated with meticulous, cryptic scribbles, and a collection of newspaper clippings that charted a course through the obscure and the arcane. Each item, a fragment of a greater enigma, seemed to mock his quest for understanding, leaving him with a pervasive sense of something vital and elusive just beyond his grasp.

Scattered across a worn wooden desk were sticky notes in a kaleidoscope of colors, each bearing cryptic messages, coordinates, and names, stuck around the edges of his computer monitor and plastered across the wall in a seemingly disordered array that only Alex could decipher. Notebooks lay open, their pages filled with dense handwriting that jumped from observations to theories, sketches of mechanical devices, and sequences of numbers that hinted at codes yet to be cracked.

In the midst of this ordered chaos, Alex's gaze fell upon a corner of his desk, cluttered with stacks of papers and miscellaneous items, where a specific notebook peeked out, almost lost among the detritus of his relentless search for truth. It was an older journal, its cover worn and edges frayed, a relic of countless nights spent in pursuit of shadows. With a spark of recognition, he reached for it, pulling it free from its accidental burial. Flipping it open to a fresh page, he began to jot down a flurry of thoughts and connections that had eluded him until this moment. Each word was a thread in the intricate web he wove, each sentence a step closer to unraveling the mystery that consumed him. As he wrote, he found himself muttering in Russian, a habit picked up from years spent decoding messages where the language was a key to understanding. "Это хорошо," he murmured to himself, the phrase a small affirmation in the solitude of his quest. "This is good," he translated silently, a rare moment of satisfaction in the midst of endless questions.

Beside the window, a sophisticated setup of camera and radio equipment stood at the ready, pointing to a world beyond the confines of the apartment. High-powered lenses capable of night vision and thermal imaging, alongside a scanner set to intercept a spectrum of radio frequencies, suggested a vigil that stretched into the small hours of the morning. This was a command center for someone who not only watched the world but also sought to peel back its secrets layer by layer. A lone picture frame stood on the nightstand, the photograph within it a reminder of a world that Alex occasionally allowed himself to remember, a contrast to the impersonal nature of the equipment that filled the rest of his space.

Drawn to the window by a movement below, Alex took his place at the command center, the lenses of his sophisticated equipment becoming extensions of his own eyes. Through the high-powered scope, he observed the usual clandestine exchange outside the nondescript storefront that had become a focal point of his surveillance. The shop owner, a man whose benign appearance belied his true activities, handed over what Alex was certain were secrets to individuals he had come to recognize as sleeper cell agents. Their interactions were brief, almost imperceptible to an untrained eye, but to Alex, each gesture was laden with significance.

As he watched, Alex also took note of the figures loitering with seeming aimlessness nearby. Dressed convincingly as prostitutes, they blended seamlessly into the urban tableau, yet Alex had discerned their true nature weeks ago: undercover police officers. Their presence had become more frequent, a silent testament to the net closing in on the shop owner's covert operations. The officers' dedication to their disguise suggested they were well aware of the shop owner's significance, perhaps more so than they let on. Alex couldn't help but admire their commitment, even as he questioned the extent of their knowledge compared to his own. They had been there for weeks now, a constant in the ever-shifting landscape of his observations, hinting at the depth of the investigation that lay hidden just beneath the surface of everyday life.

With the scene below his window momentarily still, Alex turned away from the glass, the secrets of the night momentarily left to unfold without his watchful eyes. The transition from the living tableau of the city's underbelly to the static yet complex world mapped out on his wall was jarring. The juxtaposition of the immediate, raw reality of the streets against the abstracted, analytical representation of his investigations served as a stark reminder of the breadth of Alex's quest. He moved towards the wall, where the chaos of the outside world was distilled into lines, notes, and images—a representation of order extracted from the pandemonium of global intrigue. Here, amidst the tangle of yarn and paper, lay the broader scope of Alex's vigil, each thread a narrative stretching beyond the confines of the city, weaving through the hidden corners of the world in search of patterns that eluded most.

Dominating one wall of the apartment was a sprawling tapestry of maps and clippings, a visual symphony of chaos and order. Lines of yarn—red, blue, and black—stretched across the expanse, connecting points across the globe with the precision of a mad cartographer. This web of strings formed a tangled network of connections between events, dates, and names, a testament to Alex's relentless search for patterns amidst the pandemonium of the world's hidden truths. The maps bore the scars of countless annotations, arrows pointing from one mysterious event to another, circling areas of interest with an urgency that spoke of Alex's desperate need to find coherence in the madness.

Above the din of his own disarray, the cacophony of a heated argument from the apartment overhead pierced through the thin veil of solitude that enveloped Alex's sanctum. The clash of raised voices, muffled through the aging plaster and beams of the building, served as a jarring intrusion from the world beyond his controlled chaos. Yet, paradoxically, this discordant symphony of everyday life, with its cadence of frustration and the all-too-human emotions it carried, acted as a lifeline, tethering Alex to a reality he often sought to escape. It was a stark reminder that, outside the cocoon of his apartment, life—with all its trivialities and trials—marched on unabated. This grounding force, the ordinary clatter of existence, yanked Alex back from the edge of his own consuming thoughts, firmly planting his feet in the tangible, breathing world of the here and now.

Frustrated by the incessant arguing from the apartment above, Alex's tolerance finally snapped. In a moment of irritation, he grabbed the nearest chair, positioning it beneath the most vocal point of the dispute. Standing on the chair, he clenched his fist and hammered it against the ceiling with a force that echoed through the silent spaces of his own apartment. The thuds were sharp, a clear demand for quiet, punctuating his own need for silence amidst the cacophony of external lives intruding upon his thoughts. For a moment, the arguing paused, a brief silence that felt like a victory in the small battle for peace.

As Alex stepped down from the chair, a flutter of movement caught his eye—a sticky note, dislodged by his actions or perhaps by the vibrations of his impromptu ceiling assault, glided to the floor, attaching itself to his foot. Irritated, he peeled it off, intending to toss it aside, but the scrawled message caught his attention. The moment his eyes processed the scribbled coordinates and a name he hadn't seen in years; a visceral flashback engulfed him.

He was suddenly back in a dimly lit kitchen, standing on the periphery of a volatile family argument. The air was thick with tension, voices raised in anger. Suddenly, the father, a figure known to him from a past that felt both distant and painfully close, pulled a knife from the drawer, his actions escalating the argument to a dangerous level. The man lunged at Alex, blade first, aggression in his eyes. Just as the weapon seemed destined to meet its mark, the memory shattered, leaving Alex back in his apartment, the sticky note in his hand a silent testament to the violence that seemed to shadow him, blurring the lines between past threats and present dangers.

No sooner had Alex found himself back in the relative safety of his apartment, the tension from the earlier memory still coiling like a spring inside him, than he was swept up in another whirlwind of emotion. Anger bubbled up, its source unclear—was it directed at the father from his flashback, or was it fueled by the incessant arguing of the family upstairs? The lines blurred as his heart raced, the argument's echoes amplifying his unrest, a mirror to the discord he'd witnessed, or perhaps imagined, elsewhere.

Then, as if propelled by a force outside his control, Alex found himself running, the night air cold against his skin. His hands, inexplicably, were slick with blood, its source as mysterious as the destination of his flight. Buildings and streetlights streaked past in a blur, the city around him morphing into a maze from which escape seemed both imperative and impossible. The sense of urgency was palpable, the fear of pursuit all-encompassing, yet who or what chased him remained shrouded in the shadows of his mind.

In an instant, the chaotic escape dissolved, and Alex was thrust back into the moment before chaos erupted in the dimly lit kitchen. The air was charged with anticipation, the father's hand hovering over the drawer that housed the knife. Alex could feel the tension between them like a tangible force, a prelude to the impending violence. The scene was frozen in time, a tableau of potential energy waiting to explode into action. Alex's own feelings of anger, fear, and confusion mingled with the unresolved conflict before him, creating a cocktail of emotions that threatened to overwhelm his senses.

The transition back to reality was almost seamless, a flicker in the continuum of Alex's perception that might have gone unnoticed by a less vigilant observer. Within the span of a heartbeat, the scenes of turmoil and escape folded into themselves, a series of images collapsing like a house of cards swept away by a gust of wind. To an outsider, Alex's sudden stillness might have seemed like a pause for breath, a mere moment of contemplation. Yet, within the confines of his mind, entire narratives had played out with vivid intensity, each leaving its mark upon his psyche. It was as if time itself bent to the will of his thoughts, stretching moments into lifetimes of experience that, to Alex, felt as real as the room around him.

The relentless arguing from the apartment above clawed at Alex's composure, triggering an almost mechanical response honed from years of living on the brink. Swiftly and silently, he retrieved his gun from its meticulously chosen hiding spot under the floorboard. The weapon felt familiar in his hand as he checked its readiness, a dark reassurance in the tangible weight of it. Alongside the firearm, his knives lay in preparation, their blades a cold reflection of the necessity of readiness. Methodically, he examined each one, affirming their readiness to defend, to attack, to survive.

This ritualistic preparation momentarily pushed the domestic echoes into the background, replaced by a surge of adrenaline that transported Alex to a different battlefield. He was navigating a shattered building, leading a team with stealth and precision.

They burst into a room, interrupting a familial dispute, the sudden intrusion freezing everyone in place in his memory. The air hung heavy, filled with threats and the palpable fear of the crossfire. The memory faded, bringing Alex back to the task at hand. Leaving the outcome an unspoken memory.

Shrouded in the remnants of that harrowing memory, Alex felt the weight of his past actions like a shackle. The tools of his survival, now hidden away, seemed to whisper of deeds best left unexamined. The tumult from above stirred a resolve within him, a pull towards a confrontation he could no longer ignore. With a deep, steadying breath, he steeled himself for the ascent, each step towards the door heavy with the burden of his own history and the unknowns that awaited. Alex paused, hand on the doorknob, the decision made. It was time to face whatever lay beyond his own threshold, each step a silent testament to the unresolved conflicts that guided him.

Chapter 2: Echoes of Violence

As Alex navigated through the bustling lanes of the Moroccan market, he felt the oppressive heat wrap around him like a thick, unyielding cloak. Each breath he took was heavy with the rich tapestry of aromas that colored the air, an intoxicating blend of scents that seemed almost tangible. The distinct earthiness of cumin seemed to seep into his very pores, mingling with the invigorating bite of cinnamon that danced through the atmosphere, and the regal scent of saffron that wafted around, painting everything with a hint of luxury.

Around him, the market buzzed with a vibrant life force, a dynamic showcase of human perseverance and ambition. Vendors, each with their own chorus of calls, competed in a lively discord, their voices weaving into a unique melody that defined the marketplace's rhythm. The collective motion of the crowd, a sea of individuals each contributing to the market's pulse, generated a warmth that went beyond the mere physical, filling the space with a scent that was distinctly human—sweat borne of effort and endurance under the relentless gaze of the sun. This aroma blended with the dust kicked up by countless footsteps, creating a veil that lightly coated everything, a testament to the day's hustle and endurance.

Navigating through the animated crowd, Alex found himself drawn to a stall nestled between an array of colorful fabric sellers and a spice vendor, whose offerings perfumed the air with an exotic complexity. The stall was cluttered with an assortment of handcrafted goods, but among them, a heavy wooden carving caught his eye. He picked it up, its weight substantial yet surprisingly comfortable in his grasp, as if it were meant to be held. The carving was a masterful piece of artistry, depicting a scene of Moroccan life with intricate detail—the figures carved into the wood seemed to move with a life of their own, their expressions captured in mid-gesture, telling stories of joy, toil, and the rich tapestry of daily existence. The wood itself bore the marks of the craftsman's tools, each groove and curve a testament to the time and skill poured into its creation. Despite its solidity, there was a warmth to the wood, a smoothness under Alex's fingers that spoke of the many hands it must have passed through before finding its way to him. Engaging the vendor in a mix of broken local dialect and gestures, Alex felt a connection to this piece, a tangible link to the culture and artistry that thrummed around him in the market's heart.

As Alex continued his journey through the labyrinth of stalls, the sun climbed higher in the sky, casting the market into a swelter of light and heat. It was just past noon, and the intensity of the day seemed to reach its peak, with the sun bearing down mercilessly, making the air around him shimmer with heat. Amidst his perusal of goods, from intricately woven baskets to fragrant herbs that promised to flavor any dish with the essence of Morocco, Alex couldn't shake the feeling of being observed. With each purchase, a small collection of items that spoke to the richness of the local culture, the sensation grew stronger. He noticed shadows that seemed to linger a bit too long, figures that appeared at multiple turns of his path through the market. The bustling crowd, a shield against the sun's relentless gaze, now felt like a maze trapping him with an unseen watcher. The vibrancy of the market, once an exhilarating backdrop for exploration, took on a tense atmosphere, each exchange with vendors punctuated by Alex's cautious glances over his shoulder. The realization that he was being followed, watched by eyes waiting for an unknown moment, added a layer of unease to the oppressive heat, transforming the midday market from a place of discovery to one of subtle confrontation.

Off the main artery of the market, an alleyway beckoned, offering a momentary reprieve from the sensory bombardment. Stepping into its shadows felt like entering a different realm, where the market's vibrancy was dimmed and its odors diluted, yet its essence lingered in the subtler notes that the cooler air carried. The sounds here were a distant rumble, an echo of the fervent activity just yards away. Alex was immersed in this scene, straddling the line between a vivid reality and the disquieting embrace of a memory, fully alive in the complexity of the moment.

Alex navigated the maze of the market street with a determination that felt almost foreign to him. His steps, firm and deliberate, resonated against the ancient cobblestones, creating a solitary echo amidst the cacophony of the bustling marketplace. The alley before him twisted like a serpent, a narrow passage carved into the heart of the city, drawing him deeper into its confines. As he ventured forward, the vibrant noise of the market faded into a hushed whisper, the chaotic melody of commerce replaced by the quietude of seclusion.

As Alex's steps drew him inevitably closer, the figure ahead became the sole focus of his attention, a sentinel in the shadows that marked the threshold between the bustling market and the secluded quiet of the alleyway. The scant rays of light, filtered through the dense canopy of the market's awnings, barely reached this hidden nook, casting everything in a twilight that seemed out of place with the time of day. The man stood unmoving, as if rooted to the spot, his posture one of waiting or perhaps resignation, outlined in a soft haze that blurred the edges of reality. This secluded space, far removed from the sun's glare and the market's cacophony, held a sense of suspended time, a pause filled with the weight of impending events. The charged air, thick with the dust and secrets of the ancient city, seemed to whisper of encounters and exchanges hidden from the view of casual onlookers. In this shadowed enclave, where the bright vibrancy of Moroccan life dimmed to a murmur, Alex moved forward, driven by an inexplicable pull towards the figure and the unknown drama that awaited in the soft gloom.

Drawing nearer, the silhouette of the man before Alex seemed to solidify yet remained veiled in mystery, the details of his appearance swallowed by the shadows. There was a stillness about him, a readiness that hung in the air like a charge before a storm. This was no accidental meeting; the man's posture, his very presence in this secluded alley, suggested a rendezvous with destiny—or danger— that Alex had unwittingly stumbled into. As the distance between them closed, an inexplicable force seemed to guide Alex's actions. A blunt object, its weight sudden and undeniable in his hand, seemed almost to materialize from the ether, a tangible manifestation of the tension that filled the space between the two men. With this weapon in hand, Alex felt an inexplicable drive, a compulsion that transcended thought, propelling him towards what felt like an inevitable confrontation. The cool heft of the instrument contrasted sharply with the rush of heat coursing through him, an adrenaline-fueled clarity that sharpened his senses and narrowed his world down to the space between him and the waiting figure.

The moment that followed was a whirlwind of primal instinct and suppressed violence breaking free. Their bodies collided with a force that spoke volumes of desperation and confrontation. The sound of impact reverberated through the narrow alley, a harsh symphony of human struggle culminating in a muffled cry that was as swiftly silenced as it had erupted. And then, as if the scene were too volatile for reality to hold, it fractured, leaving behind nothing but the echo of violence in Alex's senses.

Abruptly, Alex was catapulted back into the reality of his living room, the intensity of the imagined confrontation lingering like the residue of a disturbing dream. As his breathing slowed, he became acutely aware of the familiar chaos that surrounded him — and yet, a newfound dissonance threaded through the ordinariness of his apartment. His gaze inadvertently landed on the wooden carving he'd encountered in his memory, now sitting quietly on his shelf. The figure, intricate and solemn, bore scars of its own: a series of scratches marred its surface, and a noticeable chip was missing from its edge, as if echoing the violence of Alex's vision.

Around him, other mementos from his travels mingled with the everyday. A picture frame, its edges dusted with the fine sands of Morocco, held within it a captured moment of vibrant market life, a stark contrast to the solitude of his current surroundings. These items, each with their own story, now seemed to carry a weight beyond their physical presence, imbued with the echoes of Alex's recent turmoil. The wooden figure, especially, stood as a silent testament to the blurred line between his reality and the violence he had experienced in the shadowed recesses of his mind. The presence of these objects, particularly the carved figure with its tangible imperfections, anchored the surreal experience in a disturbing reality, leaving Alex to navigate the aftermath of an encounter that felt both alien and eerily personal.

Alex remained frozen, his body echoing the shock and terror that coursed through his veins like ice water. Beads of sweat formed on his brow, each one a silent witness to the intensity of the ordeal he had just experienced, even if only in the recesses of his mind. The confines of his living room, usually a sanctuary filled with the quiet companionship of books and the familiar geography of maps, now seemed to close in on him. The space, cluttered with the artifacts of his many intellectual pursuits, transformed into a prison of his own making, a tangible representation of his inner turmoil.

His heartbeat thundered in his ears, a relentless drumming that mirrored the tumultuous storm of emotions within. This discord between the man he knew himself to be—a creature of intellect and restraint—and the man capable of such violence in his visions tore at him, leaving a rift of doubt and fear. This chasm threatened to swallow him whole, challenging his understanding of his very identity. The reality of his serene existence clashed violently with the brutality of the actions he had envisioned, leaving him in a state of profound disarray, questioning the very fabric of his being.

In his efforts to piece himself back together, Alex found himself grappling with the haunting possibility that the violence in his memory might not be an invention of his psyche, but rather a dark fragment of his past breaking through. The line between imagined horrors and buried realities seemed to blur, casting him into a tumultuous ocean of doubt. This uncertainty, this inability to discern the truth of his own experiences, left him feeling untethered, floating aimlessly amidst the wreckage of his thoughts. The notion that such brutality could be a part of his history, hidden beneath layers of forgetfulness or denial, was as terrifying as the memory itself. Wrestling with these fears, Alex stood on the precipice of an abyss, peering into the depths of his own soul, searching for answers that seemed as elusive as shadows at dusk.

Driven by a need for clarity, Alex moved towards the expansive wall map that adorned one side of his room, its surface a testament to his relentless quest for understanding. His fingers traced the web of lines and notations that crisscrossed the paper, each a marker of mysteries explored and yet unsolved. With a growing sense of purpose, he turned to a journal lying open on the table, its pages filled with observations, theories, and the occasional clipping that caught his attention. Flipping through the weathered pages, he sought a correlation, a tangible link to the violent memory that haunted him.

And there it was, almost as if waiting to be rediscovered: a small, newspaper clipping, yellowed with age but distinctly familiar. It detailed an unsolved mystery, an incident that had occurred several years earlier, eerily similar to the violence of his recent memory. The event was circled on his map, a silent beacon amidst the chaos of his collected data. The clipping seemed to leap out at him, its presence both a confirmation and a conundrum, solidifying the connection between his haunting vision and a reality he could no longer ignore. As he absorbed the implications, his analytical mind racing to piece together fragments of possibility, the silence that had enveloped him was shattered.

Sounds from the neighboring apartment pierced the veil of his concentration, the abrupt intrusion jarring him from his deep dive into the past. The noises, indistinct yet unmistakably human, broke the spell of his introspection, reminding him of the world beyond his walls. In this moment of disruption, the profound solitude of his investigation was laid bare, contrasting sharply with the ordinary lives that unfolded so close to his own, yet felt worlds apart. The interruption, while brief, underscored the isolation of his quest, a solitary journey through the shadows of memory and reality.

In the solitude of his apartment, with the distant clamor from the neighbors fading into silence, Alex was confronted with an unsettling realization. Hidden beneath the surface of his conscious self were facets of his being that remained dark and uncharted. The stark and violent imagery of his flashback, though brief and hazy, starkly underscored the mind's ability to harbor deep-seated shadows. This glimpse into the violence, a spectral memory or a harbored secret, hinted at the existence of depths within him that were perhaps too profound and daunting to fully comprehend.

Chapter 3: The Neighbor's Screams

The noise from the apartment above had turned into a regular, if unwelcome, part of Alex's evenings. But tonight, the disturbance hit a new high. The sounds of dinner being abruptly interrupted, voices rising in anger, and the scrape of a chair against the floor all signaled the start of another loud argument for the Dawson family.

In his mind, Alex could see it all too well: James Dawson, large and quick to anger, standing up at the dinner table, red-faced and shouting. His wife, Maria, thin and quiet, looked down, trying to calm the situation as she always did. Their kids, Lily and Daryl, sat frozen, watching the familiar scene unfold with wide, scared eyes.

The argument grew louder, the words blending into a mess of shouting that vibrated through Alex's ceiling, making him feel like he was right there with them. He couldn't understand what they were saying, but the anger and frustration were clear as day. The indistinct clamor, though muffled, carried an emotional weight that Alex felt in his bones—a visceral reminder of his own childhood, marked by similar scenes of discord. He found himself transported back to those earlier days, sitting at the bottom of the stairs in his childhood home, knees hugged tightly to his chest as he tried to make himself invisible.

Alex saw his parents in the throes of their own tempestuous disputes. His father, a large man with a booming voice that seemed to shake the very foundations of their house, stood imposingly over his mother, who, in stark contrast, tried to diffuse the situation with a quiet, pleading tone that seldom reached his father's ears. The sharpness of his father's shouts against the softness of his mother's appeals created a jarring harmony that Alex had grown to dread.

His older sister, Sarah, would often grab his hand, pulling him further away from the epicenter of the storm, whispering reassurances that did little to quell the churning in his stomach. They would huddle together in the dim light of the hallway, sharing a silent solidarity that only those who have navigated the unpredictable waters of a tumultuous household could understand.

Even as a child, Alex felt the tension like a physical entity, a third unwelcome presence that lurked in the corners of their home, emerging with a vengeance at the slightest provocation. The residue of these confrontations lingered long after the shouting had ceased, settling over the household like a thick fog, making everything feel muted and distant.

Now, years later, the Dawson's heated exchange mirrored those long-forgotten battles, reviving feelings Alex had long buried. The frustration, the anger, and the underlying sense of helplessness transported him back to a time he had worked hard to move beyond. It was a stark reminder of how deeply those early experiences had been etched into his psyche, shaping his understanding of family, love, and conflict.

As the memories flooded in, Alex felt a pang of empathy for the Dawson children, knowing all too well the impact such an environment could have on young, impressionable minds. It was a cycle of distress and recovery, one that he recognized and wished he could shield them from. The familiarity of the situation, coupled with the distance of his own vantage point, left him feeling both connected to and helplessly detached from the unfolding drama above, a silent witness to a story that mirrored his own.

Alex suddenly found himself seated in the police interrogation room, a sharp departure from the maelstrom of his thoughts. The room was stark and unforgiving, defined by its utilitarian simplicity and the unyielding glare of fluorescent lighting overhead. These lights bathed everything in a clinical, almost surgical light, leaving no shadow untouched, no corner dimmed. The walls, painted a nondescript shade of gray, were unadorned, save for a lone, outdated clock that ticked away with an almost taunting monotony. The only furniture was the metallic table at its center, cold and impersonal, surrounded by a few chairs that had seen better days, their faux leather surfaces worn by countless previous occupants.

Detective Laura Henderson sat across from him, her presence commanding even in this austere setting. The fluorescent lighting accentuated the stern set of her jaw and highlighted the intensity of her blue eyes, which seemed to pierce through the veneer of any pretense. She leaned forward, elbows resting on the table, creating a bridge of scrutiny that Alex found himself unable to escape. Her gaze was unwavering, a clear signal that she was not merely seeking answers but demanding them. The worry lines that furrowed her brow spoke of a seasoned officer who had navigated the murky waters of human deception more times than she cared to count.

Beside Detective Henderson, her partner, Detective Marcus Reed, offered a stark contrast with his silent, stoic demeanor. Positioned slightly behind and to the side, his broad, imposing figure seemed to command the light itself, bending and recoiling to cast him in a shadow that afforded him an almost spectral presence. His eyes, a deep, unreadable shade of brown, observed the proceedings with a calm, analytical gaze that missed nothing, from Alex's slightest twitch to his every hesitant pause. Unlike Henderson's dynamic interrogation style,

Reed's silence was a strategy in itself, his stillness a counterbalance to her intensity. His short, meticulously groomed hair and the neat fold of his hands on the table in front of him suggested a man of order, one who preferred to let the quiet accumulation of facts speak louder than words. Yet, the subtle tightening of his jaw at key moments betrayed his engagement, his vested interest in the truths that Alex might be withholding. Together, the detectives presented a united front of authority and expectation, their distinct approaches converging in a singular purpose—to unravel the mystery at hand.

Every aspect of the room seemed designed to unnerve, from the relentless buzz of the fluorescent bulbs overhead to the stark, unyielding surfaces that left one feeling exposed and vulnerable. The air was thick with a tension that seemed almost tangible, a psychological weight that pressed down on Alex, making it hard to breathe, let alone think.

The room's atmosphere was a far cry from the chaotic warmth of the Dawson family's apartment or the tumultuous emotions of Alex's own childhood memories. Here, in this confined space, there was nowhere to hide, no shadows to retreat into. The interrogation room was a realm of absolute truth— or at least, the pursuit of it—where every word and gesture was scrutinized, every pause potentially incriminating.

As Detective Henderson's questions began, the room seemed to close in around Alex, the walls inching closer with each syllable uttered, each note jotted down in her notepad. The interrogation room, with its stark lighting and sparse furnishings, became an arena of mental and emotional confrontation, a place where past and present collided with the force of the questions asked and the answers desperately sought."Mr. Bennett," Detective Laura Henderson initiated, her tone straddling the delicate line between cold professionalism and an almost tangible urgency that seemed to fill the interrogation room with an unspoken tension. Her voice, though steady, carried an undercurrent of insistence that made Alex's nerves tighten, the words resonating more as a command than a question. The scent of her sharp, no-nonsense perfume subtly permeated the air, setting a backdrop of stern formality to their exchange.

As she spoke, her gaze fixed intently on Alex, her eyes—a striking shade of steely blue—bore into him with a piercing clarity that seemed to seek out the truth, or any flicker of deception. The intensity of her stare, coupled with the slight furrow of her brows, communicated a silent expectation of transparency, as if her look alone could unravel the layers of any façade Alex might have been inclined to maintain.

The atmosphere was charged with a palpable sense of scrutiny that left Alex feeling as though every word he uttered was being weighed and measured against an invisible scale of guilt or innocence. Despite the absence of explicit accusations, there was an implicit pressure emanating from Henderson that whispered of her resolve to find the threads that might lead to culpability, casting a shadow of intimidation across the room. This silent determination, paired with her authoritative presence, began to shake the very foundations of Alex's resolve, planting seeds of doubt about the impending direction of this interrogation.

"Mr. Bennett," Detective Henderson commenced, her voice a mix of professional detachment and underlying urgency, "we invited you here to tonight to help us. We need to talk about the Dawsons. What can you tell us about the night in question?"

As Detective Henderson's words hung in the air, a whirlwind of thoughts and fears began to swirl within Alex. Beside her stood another detective, his presence silent yet imposing, adding another layer of intensity to the already charged atmosphere. In the corner of the room, a figure that Alex recognized as a doctor stood by a table adorned with a polygraph machine, its wires and sensors ominously arranged as if waiting to ensnare him in their grasp. The very sight of it sent a shiver down his spine, amplifying the fear that was already coursing through him.

The room felt smaller, the walls inching closer with every passing second, a physical manifestation of the pressure building inside him. Alex's mind was a battlefield of conflicting emotions—fear of being wrongfully accused, anxiety over the unknown elements of the night in question, and a deep-seated dread of the polygraph revealing more than he intended. The idea of being hooked to the machine, with every heartbeat and breath scrutinized for truth, was terrifying. He questioned the reliability of his own memory, the blurred lines between what he had witnessed and what his mind might have construed or omitted.

In this moment, trapped in the gaze of not one, but two detectives and the silent judge that was the polygraph, Alex felt a profound sense of isolation. The fear of misremembering, or worse, revealing something he wasn't even aware of, loomed large. He was acutely aware of the gravity of his situation, caught in the intricate web of an investigation that seemed to grow more complex and threatening by the minute. The weight of expectation, the fear of the unknown, and the potential consequences of this interrogation cast a long shadow over his thoughts, leaving him grappling with a tumultuous sea of confusion and apprehension.

Alex felt the weight of her scrutiny, a tangible
pressure that seemed to demand the truth—or at
least, a version of it. His mind raced, the transition
from the vivid memory of the argument to this cold,
sterile environment leaving him disoriented. He
searched for something to say, aware that any
information could be crucial, yet uncertain of what
he actually knew.

"I heard them arguing," Alex said, feeling like his
voice came from far away. "They argue a lot, but that
night was different. It felt more serious."

Detective Henderson gave him a quick nod as she
scribbled in her notepad, which she seemed to
always have with her. "Different how?" she asked,
her eyes sharp, trying to get more out of him.

The other detective, who had been quiet until now,
showed a hint of interest in Alex's words. His look
was a mix of doubt and curiosity, as if he wasn't
quite sure what to make of Alex's statement about
the argument being different.

Even the doctor, who was setting up the polygraph
machine in the corner, paused and glanced over. His
expression changed slightly, showing he was paying
attention now, but it wasn't clear if he believed Alex
or was just curious about what he said.

Feeling their eyes on him, Alex started to doubt
himself. Were his feelings about that night just in his

head? The way they all reacted, with those looks of skepticism, made him question his own words. It was like they all expected more from him, something solid he couldn't quite grasp or remember correctly. This made him unsure, not just about what he was saying but about what had actually happened that night. The room felt like it was closing in on him, filled with doubt and the pressure to remember details he wasn't sure were real.

Alex hesitated, struggling to articulate the sense of foreboding that had settled over him that evening. "It was the silence afterward," he finally said.

As Alex tried to continue, a momentary lapse betrayed him. His voice faltered, a bead of sweat traced a path down his temple, and his eyes briefly darted away from Detective Henderson's unwavering stare. His hands, which had been steadily clasped, now fidgeted on the table's surface, betraying his inner turmoil. These fleeting signs of distress did not go unnoticed by Detective Henderson, whose sharp eyes seemed to catalog every nuance of Alex's demeanor. For a split second, Alex's behavior hinted at something unsaid, a suggestion of guilt or knowledge he was yet to disclose. However, no admission came; instead, he swallowed hard, trying to regain his composure under the heavy cloak of suspicion that seemed to settle around him.

Regaining a semblance of control, Alex's narrative found its footing once again, though his voice carried the weight of lingering uncertainty. "After the shouting stopped, there was this... absolute silence," he said, emphasizing the profound change in the atmosphere. "It was eerie." The stark contrast between the prior chaos and the sudden stillness painted a vivid picture. "Suddenly, there was nothing. An absolute silence that filled the room, unsettling, like a charged pause waiting to explode. That silence... it was unlike anything I've experienced with them before. It felt ominous." His words, carefully chosen, hung heavily in the air, evoking a sense of unease that mirrored his own. The charged stillness he described seemed to extend beyond the confines of his memory, casting a shadow over those present in the room, leaving them to ponder the significance of the silence that had followed the storm.

The detective's face was a mask of professional inscrutability, her eyes revealing nothing of what churned beneath the surface. Yet, Alex sensed a tangible change in the atmosphere, as if the very air had thickened in response to his testimony. It was an imperceptible shift, but one that he felt keenly, like a sudden turn in a road that had gone unnoticed until the landscape had irrevocably changed. He found himself suspended in a moment of transition, teetering on the edge of a precipice that divided the known tumult of the Dawson family's frequent disputes from the eerie quiet that had inexplicably ensued.

There was a palpable tension now, a charged silence that mirrored the one he had described, enveloping the room and its occupants. Detective Henderson's steady gaze, though outwardly neutral, seemed to bore into him with increased intensity, as if attempting to peel back the layers of his narrative in search of hidden truths. Alex was acutely aware of the weight of his own words, of the power they held to direct the course of the investigation. He was a bridge between the ordinary past, filled with the predictable cacophony of familial discord, and an uncertain future marked by the heavy, foreboding silence that had settled over the Dawson household.

Caught in this liminal space, Alex grappled with the enormity of what his account implied. The normalcy of the arguments he had grown accustomed to was now tainted, overshadowed by the quiet that had followed—a quiet that hinted at something far more sinister than mere absence of sound. It was as if, in speaking of the silence, Alex had unveiled a hidden layer of reality, one that both he and the detective were now compelled to confront. The room, once merely the setting for a routine inquiry, had become a crucible in which the truth, however elusive, began to simmer and take shape, demanding to be acknowledged.

As the interrogation unfolded, Alex's mind became a battleground of conflicting memories and emotions. The detective's questions, sharp and unyielding, pierced through the fog of his thoughts, pulling him deeper into a vortex of uncertainty. What had transpired in the Dawson household that night? And more critically, what part had he, Alex, unwittingly played in those events? These questions echoed in the stark room, their answers as elusive as shadows flickering on the wall.

Amidst this turmoil, a fragment of memory surfaced with startling clarity: Alex standing at his own doorstep, his hand hesitating on the doorknob, a metaphorical line between the sanctuary of his solitude and the chaos of the world outside. That moment of decision, of stepping beyond the threshold, seemed now to mirror his current predicament—caught between the known and the unknown, between the safety of ignorance and the peril of truth.

But as quickly as this memory solidified, it fragmented, replaced by an innocuous recollection of a recent, sunlit afternoon. He saw himself handing out ice cream to the Dawson children, their faces alight with simple joy, a stark contrast to the dark undercurrents of their family life. Maria Dawson, watching from a distance, offered him a grateful, if somewhat weary, smile. It was a moment of normalcy, of mundane kindness, that seemed wholly at odds with the sinister implications of the night in question.

Confusion reigned in Alex's mind. How could these disparate pieces fit together? The warmth of a sunny day and the simple pleasure of ice cream juxtaposed against the cold, accusatory atmosphere of the interrogation room. Was it possible that he had played some role in the Dawsons' plight? The very thought was anathema to him, yet he couldn't dispel the nagging suspicion that had taken root in his mind.

As the interrogation drew to a close, Alex's unease deepened. The detective's probing had unearthed more questions than answers, leaving him to navigate a labyrinth of doubts and half-remembered truths. What had truly happened to the Dawsons, and where did he fit into the narrative? The events of that night remained shrouded in mystery; a puzzle that seemed to grow more complex with each passing moment.

In the silence that followed, Alex was left alone with his thoughts, the echo of the detective's questions lingering in the air. The boundaries between past and present, between guilt and innocence, seemed to blur, leaving him in a state of profound disorientation. Had his actions—or inactions— altered the course of the Dawson family's fate? Or was he merely a bystander, caught up in the aftermath of a tragedy beyond his comprehension?

Chapter 4: Tangled Realities

In the sanctuary of Dr. Emily Carter's office, a haven of tranquility, Alex was paradoxically ensnared by an internal tempest, his psyche at odds with the serene environment. The office, bathed in soft, muted hues of pale blue, exuded a calming atmosphere. Light from the afternoon sun filtered through sheer curtains, casting a warm, gentle glow that danced across the plush armchair enveloping Alex in its embrace. Despite the comfort offered by the surroundings, Alex's mind remained a battleground, the external peace highlighting his internal chaos.

The faint murmur of the city outside, a distant symphony of car horns and the occasional laughter of passersby, barely penetrated the thick walls, creating a cocoon of silence around the office. Inside, the air was lightly scented with lavender, a deliberate choice by Dr. Carter to foster a sense of calm and focus. The temperature was carefully regulated, neither too warm nor too cool, designed to comfort without distracting from the task at hand.

Around the room, tasteful decorations adorned the space: a small, well-tended plant on the windowsill, its leaves vibrant green against the soft blue backdrop; abstract paintings that invited contemplation without imposing meaning; and a bookshelf filled with volumes on psychology, their spines a spectrum of muted colors. A small, delicate clock ticked softly in the background, its sound a reminder of the passing time yet strangely comforting in its consistency.

Despite the office's inviting atmosphere, Alex found himself adrift in a sea of confusion, the tranquil setting a stark contrast to the storm raging within. The gentle caress of the armchair and the soothing ambiance crafted by Dr. Carter were but distant realities to him, as he navigated the tumultuous waters of his thoughts. The juxtaposition of the peaceful office with his chaotic mind underscored the complexity of his struggle, a vivid reminder of the journey he had embarked upon with Dr. Carter to find clarity amidst the confusion.

"In our dialogues, we have explored the notion that stress functions as a precipitating agent for your dissociative manifestations," Dr. Carter expounded with clinical precision, her tone an anchor in the tumultuous sea of Alex's psyche. "Your experiences of temporal disorientation, characterized by an aberrant fluidity of time's sequential flow, effectively dislocate you into instances divorced from chronological continuity. This phenomenon obfuscates the boundaries separating authentic recollections, present experiences, and the fabrications of your mental landscape, rendering them indistinct."

She continued; her discourse steeped in the terminology of advanced psychological practice. "This symptomatic presentation is indicative of a complex dissociative disorder, where the psyche, in an attempt to mitigate psychological distress, compartmentalizes experiences, leading to a fragmentation of the cohesive self-narrative. It's imperative that we delve into the underlying etiology of these episodes, employing both cognitive-behavioral and psychodynamic therapeutic approaches to foster integration and resilience within your cognitive schema."

Alex listened, the depth and complexity of Dr. Carter's explanations a stark contrast to the turmoil within him. His understanding of her words was intuitive rather than intellectual, a testament to the chasm between the world of psychiatric academia and his lived reality. While Dr. Carter navigated the labyrinth of mental health with the ease of a seasoned professional, Alex found himself lost, grasping for the meaning behind the jargon, a reflection of the vast divide between patient and therapist, yet united in their pursuit of healing.

Alex, grappling with the linguistic expression of his chaotic experiences, murmured, "It feels like I'm caught in time's flow, yanked into moments without any heads-up," Alex said, his voice carrying the weight of his internal chaos. "It's like I'm on this endless ride through time, tumbling from one memory to another, or maybe even into things that never really happened at all." His gaze wandered, lost in the maelstrom of his thoughts. "Trying to figure out what's an actual memory, what's happening right now in the moment, and what might just be something my mind's cooked up—it's like trying to catch smoke. It's there, but when you try to grab it, it slips right through your fingers." Alex's words painted a vivid picture of a man adrift in his own psyche, struggling to navigate the turbulent waters of reality versus the imagined, each wave of confusion pulling him further from the shore of understanding.

"Am I truly caught in such a whirlpool of time?" he questioned, the idea visibly unsettling him, shaking the foundations of his understanding. "But how can that be? I mean, yesterday was just yesterday, and tomorrow is always tomorrow," he continued, his voice tinged with disbelief and a growing sense of unease at the thought of time being anything but linear. The very concept of disorganized timelines seemed to rattle him deeply, challenging his grasp on what he had always considered the unshakeable reality of sequential days.

Encouraged by Dr. Carter's nod, a quiet cue to explore deeper into his turbulent mind, Alex found himself recalling a distinct memory from his childhood He was back to being eight years old, in the kitchen bathed in sunlight at his family home.

The room glowed with a warm, golden hue, every surface touched by the gentle embrace of morning light filtering through the window, casting long shadows that danced across the floor with the sway of the curtains. Sounds of the outside world were muffled here, replaced by the comfortable hum of the refrigerator and the distant sounds of animals outside, a backdrop to this scene of domestic tranquility. In this moment, the kitchen felt like a sanctuary, a place of safety and warmth. His mother, always more absent than present, floated at the edges of this memory. The focus was on a glass of milk sitting dangerously close to the edge of the table.

Caught in a moment suspended outside of time, young Alex became an observer to his own actions, detached yet deeply intertwined. His hand, guided by an inexplicable impulse, moved towards the glass with a grace that belied the impending disaster. The slightest contact, a whisper of movement against the cool surface, was enough to set the glass on a path to destruction. It seemed to fall in slow motion, each second stretching into eternity as Alex watched, his heart caught in his throat, unable to intervene or look away. The glass hit the ground with a force that contradicted its silent descent, unleashing a chaotic symphony of shattering and splashing that reverberated through the tranquil kitchen. Milk splattered in every direction, droplets catching the sunlight in a display of fleeting brilliance before succumbing to gravity's pull, staining the floor with their passage.

In that instant, a surge of emotions cascaded through Alex, a tumultuous blend of fascination and horror at the consequences of his actions. Regret tangled with a child's curiosity at the physics of the fall, the way something so stable could so quickly become a force of disarray. Guilt pricked at his conscience, knowing this minor catastrophe was his doing, yet there was also a strange pride in the magnitude of the effect he'd caused with such a small action. The silence that followed, punctuated only by the drip of milk from the table's edge, was heavy with realization and the imminent reaction from his mother, turning a moment of childhood mischief into a poignant memory of cause and effect.

This memory, simple and ordinary, became a highlight against the backdrop of Alex's current mental challenges. Seeing himself as a young boy, accidentally causing a mess, stood in sharp contrast to the disturbing, more violent memories that sometimes broke through his calm. This stark difference between the two types of memories showcased the deep and complicated nature of Alex's mind, blending innocence with the undercurrents of unrest. It painted a picture of a mind caught between the light of simple, childhood errors and the shadows of more troubling experiences. This mix shows how complex Alex's thoughts are, balancing the straightforward mistakes of youth with the dark, unresolved issues that sometimes surface.

In this memory, the simple act of spilling milk turned into a strong reminder of how unpredictable life can be, with each spill reflecting those small but significant moments that influence our lives. As Alex thought back on this, he could see the clear difference between the innocent times like these and the darker, more troubling memories. This contrast shed light on the complex world of his thoughts, showing a place where the gentle memories of simpler times meet the heavier, more complicated parts of his experiences.

This seemingly harmless recollection was violently interrupted by an entirely different kind of memory—a chilling wave of darkness that seemed to swallow him whole. Suddenly, Alex found himself caught in the grip of an instinctual fear, his entire being screaming for escape from an unseen threat. The atmosphere around him thickened with dread, every shadow seemed to move with sinister intent, and the air felt charged with impending doom.

Into this oppressive darkness, a scream shattered the silence, cutting through the night with a sharpness that felt almost physical. It wasn't just any scream—

it was one filled with such terror and desperation that it seemed to echo endlessly in his mind, leaving a trail of cold fear in its wake. Alongside this haunting cry, there was a distinct, harrowing sound of something breaking—bone, or perhaps something equally as vital. This sound, dreadfully final, underscored the nightmare with an undeniable reality of violence.

This memory, if it could indeed be called that, was drenched in an intense atmosphere of fear and danger, starkly contrasting with the simple, innocent accident of spilled milk. Whereas the earlier memory was tinged with the light of a sunny kitchen and the minor guilt of a child's mistake, this new vision plunged Alex into a world of shadow and fear, where every sense was heightened by the survival instinct, and every moment felt stretched by adrenaline.

The memory, real or imagined, stained the innocence of his earlier recollection, overlaying it with a layer of darkness that was hard to shake off. The juxtaposition of these two memories— one so mundane and the other so terrifyingly vivid— highlighted the complex tapestry of Alex's psyche, where moments of innocence and trauma were intertwined, casting long shadows over his present reality.

As Alex resurfaced from the depths of his memories, he felt the abrupt transition from the dark, tumultuous sea of his psyche to the calm, soothing shores of Dr. Carter's office. The room, with its soft lighting and serene ambiance, felt like a sanctuary, a stark contrast to the chaos of his mind. Dr. Carter's face, marked by an expression of deep concern and professionalism, was a beacon in the fog of his confusion, grounding him in the present.

"Alex?" Dr. Carter's voice, gentle yet insistent, cut through the haze of his thoughts, a lifeline pulling him back from the edge of his mental precipice. "It seemed as if you were somewhere far away. Can you tell me what you were experiencing?"

Caught between the innocuous memory of a childhood mishap and the sudden, dark intrusion of a potential trauma, Alex felt the weight of both worlds pressing upon him. "I remembered something... trivial, from when I was a kid. Knocking over a glass of milk," he began, his voice a whisper of vulnerability in the safety of the room. "But then... it changed. It was as if that simple moment peeled back a layer, revealing a glimpse of something much darker beneath. It's like I stumbled into a memory—or a nightmare—that I can't be sure ever really happened."

In the secure confines of Dr. Carter's office, with its atmosphere of understanding and non-judgment,

Alex confronted the juxtaposition of his experiences. The dichotomy of his memories, one bathed in the innocent light of childhood and the other shrouded in the shadows of fear, encapsulated the battle waging within him. The serene environment of the office, a marked departure from the turmoil of his recollections, provided a haven in which Alex could navigate the murky waters of his psyche. Dr. Carter's patient, attentive presence offered not just a professional anchor but a compassionate witness to his struggle, underscoring the complexity of his journey toward understanding and healing.

Dr. Carter, with a posture embodying both acute focus and deep empathy, leaned forward, her intense concentration mirroring the gravity of the conversation. "Alex, in the realm of your psyche, particularly when besieged by stress, there exists a tendency for the mosaic of your memories to blend disparate elements, thus obscuring the boundaries between concrete reality and the more ephemeral remnants of the past," she began, her voice a harmonious blend of clinical precision and soothing reassurance. "This amalgamation of experiences, especially under duress, often results in a conflation of divergent strands of your life's narrative, blurring the distinction between the tangible and what might merely be spectral echoes of bygone moments."

She continued; her gaze fixed upon Alex with an intensity that underscored her words. "It is of paramount importance to acknowledge these confluences as nothing more than phantasmagorical reflections, bereft of any capacity to wield influence over your present circumstances. Such recognition is a fundamental step on the path to reclaiming mental stability and achieving a state of equilibrium," Dr. Carter elucidated further. "Viewing these episodes as mere specters, devoid of the potency to exact change or inflict distress in your current existence, is essential to navigate through the labyrinth of your mind and emerge unscathed."

She paused, ensuring her words had taken root, then continued, "Let us consider employing strategies to anchor you firmly in the now, techniques designed to differentiate the palpable immediacy of the present from the intangible wisps of memory. Mindfulness exercises, for instance, can serve as a beacon, guiding you back to the safety of the present whenever the past's shadows grow too insistent."

Dr. Carter's suggestions flowed with the precision of someone well-versed in navigating the complexities of the human psyche. "Additionally, journaling your experiences might provide clarity, transforming nebulous thoughts into concrete expressions that can be examined and understood in the light of day. Through such practices, we aim to fortify your ability to discern reality from the figments conjured by stress or dissociation, thereby reclaiming the autonomy over your mental landscape."

In the sanctity of her office, surrounded by books and certificates that spoke of her expertise, Dr. Carter represented a beacon of hope. Her guidance, steeped in the wisdom of psychological science, promised a pathway through the fog of confusion, a means for Alex to untangle the Gordian knot of his memories and perceptions.

As Alex processed Dr. Carter's explanations, he found himself grappling with a lingering skepticism. The seed of doubt that had embedded itself in his mind seemed to flourish amidst the unsettling vividness of the more ominous memory. To him, the visceral nature of this recollection—its sharp edges and cold dread—felt as tangible as the chair he sat in, challenging the notion that it could simply be dismissed as a phantom of his psyche.

The authenticity of this darker memory, felt so keenly through every nerve, presented Alex with a daunting puzzle. How could he sift through the entangled threads of his consciousness to separate the genuine from the imagined? This question loomed large, casting a shadow over the therapeutic insights Dr. Carter had offered.

Alex found himself at a crossroads, caught between the clinical detachment suggested by his therapist and the raw, undeniable reality of his experiences. The disparity between the two left him adrift in a sea of confusion, searching for a lifeline that could anchor him to a semblance of truth. The very task of untangling the web of his psyche, of discerning the real from the fabricated within the labyrinthine recesses of his mind, seemed Herculean in its complexity.

And yet, the necessity of this endeavor was clear. If he were to navigate his way back to a place of mental clarity and stability, Alex understood he must somehow bridge the gap between his visceral experiences and the clinical perspectives offered by Dr. Carter. The journey ahead, fraught with uncertainty and the potential for revelation, promised to be both challenging and transformative, demanding a level of introspection and courage Alex was only beginning to muster.

Throughout the session, the exchange between Alex and Dr. Carter undulated like the ebb and flow of an uncertain tide. Dr. Carter offered techniques and insights designed to ground Alex in the present, employing a lexicon steeped in psychological expertise. Yet, each concept introduced seemed to orbit just beyond Alex's full grasp, leading to moments of palpable frustration and misunderstanding.

"Imagine yourself tethered to the current moment by a series of grounding exercises," Dr. Carter suggested, presenting mindfulness as a tool to navigate his temporal disarray. Alex, however, found his mind adrift, caught in the whirlpool of his thoughts, misinterpreting her guidance as a call to suppress rather than acknowledge his experiences.

This cycle of communication and miscommunication played out repeatedly. Dr. Carter patiently redirected the conversation each time, her voice a constant beacon amidst the fog of Alex's confusion. "No, Alex, it's not about denying your experiences. It's about acknowledging them without letting them consume you," she clarified, steering him back towards understanding.

For every step forward, there seemed to be a half-step back, as Alex grappled with integrating the therapeutic strategies into his lived experience. The session felt like navigating a complex dance—two steps forward, one step back—each misstep a learning opportunity, each correction a chance for deeper insight.

Despite the occasional misalignment, breakthroughs shimmered on the horizon. Alex began to grasp the essence of Dr. Carter's guidance, finding brief moments of clarity amid the chaos. These fleeting instances of connection, where therapist and patient found themselves perfectly aligned, offered glimpses of potential progress, illuminating the path forward through the dense underbrush of Alex's psyche.

As the session drew to a close, a palpable shift had occurred. The initial dissonance that marked their exchange had given way to a more harmonious dialogue. Dr. Carter's steadfast patience and Alex's burgeoning understanding had forged a bridge over the chasm of misinterpretation that had separated them. "You're learning, Alex. It's a process, one that takes time and patience, but you're making strides," Dr. Carter affirmed, her words imbued with genuine encouragement.

Emerging from Dr. Carter's office into the muted light of the corridor, Alex felt a weight lift, if only momentarily. The disquiet that had shadowed him into the session had receded, replaced by a nascent sense of empowerment. Dr. Carter's strategies, though still nebulous in his turbulent sea of thoughts, now felt like potential lifelines—threads he could grasp to pull himself back to the present, to reality.

Alex paused at the threshold of the office, turning back to offer Dr. Carter a nod of gratitude. "Thank you," he murmured, his voice reflecting a newfound resolve mingled with vulnerability. Dr. Carter's smile in response was both acknowledgment and encouragement, a silent testament to the progress made and the journey ahead.

As he was escorted out, the clinical sterility of the hallway seemed less oppressive, the outside world less daunting. Though the mysteries of his mind remained largely uncharted, the session had bestowed upon Alex a critical tool: hope. Hope that, with guidance and effort, the tangled realities that ensnared him could be unraveled, that he could find his way through the labyrinth to a place of understanding and peace.

This tentative optimism was a fragile bloom in the garden of his recovery, but it was a start—a promise of spring after the longest, coldest winter.

Chapter 5: The Discovery

Alex's nights had become an intriguing tableau of shadows and whispers, his living room a clandestine vantage point from which he meticulously charted the comings and goings of the street below. His gaze often lingered on the shopkeeper across the way, a figure he had come to suspect as a covert operative, engaging in the subtle trade of secrets under the guise of mundane transactions. The local officers, regulars in this nightly dance, seemed to him not just patrollers of peace but potential players in a deeper game, their casual stops at the shop a cover for exchanges far more significant than they appeared.

This evening's calm was shattered not by the expected clandestine exchanges but by the sudden, sharp intrusion of sirens, slicing through the night with the urgency of a crisis unfolding. Alex, his mind a whirlwind of suspicion and speculation, watched the drama escalate. The swift passage of the police cruiser and ambulance beyond the shop's facade hinted at a turn of events far removed from his theories of espionage and undercover operations.

The absence of the women who had become a fixture of the nighttime landscape, whom Alex had fancifully cast as skilled agents in disguise, now seemed an ominous prelude to the night's emergency. Their disappearance, previously a puzzle piece in his imagined intrigue, now took on a new, more urgent significance as the emergency vehicles halted not at the shop but at his own building.

As the vehicles bypassed the shop, instead stopping abruptly at his building, a surge of confusion unsettled Alex's thoughts. The reality of emergency responders converging at his doorstep starkly contradicted his earlier suspicions, dislodging any preconceived scenarios he had woven into the fabric of the night. The pulsating red and blue lights, splashing across his living room, shifted the atmosphere from one of speculative observation to the forefront of an unfolding real-world drama, casting his space in the uncertain light of unfolding events.

Compelled by a swirling mix of curiosity and a deep, unspoken sense of obligation, Alex felt himself irresistibly drawn towards the epicenter of the turmoil. With each deliberate step he took towards the staircase, the weight seemed to multiply beneath his feet, as if the very fabric of the building conspired to slow his approach, echoing the mounting dread that began to encase his heart like a vice. The ordinary sounds of the night had been replaced by the urgent cacophony of first responders; the staccato rhythm of boots on concrete, the sharp, authoritative commands cutting through the air, and the distant, underlying murmur of a crowd gathering beneath the pulsating glow of emergency lights.

This was no longer the detached routine of his nightly vigil. Instead, it had transformed into a precipitous journey into uncertainty, with each step forward amplifying the sense of apprehension that clouded his thoughts. The once familiar pathway now felt like a corridor to the unknown, every sound and movement intensifying the sense of unease that threatened to overwhelm him. It was as though the very atmosphere had thickened, charged with the electricity of anticipation and the heavy scent of fear, pulling him forward with the force of an unseen hand guiding him towards a destiny that remained shrouded in shadow.

As he ascended, the world around him felt both intensely vivid and eerily detached, as if he were moving through a dream. The usual sounds of life — of neighbors' doors closing, of distant laughter, of life being lived — were conspicuously absent, replaced by the ominous hum of a scene yet unseen but palpably charged with urgency and despair. It was in this surreal procession towards the unknown that Alex's role shifted from passive observer to reluctant participant, drawn into the vortex of an event that would indelibly mark the canvas of his life.

As Alex reached the final step, the air around him seemed to thicken with an ominous tension, heralding the unfolding of a catastrophic event. The door to the Dawsons' apartment, typically closed and secretive, stood eerily open, beckoning him into a realm that had irrevocably shifted from the familiar to the nightmarish. The sight that greeted him was so profoundly shocking that it seized his breath, embedding a moment of pure terror deep within his consciousness.

Contrary to the tumult of emotions and the expected disorder stemming from James Dawson's often volatile temperament, the scene that greeted Alex was one of unnerving order and cleanliness. The living room, far from the anticipated disarray, was meticulously organized, with every piece of furniture in its rightful place, and surfaces gleaming with the touch of recent cleaning. This stark sterility contrasted sharply with the home's usual atmosphere, one often punctuated by James's loud and aggressive demeanor, suggesting a backdrop of underlying tension and unrest.

Amidst this almost clinical precision, James Dawson's body lay out of place, an anomaly in the otherwise impeccable environment. His form, disturbingly still and silent, was the sole indicator of the tragedy that had unfolded. No signs of struggle or chaos marred the surrounding space, only the stark, final presence of James, whose life had been abruptly and violently ended. This incongruity between the expected chaos and the actual, almost surgical neatness of the scene deepened the mystery, leaving Alex to ponder the unsettling calm that now enveloped the apartment, a silent testament to the complexity and hidden depths of the household he had thought he knew.

The atmosphere was charged, a palpable tension filling the room, enhanced by the sporadic flicker of emergency lights from outside that penetrated the sterile environment of the apartment. These intermittent flashes of red and blue light cast sharp, elongated shadows across the space, lending an otherworldly aspect to the scene before Alex. In this eerie silence, so at odds with the chaos that had once defined the household, the lack of sound weighed heavily, amplifying the sense of sterility and order that now reigned.

Within this ordered silence, a nebulous memory surfaced in Alex's mind, a sensation of driven anger and unfocused intent. It was as though he could see himself approaching the Dawson's apartment, propelled by an anger that seemed alien to the man currently caught in the grip of shock and disbelief. This shadowy memory, vague and disconcerting, hovered at the periphery of his awareness, offering no clarity or context, only adding layers to the enigma of his involvement in the night's tragic events.

The shock of the scene before him, coupled with the elusive memory of anger, left Alex adrift in a sea of confusion and dread. He stood on the threshold of a nightmare, the reality of James Dawson's lifeless form before him colliding with the ghost of a memory too fragmented to grasp. In this moment, the tension in the air was almost tangible, a heavy, oppressive cloak that seemed to settle over everything, marking the point of no return in a night that had irrevocably changed the course of Alex's life.

Rooted to the spot, Alex's senses were assaulted by the chaos before him. How had circumstance conspired to place him here, a voyeur to the macabre, standing sentinel over the remnants of his neighbor's existence? His mind churned, attempting to bridge the chasm between his last moment of mundane normalcy and the horror that now confronted him. No thread of memory offered guidance through the labyrinthine events that had culminated in this moment of shock and disbelief.

The moment the police entered; the dynamics of the scene shifted dramatically. Their presence, assertive and resolute, cut through the air with undeniable authority, transforming the building's undercurrent of whispers into a focused stream of action and inquiry. Commands issued forth from the officers became the new rhythm to which everyone present instinctively attuned, a stark contrast to the prior confusion and whispers of speculation that had filled the hallway.

As they moved with purposeful strides, assessing the scene and cordoning off areas with the swift efficiency of practiced professionals, the neighbors' reactions evolved from shock to a guarded wariness. Their eyes, wide with the fear and curiosity that tragedy inevitably draws forth, found a common focal point in Alex. Whispers swirled around him like leaves in an eddy, each glance laden with the heavy cloak of suspicion and the unvoiced question of his involvement in the night's events. It was as if his mere presence at the scene painted him with a brush of culpability, coloring their perceptions with hues of doubt and accusation.

Alex felt the weight of those speculative glances as if they were tangible, each one a silent indictment that added to the surreal nature of the situation. Standing there, amidst the controlled chaos orchestrated by the responding officers, he became acutely aware of the narrative being constructed around him. The reclusive, solitary figure from the apartment below, now inexplicably linked to an act of violence that shattered the mundane reality of their residential community.

This palpable shift in perception, from neighbor to suspect, was a burden that Alex felt keenly. The air seemed to thicken with judgment, every sidelong look and hushed whisper a thread weaving him tighter into the fabric of the tragedy that had unfolded. The police, with their questions and their methodical gathering of evidence, only served to solidify his position at the heart of the investigation. Alex, caught in this storm of circumstance and suspicion, could only stand as a silent witness to the rapid unravelling of the life he knew, propelled into the eye of a storm he had never seen coming.

"Sir, I need you to move back," an officer said firmly, advancing toward Alex with a demeanor that brokered no argument. In that moment, the gravity of his situation settled upon him with the weight of the world, a sudden and profound realization that he had unwittingly stepped into the heart of a crime scene, a collage of tragedy he had no memory of entering. The previously indistinct murmurs of the assembled crowd seemed to solidify into a chorus of silent judgment, their speculative whispers weaving a net of suspicion that ensnared him tightly.

The room, bathed in the stark, artificial light of emergency, felt surreal to Alex. Time seemed to dilate, stretching the seconds into minutes, each one laden with the heavy significance of his presence in this place of death. The onlookers, once just neighbors living their separate lives, now bore witness to his inexplicable involvement in the night's grim proceedings. Their eyes, a mix of curiosity, fear, and judgment, followed his every move, casting him in a role he had no script for.

Overwhelmed by the sudden shift from observer to participant in the unfolding drama, Alex's mind raced for a rational explanation, a lifeline to throw to the officers and the silent jury of his peers. Yet, as he opened his mouth to speak, to protest his innocence and confusion, he found that words eluded him. The attempt to articulate his thoughts, to bridge the chasm between his experience and their expectations, was thwarted by a maelstrom of emotions. Shock, disbelief, and a nascent fear rendered him mute, his voice lost amid the cacophony of emergency response and the low rumble of speculation.

The officer's hand on his arm, guiding him away from the threshold of the Dawson's apartment, felt both grounding and alien, a physical reminder of the new reality Alex found himself thrust into. As he was led past the threshold of his own understanding, stepping back into the role of a spectator in his own life, Alex couldn't shake the feeling of being adrift. The murmured speculations of the crowd, once just background noise, now carried the weight of an impending judgment, marking him as a figure of intrigue and suspicion in the tragedy that had overtaken the building.

In a disjointed haze, Alex felt the cold, unyielding grip of handcuffs encircle his wrists, a harsh prelude to the nightmare that ensued. The memory, fragmented and harrowing, surged forth with visceral intensity. He was dragged away, not to the sanctuary of reason and law, but into the shadowed depths of an undisclosed location, where the promise of interrogation twisted into the reality of torment. The staccato rhythm of his heartbeat thundered in his ears, drowning out the muffled sounds of his own pleas as unseen hands wielded pain with methodical precision. Each flash of agony sought to pry open the vaults of his mind, to extract truths that Alex himself could not grasp. This dark tableau of torture ebbed as suddenly as it had engulfed him, leaving behind a residue of fear so potent it threatened to fracture his already tenuous hold on reality.

Snap back to the sterile light of the interrogation room, the metallic chill of handcuffs still biting into his skin, a cruel reminder of the ordeal's lingering shadows. Detective Henderson stood just beyond the barrier of reinforced glass, her silhouette a silent sentinel. There was no dialogue, no exchange of words to bridge the gulf of understanding between them; only the weight of suspicion that filled the space with its oppressive silence.

The room itself was austere, devoid of any semblance of warmth or comfort. The harsh fluorescent lighting cast stark shadows, painting Alex's surroundings with a grim palette of grays and blacks. Every detail, from the unyielding hardness of the chair to the one-way mirror reflecting his haunted visage, seemed designed to disorient, to strip away layers of identity until nothing remained but the bare essence of guilt or innocence.

Outside, the world moved on, oblivious to the drama unfolding within these walls. Inside, Alex was subjected to a barrage of procedural formalities. Fingerprints were taken, each press of his skin against the cold ink pad a stark reminder of his precarious position. Photographs captured his image from every angle, the camera's flash searing his likeness into the official narrative of the night's events. The mundane act of cataloging his possessions felt like an erasure of his identity, each item logged and sealed away, leaving him feeling more like evidence than a man.

Intermittent glimpses of James Dawson's lifeless form haunted Alex, each flashback a visceral jolt that tethered him to the horror of the crime. The image of Dawson, so vivid and accusing in its silence, became a specter that haunted the periphery of his vision, blurring the lines between past and present, reality and nightmare.

As he was led away, Alex couldn't help but look back at the Dawsons' door. It felt like a line had been crossed in their home, changing everything. Maria Dawson's face, full of sadness and shock, stuck with him. Her look was a powerful reminder of how quickly life can change, marking the moment as a stark example of how close normal life is to something much darker. This brief look between them, filled with so much emotion, made the night's events even more real and heartbreaking.

As hours stretched into an indeterminate expanse of time, Alex sat in the interrogation room, a man suspended between the world he knew and one irrevocably altered by the night's events. Detective Henderson's presence outside, silent and inscrutable, offered no solace, only the stark realization that, in the eyes of the law, he was inexorably linked to a tragedy he could not remember, a suspect in a narrative he could not comprehend.

The procedural events unfolded with mechanical efficiency, each step further entrenching Alex in the role of the accused. The reality of his situation was inescapable, each moment in that room a tightening noose around the concept of his innocence. As the door finally opened, signaling the next phase of this Kafkaesque ordeal, Alex braced himself, the remnants of his resolve hardened by the ordeal. The interrogation, with its promise of answers and accusations, loomed ahead, a critical juncture on the path to uncovering the truth or cementing his fate.

Caught in the swirling currents of suspicion and incredulity, Alex became the unwitting centerpiece of a macabre scenario, cast as the lead in a story that defied understanding and challenge. Stripped of any recollection or rationale, he teetered on the brink of an unfathomable existence, grappling with the harrowing notion that the brutality that stalked his innermost thoughts could have breached the confines of his mind to materialize in a chillingly tangible form.

Without a thread of memory to cling to or a clear motive to claim, Alex faced the terrifying prospect that the shadows of aggression that had long lurked in the corners of his subconscious had somehow found their way into the physical world, leaving behind a scene as real as it was dreadful. This stark confrontation with a possibility so gruesome thrust him into a realm of confusion and fear, where the lines between imagined nightmares and stark reality blurred, leaving him stranded in a nightmarish limbo that threatened to consume him whole.

Within the sterile confines of the interrogation room, under the unwavering gaze of law enforcement, Alex found himself ensnared in a constrictive cocoon of circumstance and suspicion. His hands were cuffed securely to the arms of the chair, an unyielding metal grasp that rendered him immobile, a physical manifestation of his current predicament. This stark restraint served as a constant, tangible reminder of his precarious position—trapped, both physically by the cuffs that bound him and metaphorically by the web of evidence and unanswered questions that ensnared him.

Confronted with the monumental task of dissecting the complex tapestry of events that had led to that night's horrors, Alex grappled with the elusive truth that danced just beyond the reach of his comprehension. The reality of the situation lay hidden within the murky depths of his own psyche, a labyrinth rife with shadowed corridors of memory and mirages of recollection that mocked his attempts at navigation.

As he sat, immobilized by the cold steel that encircled his wrists, the weight of his situation pressed down upon him with crushing intensity. Was he simply a bystander, caught in the tumultuous wake of his own fragmented psyche, or was he indeed the mastermind behind the gruesome tableau that had been laid bare in the apartment above his own? This internal struggle, a ceaseless battle between the perceived innocence of his intentions and the potential darkness of actions unremembered, tormented him.

In this moment of profound isolation, the line between victim and perpetrator blurred, leaving Alex adrift in a sea of uncertainty. The paradox of his own identity—a man cleaved in two by the schism between reality and perception—loomed large, a riddle wrapped in the enigma of a night shrouded in shadows.

Chapter 6: Fragmented Investigations

The interrogation room felt cold and unwelcoming, lit by harsh fluorescent lights that flickered occasionally, casting odd shadows across the room. This was where Detective Laura Henderson faced her newest puzzle: Alex Bennett. He sat across from her, seemingly calm but with a hint of restlessness in his movements. His answers jumped from one topic to another, making it hard to follow his train of thought.

"Mr. Bennett," Detective Henderson started, her tone striving for an even, professional cadence as she leaned forward slightly in an attempt to bridge the gap between them. She sought to capture Alex's gaze; a man seemingly adrift in his own tumultuous sea of thoughts. "Can you tell me exactly where you were last night?" she prodded, not just for an answer but to gently reel him back from the edge of his own world. Without waiting for the confusion to settle in his eyes, she pressed on, her voice now tinged with a mix of professional duty and a hint of intrigue sparked by his previous, scattered answers. "Let's anchor ourselves in the now, Mr. Bennett. Leave aside Paris, Berlin, or any impending cities engulfed in flames. Focusing on last night, within the confines of this reality, what memories can you bring to the surface? What details linger in your mind?" Her question, aimed like a lifeline, was designed to coax him back from the precipice of his vast, tangled thoughts to the solid ground of the present moment.

Alex's fingers intertwined nervously, betraying the outward appearance of calm he attempted to project. "Last night," he began, his voice faltering as if each word navigated a maze of uncertainty. "There were voices, not singular but plural, a cacophony of whispers overlapping, interweaving, speaking of danger, of secrets buried deep beneath the city..." His voice tapered into a silence charged with tension, an echo of the confusion that seemed to grip him. Almost as quickly as the vulnerability appeared, it vanished as Alex's eyes, which had flickered towards Detective Henderson and then skittered away as if direct eye contact was an unbearable intensity, found focus again. "I was at home," he corrected himself after a heavy pause, the lines on his forehead deepening as he sifted through the fog of his recollections. "But it felt like I was elsewhere, somewhere distant, beyond the confines of my apartment." A visible struggle played across his face, a tug-of-war between confusion and clarity, until suddenly, his expression smoothed into a mask of certainty. "No, I was definitely at home. Reading," he concluded, the fleeting glimpses of clarity and disarray painting a complex portrait of a man wrestling with the elusive nature of his own memories.

Detective Henderson observed the fluctuation in Alex's tone, a journey from uncertainty to conviction and then back into the realm of doubt. It was akin to witnessing someone traverse a labyrinth within their own thoughts, each twist and turn marked by a change in his voice. Beside her, Detective Jameson, who until that moment had maintained a posture of silent skepticism, shifted his attention more directly towards Alex. Leaning forward, interest piqued by the latest revelation, he interjected, "Voices? Mr. Bennett, were these individuals you're familiar with? Were they physically present with you?" This question, poised between curiosity and investigative probing, sought to peel back another layer of the enigmatic narrative that Alex was struggling to convey.

Alex's reply came tinged with a mixture of introspection and perplexity, his gaze drifting towards some unseen horizon only he could discern. "No, not physically with me, not in the tangible sense you're implying," he elaborated, the words seeming to catch and drag, as if he were pulling them from a deep, obscured well within himself. "They're like whispers, ethereal and elusive, emanating from the fringes, from the barely perceptible fissures in what we collectively agree to call reality. These voices, they oscillate between being my wardens and my guides, sowing seeds of guidance mingled with disarray in my mind." His hands, previously intertwined in a display of nervous tension, now moved with a slight, almost imperceptible tremor, tracing patterns on the table as if to outline the source of these spectral murmurings. The room, already charged with the undercurrents of unsolved mysteries, seemed to contract around his words, lending a weight to the air that made each breath feel like an inhalation of deeper truths, or perhaps, deeper illusions.

The detectives shared another glance, their eyes communicating a silent dialogue that spoke volumes of their growing unease. In the realm of their professional experience, the concrete evidence and logical sequences of criminal behavior were familiar territories, domains they navigated with confidence and acumen. However, the path that Alex Bennett was charting through his disjointed narrative ventured far beyond these bounds, into the murky waters of psychological complexity and the shadowy nuances of potential mental health concerns. This unspoken exchange between Detective Henderson and Detective Jameson was fraught with the recognition of their venture into uncharted territory—a realm where the signposts of motive and rationale were obscured by the mists of the mind.

Detective Henderson's eyebrows knitted slightly, a subtle indicator of her concern, not just for the integrity of their investigation but for the well-being of the man before them, whose reality seemed fragmented by unseen forces. Detective Jameson's posture shifted almost imperceptibly, leaning slightly forward, his skepticism tempered by a growing awareness of the depth and intricacy of the psychological labyrinth they were being asked to navigate. In this moment, their shared glance was not merely an exchange of professional assessment but a mutual acknowledgment of the delicate balance they needed to maintain—pursuing the truth of the crime while navigating the delicate psyche of a man whose experience of reality was profoundly disjointed. This interplay of glances, brief yet laden with meaning, underscored the complexity of the task at hand, blending the rigor of detective work with the nuanced understanding required to tread the fine line between investigation and empathy.

Henderson, with a practiced patience that betrayed none of her internal concern, sought to steer the interrogation towards the solid ground of tangible evidence and credible witness testimony. Despite her efforts, the gap between the ethereal world Alex described and the concrete details required for their investigation seemed to stretch further with each exchange. Her voice, steady and imbued with a professional insistence, pierced the strange fog of Alex's narrative. "Mr. Bennett," she pressed on, her words sharpened by the necessity of clarity, "despite these whispers or visions you speak of, our investigation demands something more substantial. According to multiple witnesses, you were seen entering the Dawsons' apartment on the night in question. How can you account for your presence there?"

Her question hung in the air, a bridge between the realms of the intangible and the evidentiary. The room, with its sterile light and oppressive silence, seemed to contract around them, focusing the entirety of its attention on Alex's response. Henderson's posture, a subtle alignment of determination and inquiry, mirrored her approach—direct yet open, ready to navigate through the maze of Alex's recounting towards a truth that remained shrouded in ambiguity.

Alex's reaction to her query was a complex interplay of emotions and cognition, his face a canvas where doubt, realization, and the struggle for recall played out in fleeting expressions. For a moment, he appeared to sift through the layers of his fractured memories, searching for a strand of reality that could connect him to the tangible world of evidence and alibis that Henderson inhabited.

The detective watched him closely, her gaze not just analytical but tinged with a hint of empathy for the man caught in the throes of his own bewildering experiences. This moment, a delicate balance between the pursuit of justice and the human complexities of the mind, underscored the unique challenges of their profession—navigating the murky waters where human psychology and criminal evidence intersect, each clue a steppingstone towards understanding the unfathomable.

Alex's sigh filled the sparse interrogation room, a tangible manifestation of his inner turmoil. The sound was heavy, resonating with the fatigue of a man burdened not just by the situation at hand but by the constant battle within his own mind. "Detective," he began, his voice tinged with a deep-seated weariness, "I wish... I truly wish I could lay out a clear, linear account of my movements for you. But the fabric of my reality isn't so easily stitched together. It's more akin to a tapestry fraying at the edges, threads coming loose and patterns becoming obscured."

He paused, collecting his thoughts as if they were tangible objects that could escape if not held tightly. "I remember ascending those stairs, each step fueled by an impulse that seemed to bypass rational thought—a compulsion that gripped me, pulling me towards an unknown fate. And then, there was nothing. A darkness enveloped me, a void where time and sense lost all meaning." Alex's hands gestured vaguely, mimicking the ebb and flow of his fractured recollections.

His gaze, previously unfocused, sharpened as he continued. "But it was the aftermath, the stark, gruesome clarity of stumbling upon... upon that scene." The words seemed to catch in his throat, the memory of James Dawson's lifeless body a vivid image that refused to be dimmed by the mists of confusion. "It was as if I was abruptly wrenched from the void into a reality too harsh, too brutal to comprehend fully."

The detectives observed Alex closely, noting the fluctuation in his tone, the way his hands moved with his narrative, painting a picture of a mind grappling with the slippery nature of perception and memory. The room itself, with its clinical austerity, seemed to press in on them, a silent observer to the unfolding drama of a man trying to navigate the fragmented corridors of his consciousness, searching for a truth that remained just out of reach.

The atmosphere in the interrogation room seemed to thicken, charged with the heavy silence that followed Alex's account. Detective Laura Henderson, with years of experience dissecting the most convoluted of criminal minds, felt an unfamiliar sense of disorientation. It was as if the very air had become saturated with the complexities and contradictions of Alex's narrative, making it difficult to breathe, to think with the clarity that her profession demanded.

Around her, the sparse furnishings of the room—the stark table, the unyielding chairs, the harsh fluorescent lights overhead—suddenly seemed oppressive, as though they too were bearing witness to a puzzle that defied easy resolution. The pieces of the story that Alex had laid out before them, each one imbued with its own peculiar weight and texture, refused to come together into a coherent whole. Instead, they floated in the space between the detective and the suspect, tantalizingly out of reach, obscured by the dense fog that seemed to have settled over Alex's recollections.

Detective Henderson leaned back in her chair, the motion slow and deliberate, as she attempted to marshal her thoughts. Her gaze lingered on Alex, observing the subtle shifts in his expression, the way his hands now lay still on the table, as if they too had given up on trying to articulate the inarticulable. Beside her, Detective Jameson remained silent, his presence a steady constant, yet even he seemed to be grappling with the unsettling undercurrents of the conversation.

In her mind, Henderson replayed the fragments of Alex's testimony, searching for a foothold, a point of entry that might allow her to penetrate the veil of confusion and reach the bedrock of truth beneath. Yet, the more she pondered, the more elusive any sense of understanding became. It was as if Alex's reality, fractured and refracted through the prism of his disturbed psyche, had become a mirror maze, reflecting back at her a multitude of distorted images, none of which she could trust to be true.

The silence stretched on, becoming a palpable entity in the room, a testament to the complexity of the human mind and the mysteries it could harbor. Detective Henderson realized then that this was no ordinary interrogation. It was a journey into the unknown, a tentative exploration of the shadowy realms that lay at the edges of consciousness. The challenge before her was not just to solve a crime, but to navigate the labyrinthine pathways of a mind in turmoil, to find a way through the fog that enshrouded Alex's memories and, perhaps, to discover the truth that lay hidden within.

In the quiet of the interrogation room, as Detective Henderson pondered the depths they were delving into, the evidence collected from Alex's apartment was brought in, each item a tangible piece of the puzzle they were desperately trying to solve. The transition from the intangible, from Alex's fragmented recollections and the psychological expedition they necessitated, to the physical evidence of his life outside the interrogation room was stark. It was as if they were crossing a bridge from the realm of the mind to the realm of the material, where every object could potentially offer a clue, a connection, a way to anchor the ethereal whispers of Alex's narrative to the solid ground of reality. Yet, as Henderson looked over the items, the bridge seemed to waver, the connection between mind and matter not as straightforward as hoped. The challenge was not merely to interpret the physical evidence but to weave it into the complex tapestry of Alex's mental landscape, to find the points where the tangible and the intangible met, where the mystery of the Dawson family's tragedy and the enigma of Alex Bennett's psyche intertwined.

The contents of Alex's apartment laid out before the detectives formed a mosaic of enigma and peculiarity. An array of keys, each belonging to no known door within the vicinity, hinted at passages to hidden or forbidden places, or perhaps they were merely symbolic, representing access to the locked away corners of Alex's psyche. Scattered across the cluttered space were notes, penned in a cipher that defied immediate decoding, suggesting secrets so profound or dangerous they required concealment even from the casual observer.

Among these items, the drawings stood out with particular intrigue. They depicted machines of a complexity and design that bordered on the fantastical, machines that could not exist in the known laws of physics and engineering. These were not the idle doodles of a bored tenant but the deliberate creations of a mind that seemed to operate within a different realm of possibility.

Each piece of evidence, when considered individually, appeared as a curiosity, an oddity that might be dismissed as the product of an eccentric mind. Yet, taken together, they wove a narrative that suggested Alex's reality was one dramatically divergent from the norm, a world where the lines between the possible and the impossible were not just blurred but altogether erased.

Detective Henderson found herself pondering the implications of these findings. Was Alex a genius ensnared by his own intellect, crafting a world beyond the understanding of those around him? Or were these artifacts the detritus of a mind losing its grasp on the anchors of reality, adrift in a sea of delusion and fantasy?

The evidence from the apartment, rather than providing clarity, only served to deepen the mystery, painting a picture of a man who lived at the edge of reality, where the mundane and the extraordinary intertwined in ways that defied easy explanation. The challenge for the detectives was not only to decipher the physical evidence before them but to bridge the chasm between their own understanding of the world and the unfathomable depths of Alex's mind.

The interrogation room, heavy with the tension of unanswered questions, became a crucible where fact and fiction seemed to merge. Detective Henderson, her skepticism tempered by a growing intrigue, found herself pondering the labyrinthine tale spun by Alex Bennett. His account, a patchwork of reality and illusion, challenged the very framework of their investigation.

As Henderson and her partner, Detective Jameson, exchanged glances, a silent conversation unfolded between them. Their years of experience had taught them to seek the truth in the weave of lies, to find the thread that led to clarity. Yet, Alex's story, with its seamless stitching of disparate realities, presented a new kind of puzzle.

"Could there be a kernel of truth amidst the fantasy?" Henderson mused, her gaze lingering on Alex, who sat before them, a figure at once pitiable and perplexing. His testimony had traversed the realms of time and space, touching on truths known only to him. Yet, in the maze of his narrative, could there lie a path to the heart of the mystery surrounding the Dawson family's tragedy?

Jameson, ever the pragmatist, remained unconvinced. "Or perhaps we're being led on a wild goose chase, chasing shadows instead of evidence," he countered, his voice a grounding force in the room's speculative atmosphere.

The detectives were left at a crossroads, between the tangible evidence that painted Alex as a suspect and the ethereal clues that suggested something beyond their comprehension. The interrogation had opened more doors than it closed, leaving them to wonder if the answers they sought were hidden in the conventional corners of motive and opportunity or if they lay somewhere along the uncharted borders of Alex's fractured reality.

As they prepared to conclude the session, both detectives were acutely aware that the investigation had taken an unexpected turn. The path forward was obscured, shrouded in the mysteries of a mind that defied easy understanding. The question that hung in the air, unspoken but palpable, was whether the key to solving the Dawson family's murder lay locked within Alex's enigmatic mind or if the true solution was grounded in the mundane world they knew all too well.

The interrogation room, silent now save for the hum of the fluorescent lights, felt like a stage upon which a drama of the human psyche had been played out. For Henderson and Jameson, the challenge was not only to decipher Alex's testimony but to navigate the shadowy terrain it had revealed, where the boundaries between truth and deception, sanity and madness, were blurred. As they stepped out into the corridor, the weight of the unsolved case rested heavily upon them, a reminder of the complex web of human motives and mysteries they had pledged to unravel.

Detective Henderson, her determination unwavering, faced Alex with a steely gaze. "This isn't the end, Mr. Bennett. We'll keep digging, untangling this web until the truth comes to light," she asserted, her statement not just a vow to solve the case but an assurance that they would navigate through the complexity, the ambiguity, to shed light on the darkness that enveloped the Dawson family's murder.

Alex offered a nod, his face a canvas of mixed emotions—resignation shadowed by a barely perceptible spark of hope. As the detectives withdrew from the sterile confines of the interrogation room, abandoning him to the oppressive silence punctuated only by the sporadic flicker of overhead lights, the complexity of the investigation stretched out before them, resembling a vast, uncharted expanse. The way forward remained veiled in ambiguity, riddled with psychological complexities and pivotal evidentiary decisions that would demand their utmost attention. Laura Henderson, however, was undaunted by the daunting intricacies of the case. There was a determined glint in her eye—a silent proclamation of her unwavering commitment to piercing through the layers of confusion and ambiguity that shrouded the truth. The Dawson family's cry for justice echoed in the silence, and she was determined to answer that call, no matter how convoluted the path to uncovering the truth might be.

In that moment, Alex felt the weight of Henderson's unspoken accusation—a heavy gaze that seemed to probe the depths of his soul, seeking the guilt that she seemed convinced lay buried within. His own mind, a turmoil of conflicting emotions and fragmented memories, seemed to betray him, flitting between coherence and a maddening sense of disarray. With every flicker of the fluorescent lights, his thoughts spiraled further into a vortex of doubt and self-questioning. Had his presence at the scene, his fragmented recollections, inadvertently woven a narrative of guilt around him? The uncertainty was suffocating, a thick fog through which he struggled to find clarity or absolution.

Chapter 7: An Alarming Pattern

Immersed in an oppressive darkness, Alex found himself in the confines of his small, cluttered apartment, the only light emanating from the dim glow of streetlamps filtering through the thin curtains. Surrounded by walls that seemed to close in on him, the room was filled with the echoes of his ragged breaths, the occasional distant siren, and the persistent drip of a leaky faucet—a soundtrack to his isolation. His body was perched on the edge of a threadbare sofa, hands clasped tightly together as if to hold himself in one piece, his eyes staring into the void that had enveloped him. The air was thick, charged with an electric current of anticipation and dread, as if the very atmosphere was waiting for the dam within him to break.

Alex's heart raced, its rapid beats a stark counterpoint to the room's oppressive silence, each thud reverberating against the walls like a drumbeat of his inner turmoil. With every heartbeat, he teetered on the edge of understanding, grappling with the tantalizing fragments of clarity that occasionally pierced his confusion. Yet, for each fleeting moment of comprehension, there was an overwhelming sense of being utterly lost, as if he stood on the brink of an abyss, the ground crumbling beneath his feet.

The fear that gripped him was palpable, a living entity that seemed to wrap its cold fingers around his throat, threatening to drag him into the darkness that clouded his mind. It whispered promises of oblivion, of an end to the ceaseless storm of emotions that tormented him, yet a part of Alex rebelled against the seductive call of despair. Deep within, a flicker of hope persisted, stubborn and defiant, a beacon urging him to fight for the sliver of light that might dispel the shadows obscuring his past.

His surroundings, a cluttered apartment that had become his refuge and prison, mirrored the chaos that reigned within him. The detritus of his life lay scattered around—the papers covered in frantic, indecipherable scribbles that seemed to mock his search for answers, photographs of people with averted gazes, as if ashamed of the stories they could tell. Each object was a reminder of a life half-lived, a story half-told, suspended in the limbo of his fragmented memories.

The air itself seemed thick with the residue of his broken dreams, each breath a reminder of what had been lost. The dust of years lay heavy on surfaces untouched by care, mingling with the acrid bite of despair that hung in the air like a noxious fog. This scent, the olfactory hallmark of his isolation, had seeped into the very fabric of the place, a constant companion in his solitary confinement within these four walls.

In this space, where the past and present collided in a tumultuous dance, Alex found himself at war with his own mind. The room, with its chaotic sprawl of personal artifacts, stood as a testament to the battle being waged—a battle for understanding, for redemption, for a semblance of peace in the storm that raged within. It was here, in this arena of his own making, that Alex faced his greatest challenge: to confront the demons of his past and forge a path through the darkness towards the uncertain light of truth.

As Alex sat, a solitary figure dwarfed by the shadows that danced upon the walls, the barrier between the present and the past began to thin. Memories, those elusive specters, began to coalesce from the darkness, each one a fleeting glimpse into a life that seemed both intimately his and profoundly alien. They came to him not as a gentle flow but as a deluge, breaking over him with the force of a tidal wave, leaving him gasping for breath, for sanity, for anything that might anchor him to reality.

Yet, within this storm of recollection and emotion, there was a thread of something else—something that whispered of truths yet uncovered, of stories yet to be told. It was this whisper that held him captive, a siren call beckoning him deeper into the abyss of his own mind, urging him to confront the phantoms that lurked within the darkness. As the first of these phantoms emerged from the void, Alex braced himself, a soldier at the precipice of battle, knowing that the war for his soul was about to begin anew.

In the midst of his confusion and fear, Alex sensed something else stirring—a faint glimmer of something deeper, like a buried secret trying to surface. This faint glimmer was like a distant call, drawing him further into the depths of his own psyche, urging him to face the shadows that danced at the edges of his memory. As he prepared to confront these shadows, Alex felt both dread and a strange sense of readiness. The echoes of past conflicts were about to resurface, bringing with them the pain and the possibility of understanding.

In the chill of the winter afternoon, Alex stood, isolated in the center of a makeshift arena formed by his classmates. Their breaths formed clouds of mist in the cold air, each puff punctuated by laughter and jeers that sliced through the wintry silence like shards of ice. The boy who dared confront him, a known bully with a sneer permanently etched into his features, advanced. His taunts sliced through the cold air, each word a barb designed to wound. "What's the matter, Alex? Too scared to fight back?" the bully jeered, his voice loud enough to draw the attention of even those lingering on the playground's fringes. "Come on, show us what you're made of, or are you just a coward?"

The playground, a desolate field of frostbitten grass and skeletal trees, stood as a silent arena for this winter confrontation. The circle of children, their breath fogging in the crisp air, tightened around Alex and his antagonist, a living barrier fueled by anticipation and the thrill of impending conflict. Wrapped snugly in their coats, they were a chorus of instigation, their youthful voices blending into a singular chant of provocation.

"Fight! Fight! Fight!" they chanted, rhythmically pushing the situation towards its inevitable boiling point. The bully, emboldened by the crowd's support, stepped closer, his face a mask of mock concern. "Aw, is little Alex gonna cry? Can't handle a bit of fun?"

Alex's fists clenched at his sides, his jaw set in a line of rising fury. The circle of onlookers, their faces eager and expectant, seemed to close in further, the space between him and the bully shrinking under the weight of their anticipation. The cold, which had been a mere background discomfort, now seemed to seep into his very bones, a chill that matched the icy fear and burning anger that warred within him.

In that moment, the playground transformed from a place of innocent play into an arena of judgment, the barren trees and frost-covered ground bearing witness to a scene as old as time—the trial by combat, where words give way to fists, and the currency of respect is the willingness to stand one's ground. Amidst the jeers and taunts, Alex felt a surge of defiance, a refusal to be cowed by the bully's words or the crowd's expectation. It was this defiance, fueled by a mixture of pride and primal instinct, that propelled him forward, out of the circle of spectators and into the annals of playground legend.

Alex, for a moment, felt as if he were outside his own body, observing the scene from a distance. The laughter echoed in his ears, a discordant symphony that fueled a rising tide of anger within him. With a suddenness that surprised even himself, he lashed out, his fists moving with a life of their own. The impact of his blows, muffled by the bully's winter jacket, felt distant, as if he were punching through water.

"Alex! What has gotten into you?" one teacher exclaimed as they made their way through the throng of children, their breath visible in the chilly air.

"Enough of this nonsense, both of you!" another added sternly, her hands firmly grasping Alex's shoulder, pulling him back as the crowd began to disperse, their excitement dampened by the arrival of authority.

The bully, now standing a safe distance away, wore a smirk that seemed to infuriate Alex even more, but the teacher's grip ensured he could not act on his impulse. "He started it," Alex muttered under his breath, a futile attempt to deflect some of the blame, his eyes darting from the teacher's disapproving gaze to the ground below.

"We saw what happened, Alex. This isn't like you," the teacher responded, her tone softening slightly, sensing the turmoil behind Alex's flushed face. "You're better than this. Let's talk about what led up to this, okay?"

But Alex was far away, the teacher's words barely piercing the fog of his adrenaline and shock. His fists remained clenched, as if holding onto the fight was his only anchor in the storm of emotions that threatened to engulf him. The sound of the other kids' voices, now a mix of whispers and fading laughter as they returned to their games, seemed like a distant echo, a reminder of the normalcy that had been so abruptly shattered.

The incident, though quickly resolved by the teachers' intervention, left a lingering tension in the air, a palpable reminder of the fine line between playground antics and the deeper, more complex battles being fought within Alex. As he was led away, his steps reluctant, the playground resumed its usual rhythm, but for Alex, the echoes of the confrontation would resonate far longer, a stark testament to the battle between the person he was expected to be and the person he feared he might become.

In the aftermath, as the crowd dispersed, leaving behind only the trampled snow and the lingering echo of their jeers, Alex felt a profound sense of disconnection. The anger that had consumed him moments before now seemed like a stranger's emotion, leaving him to wonder at the force that had possessed him. He stood alone in the fading light, the cold seeping through his clothes, a sense of isolation wrapping around him as tightly as the winter air.

Suddenly, Alex was transported back to his adolescence, a period marked by rebellion and inner chaos. He found himself in the confined space of his bathroom, facing the mirror that had always felt more like an adversary than a reflection. The face staring back at him was one he recognized but couldn't fully accept as his own, its calmness at odds with the storm raging inside him.

The air was thick with tension, every surface in the bathroom echoing back his rapid, uneven breaths. In a moment that seemed suspended in time, a surge of despair washed over him. It was as if the mirror held not just his reflection but the weight of expectations and self-doubt he could no longer bear. With a sudden, impulsive fury, his hand shot out, the mirror cracking with an almost surreal clarity, spiderwebs of glass spreading from the point of impact.

The sound of shattering glass reverberated through the small room, a violent release of pent-up emotions. Alex stared at the broken mirror, each fragment reflecting a piece of him, disjointed and distorted. Blood dripped from his hand, the sharp sting of it barely registering over the tumult of his thoughts. He watched the droplets fall, their crimson stark against the white of the sink, a visceral reminder of the moment's reality.

For a brief instant, the world seemed to narrow to the space between him and the remnants of the mirror, each shard a testament to his inner conflict. He was detached from the pain, from the sight of his own blood, caught in a vortex of alienation and self-recrimination. The mirror, now a kaleidoscope of broken images, seemed to mock him with its disarray, a mirror to the chaos he felt within.

As he stood there, the aftermath of his action settling around him like dust, Alex was engulfed in a profound sense of isolation. The shattered mirror, with its jagged edges and scattered pieces, was a stark, physical echo of his splintered sense of self, a visual echo of the fractures that ran deep through his psyche.

Yet, this act of defiance, this momentary escape, offered no true solace. The shattered mirror, now a kaleidoscope of broken reflections, served only to underscore the multiplicity of his inner turmoil. Each shard reflected a fraction of his face, a fragment of the self he could neither fully understand nor accept. The bleeding from his hand, though superficial, marked a deeper wound within—a scar upon his psyche, emblematic of the internal battles that raged unchecked. In the silence that followed the mirror's demise, amidst the sharp echoes of his own distress, Alex confronted the undeniable truth that the pieces scattered before him were a mirror in their own right, reflecting the complexity of a soul fractured by its own unresolved conflicts and the elusive quest for a wholeness that seemed perpetually just out of reach.

The darkness seemed to pulse around him, a living entity that breathed unease into the night. Alex found himself in an alleyway, the shadows stretching long and sinister from the few sputtering streetlights. His own shadow merged with the darkness, a part of the night itself, as he faced the indistinct figure before him. The details of this other were blurred, as if smeared by the damp, heavy air that hung between them, thick with anticipation.

Words were exchanged, their exact nature lost to the whirlwind of emotions that engulfed Alex. The dialogue, if it could be called that, was charged with an undercurrent of anger and fear, a prelude to the inevitable clash. The air felt charged, electric, as if the very atmosphere anticipated the forthcoming eruption of violence.

And then, without warning, the tension broke. The confrontation, brief yet intense, unfolded with a violence that seemed at odds with the silent, shadowy world they inhabited. Movements were swift, almost frantic, a dance of shadows and echoes in the confined space of the alley. The sound of flesh meeting flesh, a symphony of desperation and defiance, filled the air, a stark contrast to the oppressive silence that had preceded it.

As quickly as it had begun, the altercation ended. Alex stood alone, panting, the other figure now nothing more than a heap at his feet. The sudden return to silence was jarring, the echo of their clash hanging in the air like a question left unanswered. Alex's heart hammered in his chest, a relentless reminder of the violence he had partaken in.

Yet, even as he stood there, the details of the encounter began to slip away, like water through clenched fists. The identity of his adversary, the cause of their conflict, even the outcome—all were lost to the shadows from which they had sprung. The alleyway, with its damp cobblestones and looming walls, seemed to swallow the event whole, leaving Alex with nothing but the lingering taste of adrenaline and a deep, unsettling sense of disquiet.

The darkness closed in once more, a curtain drawn over the scene, leaving Alex to wonder at the reality of the encounter. Was it a memory, a dream, or something else entirely? The only certainty was the solitude that enveloped him now, as complete and impenetrable as the night that hid the alleyway from prying eyes.

The scream echoed in his mind, a harrowing reminder of a past shrouded in shadows. Lying in the darkness, Alex's heart thudded heavily against his chest, each beat echoing the distress of the cry that had shattered his sleep. The room around him felt oppressively silent in the aftermath, as if the very walls were holding their breath, waiting for what would come next.

Confusion clouded his thoughts as he struggled to distinguish between the remnants of a nightmare and the haunting specter of reality. The scream had felt so real, so immediate, yet now there was nothing but the oppressive silence and the rapid beat of his own heart. Slowly, a memory began to surface through the fog of confusion—a memory of another night, one that bore the weight of truth and the stain of guilt.

He remembered the heat of anger, the kind that simmers and grows until it consumes all reason and compassion. There had been words, harsh and unforgiving, that escalated into a confrontation fraught with tension. And then, the release of that pent-up fury, a moment where control slipped through his fingers like sand, giving way to an outburst that left nothing but regret in its wake.

But as quickly as the memory surfaced, it slipped away, leaving Alex grappling with the ambiguity of his own past. The details of that night, the identity of the person who had borne the brunt of his wrath, even the reason behind the altercation—all faded into the recesses of his mind, as elusive and intangible as the shadows that danced at the edge of his vision.

The scream, whether a remnant of a dream or a ghost from his past, left Alex with a profound sense of unease. It was a reminder of the potential for violence that lurked within him, a dark counterpart to the person he believed himself to be. As the night stretched on, endless and immutable, Alex lay awake, wrestling with the duality of his nature and the unsettling possibility that the capacity for harm was an integral part of his being.

As the echoes of these fragmented memories faded back into the dark corners of his mind, Alex found himself ensnared in a web of confusion and introspection. The unfolding narrative of his life, as revealed through these sudden, jarring flashbacks, painted a picture of intermittent aggression, each instance brief in duration but profound in its impact.

The episodes, though vivid, left behind a trail of ambiguity, their aftermath shrouded in the mists of uncertainty, their true motives obscured by the fog of time.

Striving for clarity in the chaos of his thoughts, Alex attempted to piece together the disjointed chapters of his past. Each memory, a fleeting glimpse into moments of unbridled anger, seemed to form a pattern—a mosaic of emotional outbursts that hinted at a deeper, more volatile undercurrent within him. Yet, as he delved deeper, seeking answers in the fragmented tableau of his recollections, the narrative remained elusive, the pieces of the puzzle refusing to coalesce into a coherent whole.

The pattern that emerged was one of potential violence, a series of snapshots that suggested a capacity for aggression lurking beneath the surface. However, the evidence of his own guilt, the tangible proof of culpability in these scattered episodes of anger, remained tantalizingly out of reach. The memories themselves, while rich in emotional detail, offered no clear verdict, no definitive confirmation of wrongdoing.

In this labyrinth of half-remembered moments and unresolved questions, Alex found himself at a crossroads. The more he sought to understand the nature of his past outbursts, the more elusive the truth became, a mirage in the desert of his psyche.

The possibility of violence, implied by the very pattern of his memories, cast a shadow over his sense of self, leaving him to wonder if the fragments of recollection that haunted him were mere phantoms of his imagination or harbingers of a hidden truth yet to be uncovered.

As the vestiges of his past receded, leaving behind a tangled mess of emotion and speculation, Alex was confronted with the profound uncertainty of his own narrative. The search for clarity had only deepened the enigma, the clarity he yearned for remaining an intangible specter, just beyond the grasp of his outstretched fingers.

The question loomed large in Alex's troubled mind, casting long shadows over his quest for understanding. Was he the mastermind behind the acts hinted at by these fragmented recollections? Or were these memories simply the fevered imaginings of a psyche in distress, a soul in turmoil seeking redemption for transgressions it couldn't quite grasp? This internal struggle propelled Alex towards a precipice, beyond which lay a realm of darkness more profound than the abyss from which his memories sporadically surfaced. It was a path fraught with peril, leading him into the depths of his own conscience, where the distinction between perpetrator and prey blurred into obscurity, obscured by the fog of his own uncertainty.

As he stood at the edge, peering into the murky depths of his own psyche, Alex felt the weight of his unresolved past pressing down upon him. The flashbacks, each a jigsaw piece of a puzzle he was desperately trying to solve, seemed to both illuminate and obfuscate the truth of his nature. Could it be that within him resided the potential for violence, a shadow self-capable of actions that his conscious mind recoiled from? Or were these memories mere phantoms, specters of a disturbed mind grappling with guilt and confusion over deeds imagined rather than committed?

This journey into the heart of his own mystery was not just a search for answers but a confrontation with the very essence of his identity. With each step forward, the path seemed to twist and turn, leading him further into a labyrinth where echoes of his past mingled with the specters of doubt and fear. The quest for clarity became a voyage into uncharted territories of the soul, where the line separating the victim from the villain wavered like a candle flame in the dark, casting an ever-changing interplay of light and shadow upon the walls of his inner sanctum.

In this twilight realm of self-examination, Alex found himself wrestling with the duality of his own nature, caught in a dance with shadows that mirrored the complexities of the human heart. It was a dance that offered no easy answers, only the promise of deeper revelations to come. Each glimpse into the recesses of his memory, each flicker of insight, served to deepen the mystery, weaving a tapestry of questions that beckoned him ever onward, into the heart of darkness where the true nature of his soul awaited discovery.

Chapter 8: Worlds Collide

In the subdued aftermath of the calamity that had unsettled the small apartment complex, a whispering undercurrent of doubt and unrest threaded its way through the corridors, as palpable as the cold draft that occasionally seeped under the doors. Amid this atmosphere of whispered speculations and shadowed glances, Clara Jenkins emerged as a particularly distinct figure—a beacon of continuity in an environment rife with transient shadows. Her association with the building, marked by the passage of countless seasons, rendered her almost a part of its very structure, a living testament to its history.

Clara, ensconced in the familiar confines of her modest living space, surrounded by the tangible memories of years gone by, presented a portrait of understated permanence. Her appearance, marked by the gentle wear of age, carried the subtle signs of a life measured in experiences rather than years. Her hair, silvered by time, was invariably drawn back in a simple, unassuming style, the soft wisps framing her face lending her an air of approachable wisdom. The lines etched upon her visage spoke of laughter, sorrow, and the myriad expressions in between, each a silent storyteller of the chapters of her life.

Her attire, consistently unpretentious and practical, seemed a deliberate choice for comfort over fashion, often consisting of plain, well-worn garments that hinted at a preference for simplicity and routine. This subtle repetition in her wardrobe—a palette of muted colors and uncomplicated patterns—suggested a life of minimal change, a routine existence that mirrored the unchanging nature of her surroundings. Yet, to the observant eye, this consistency also whispered of something more, a veiled clue to the depths of Clara's connection to the world around her, perhaps indicative of a reality perceived differently from those around her.

Clara's mannerisms, a blend of deliberate movements and serene gestures, conveyed a sense of quiet contemplation. Her voice, when she spoke, carried the richness of age, imbued with a timbre that was both comforting and authoritative, its cadence a gentle echo in the stillness of her apartment. The air around her was suffused with the faint, comforting scent of lavender and old paper—a combination of her preferred soap and the omnipresent books that lined her shelves, each tome a silent guardian of her solitude.

As she engaged with Detective Henderson, Clara's demeanor was one of composed reflection, her hands occasionally folding and unfolding in her lap, a rhythm to her thoughts. The atmosphere of her home, marked by the soft, ambient sounds of a building long familiar with its inhabitants' rhythms, enveloped the conversation in a cocoon of introspective calm.

In this setting, Clara Jenkins recounted her observations and insights regarding Alex Bennett, her narrative weaving through the tapestry of past and present with a fluidity that mirrored the enigmatic subject of their discussion. To Detective Henderson, Clara presented a conundrum—a figure so intertwined with the fabric of the building and its history, yet suggesting, through subtle nuances and unspoken hints, a reality far more complex than the visible threads of her existence.

Clara, comfortably ensconced among cushions that had gently molded to the contours of countless moments spent in reflection, articulated her thoughts with the distinct lucidity that comes from decades of quiet, watchful living. "There's something about that boy, Alex, a certain unease that seems to cling to him," she began, her voice a blend of warmth and wistful concern, echoing softly in the room filled with the quiet companionship of her possessions. "He's like a ship caught in a relentless gale, invisible to all but him, perpetually tossed by waves unseen," she continued, her gaze drifting towards the window, as if expecting to catch a glimpse of Alex battling his unseen tempests right there on the street below.

"I remember, not too long ago, perhaps last spring or the one before, he helped me carry my groceries up these very stairs," Clara recounted, a small smile playing at the corners of her lips, the memory bringing a transient light to her eyes. "It was such a simple act, the kind of small kindness that's all too rare these days. Yet, it wasn't the action itself that imprinted upon my memory, but rather, the look in his eyes as he did it." She paused, searching for the words to encapsulate the complexity of that fleeting interaction. "There was a distance in his gaze, a sort of profound disquiet, as if his mind was navigating some far-off, stormy sea even as he stood there in my hallway, groceries in hand."

Her fingers traced the patterns on the fabric of the cushions, a tactile memory of textures that seemed to anchor her to the moment. "That brief encounter, it left an impression on me, you see. Beneath the veneer of his everyday politeness, there was a turbulence, a restless energy that seemed almost... out of place, out of time," she concluded, her words hanging in the air, imbued with a poignant blend of empathy and unspoken concern for the young man who, even in his attempts at normalcy, seemed perpetually ensnared by inner tumults.

Leaning forward, Clara's movement caused the old sofa to emit a soft, familiar creak, a sound as much a part of her home as the walls themselves. This slight adjustment in her position seemed to draw her closer into the narrative she wove, as if by narrowing the physical space between herself and Detective Henderson, she could bridge the gap between her observations and the detective's understanding. "And then there were the nights," she continued, her voice dropping to a near whisper, as though relaying a closely guarded secret, "when the quiet of the building was shattered by the sound of his restless movements. Back and forth he would pace, across the creaking floorboards of his apartment, each step a muted echo in the otherwise silent hours."

As Clara recounted her observations and insights about Alex Bennett, her narrative wove through past and present with the fluidity that mirrored the enigmatic subject of their discussion. Comfortably ensconced among cushions bearing the indents of many such reflections, she articulated her thoughts with a lucidity honed over decades of quiet observation. Her voice, a warm blend of concern and nostalgia, filled the room, complemented by the soft, ambient sounds of the building—a familiar backdrop to the introspective calm of her apartment.

"There's something about that boy, Alex," she began, her gaze momentarily wandering towards the window, as if in search of Alex's shadow. "A restlessness, a storm perpetually brewing within him, visible to none but him." She shared a memory of Alex assisting with her groceries—a simple act that left a profound impression not for the deed itself but for the distant turmoil she glimpsed in his eyes.

Her narrative paused as she glanced towards her bookshelf, a gesture seemingly inconsequential but laden with intent. A heavy tome, untouched for years and previously ensconced in the far corner of the shelf, now conspicuously lay upon her coffee table. Its presence, as inexplicable as the phantom arguments and restless wanderings of Alex, hinted at unseen disturbances mirroring those she attributed to the young man.

"And then there were the nights," Clara's voice dropped to a near-whisper, recounting episodes of Alex's restless movements and one-sided dialogues that filled the silence of the building. These narratives, punctuated by the creak of the old sofa as she leaned forward, bridged the gap between her observations and the detective's understanding, suggesting a deeper, shared turmoil between the observer and the observed.

Clara's observations extended beyond mere behavior, touching upon the unseen and unheard. She recounted how items within her own apartment seemed to shift inexplicably, mirrors reflecting unseen movements, and clocks that hinted at lost time—phenomena that resonated with the mysterious aura surrounding Alex.

As she delved into these peculiar occurrences, her narrative subtly shifted, blurring the lines between Alex's perceived reality and her own experiences.

This convergence of experiences, Clara's narrative suggested, might not be mere coincidence but a reflection of a deeper, interconnected mystery that enveloped both her and Alex—a mystery woven into the very fabric of the building and its history.

Her hands clasped together, fingers intertwining as she recalled the unease those nights brought. "He wasn't alone in those moments, or so it seemed," she added, a hint of mystery threading through her words. "Arguments would spill out into the stillness, his voice mingling with others that weren't there. To an outsider, it might've seemed like a simple case of talking to oneself, but there was an intensity to it, a fervor that suggested a dialogue with unseen entities."

Clara's eyes, reflecting a lifetime of witnessing human peculiarities, held a depth of concern as she described the disconcerting atmosphere those episodes created. "It was unsettling, the sheer force of the emotions involved. You could feel the tension, a tangible presence in the air, like the distant rumbles of a storm yet to break. Those walls of his, thin as they may be, contained worlds of turmoil, private tempests that raged unchecked and unseen."

She paused, letting the imagery of her words hang between them, a vivid painting of a young man ensnared in battles both internal and external. "One couldn't help but be put on edge by it, the sense of being an unwitting witness to a solitary struggle. It was as though the very fabric of the building became a reluctant confidant to his unrest, echoing back his words and footsteps in a somber chorus of shared solitude. The nights when his pacing ceased were almost as troubling as those filled with his restless wanderings, the silence left in their wake not a reprieve but a haunting reminder of the unseen conflicts that lay just beyond the reach of comprehension."

Clara's gaze shifted, drawn inexorably towards the window, her eyes narrowing as if attempting to pierce through the gathering twilight to discern shapes and movements in the shadows that none but she could see. "Oh, many's the time I've seen him, that boy Alex, standing there by his window," she remarked, a reflective note in her voice as she pondered the scenes she had witnessed. "He'd be so still, so utterly absorbed, that you'd swear he was a statue, save for the occasional twitch or nod, as if in response to a voice only he could hear."

Her fingers traced a pattern on the armrest of her chair, a subconscious mimicry of the watchful vigil Alex held at his window. "There was a kind of intensity in his gaze, a focus that seemed to stretch far beyond the confines of our little street. It was as though he was on the lookout for something, or someone. Or maybe," she mused, her tone dipping into speculation, "he was haunted by the specter of an event that had left its mark on him, tethering him to that spot with chains made not of iron, but of memory and regret."

Clara's eyes, now reflecting the dim light filtering through the curtains, held a distant sadness as she considered the young man's plight. "It was a peculiar sight, I'll grant you. At times, he looked as if he expected the world to come crashing through his window, bringing with it answers to questions we couldn't even begin to fathom. And at others, he seemed trapped in a loop of recollection, replaying moments of significance known only to him."

Leaning back, her focus returned from the world outside the window to the safety of her living room, yet her thoughts remained on the young man's solitary vigils. "Whatever it was that held his attention so, it bore the weight of something momentous. It wasn't the idle gaze of someone simply watching the world go by but the keen observation of a sentinel on the brink of discovery, or perhaps on the edge of despair. In those moments, he was both profoundly present and impossibly distant, a contradiction embodied in the silhouette of a young man framed against the glass."

Detective Henderson, intrigued by Clara's detailed observations and the implicit undercurrents of mystery they carried, subtly shifted her position to engage more directly with the elderly witness. The detective's demeanor, a blend of professional inquisitiveness and genuine concern, was evident as she leaned forward, bridging the physical and metaphorical gap between them. Her eyes, sharp and assessing, sought to glean not just information but understanding from Clara's narrative tapestry.

"Mrs. Jenkins," she began, her voice modulated to convey both her authority and her willingness to listen, "in all the time you've spent watching over this building, and in your observations of Alex, did you ever witness anything...out of the ordinary? Any behavior or incident that might hint at a tendency towards violence?" Her question, carefully phrased, invited not just an answer but a reflection on the nuances of human behavior that Clara might have noticed.

Clara paused, considering the detective's question with the seriousness it warranted. Her fingers, which had been idly tracing the floral pattern on her cushion, stilled as she collected her thoughts. "Well, Detective," she started, her voice taking on a contemplative tone, "it's not easy to say. Alex, he always seemed more at war with himself than anyone else. But there was this one time, a peculiar incident that did give me pause."

She recounted an observation, a fragment of time captured from her window — a glimpse of Alex returning home under the cloak of night, his movements hurried, almost frantic. "It was late, well past the hour when the street falls silent," she continued, her voice dropping to a whisper as if to share a secret. "He looked disheveled, his clothes a bit worse for wear, and there was something in his gait, a heaviness, as if he was carrying the weight of the world on his shoulders."

"Then there were the bruises," Clara added, her eyes locking with Henderson's to emphasize the significance of her statement. "Not often, but enough to make you wonder. On his knuckles, like he'd been...well, you know. He'd brush it off as clumsiness, but one does start to wonder about the nature of such accidents."

Detective Henderson, absorbing every detail, noted the mixture of concern and suspicion in Clara's voice. The mention of bruises, of a hidden turmoil possibly manifesting in physical altercations, added a new layer to the evolving profile of Alex Bennett—a layer that warranted further investigation.

"As for outright violence, no, I can't say I've seen him lash out at anyone," Clara concluded, her gaze drifting off as if scanning her memory for any missed detail. "But there's an energy about him, something pent up, like a storm brewing on the horizon. It's all under the surface, but it makes you wonder what might happen if it ever found its way out."

Detective Henderson, her notebook filled with Clara's insights, nodded thoughtfully. The elderly woman's observations provided valuable pieces to the complex puzzle of Alex Bennett's character and actions. Each detail, from the mundane to the mysterious, contributed to the broader picture they were attempting to assemble—a picture that, with each new piece, seemed to grow more intricate and enigmatic.

Clara's response, reflective and deliberate, carried the weight of careful observation. With a gentle, almost imperceptible shake of her head, she conveyed her uncertainty and concern. "Direct violence? No, I haven't witnessed that. But there's always been a sense of something... turbulent, just beneath the surface with him," she began, her voice low and imbued with a hint of worry. "It's as though he's perpetually wrestling with something inside him, something hidden from the rest of us."

She leaned back slightly, her gaze momentarily distant as she summoned the memory with clarity. "I did see, on a few occasions, bruises across his knuckles. Quite noticeable they were," Clara recalled, the lines on her face deepening with the gravity of her recollections. "He dismissed them as the result of some clumsy mishap when I asked. Yet, his explanation, while plausible, always seemed a bit... off to me."

Her eyes, sharp despite her years, fixed on Detective Henderson, communicating the depth of her intuition. "Those marks, they spoke of more than just an accidental stumble or a carelessly slammed door. They hinted at a struggle, a physical manifestation of the internal conflict I sensed in him." Clara's hands, now still in her lap, underscored the seriousness of her observation. "It's the kind of thing that nags at you, Detective. Leaves you wondering about the real story behind those so-called accidents."

The room was silent for a moment as the weight of Clara's words hung in the air, a testament to her keen insight into human nature—a skill honed through years of quiet scrutiny from the sidelines of life. Her ability to notice the subtlest of cues, to read the unspoken stories etched in the bruises of a young man's hands, offered a glimpse into the complexity of Alex's situation, one that transcended the simple narratives of accident and coincidence.

Detective Henderson, her interest piqued by Clara's observations, made a mental note of the implied volatility in Alex's character as described by the elderly woman. The mention of bruises, dismissed by Alex but questioned by Clara, added a nuanced layer to the detective's understanding of the young man in question. It was a piece of the puzzle that, while not conclusive on its own, suggested a depth to Alex's struggles that warranted further exploration.

"As you've watched him over the years, Mrs. Jenkins, have you noticed any other signs, anything at all that might help us understand the full scope of what we're dealing with here?" Detective Henderson asked, her voice a blend of professional curiosity and genuine concern for the truth that lay buried in the heart of the complex web surrounding Alex Bennett.

As the conversation took a turn toward the speculative, Clara leaned back into the embrace of her time-worn sofa, her eyes reflecting the glow of a setting sun that filtered through the lace curtains. Her hands, previously animated in recounting her observations, now rested softly on her lap, her fingers occasionally fidgeting with the edge of a faded throw blanket. There was a noticeable shift in the atmosphere, as if the room itself held its breath, awaiting her next words.

"It's like walking through a fog," she continued, her voice lower now, imbued with a hint of foreboding. "You sense more than you see. With Alex, it's the shadows behind his eyes, the tension in his smile. It's not the acts he's committed, but the potential for what he could do that keeps me awake at night." Clara's gaze drifted away, lost in contemplation, her thoughts wandering to the unseen and unspoken fears that Alex's presence invoked in her.

She turned to face Detective Henderson directly, her eyes searching the detective's for understanding. "Imagine, if you will, a tightly wound spring, coiled with years of restraint and silence. What happens when that restraint snaps? What chaos could be unleashed from such a well of suppressed energy?" Clara's question hung in the air, a rhetorical musing that invited not an answer but a shared reflection on the complexity of the human psyche.

"There's a moment," Clara added, "a fleeting second, where you glimpse the precipice he stands upon. It's in the way he pauses mid-sentence, the abrupt halts in his laughter, as if he's suddenly aware of the edge. It's those moments that reveal the true battle raging within him—a battle between the man he is and the darkness he fears he may become."

Detective Henderson listened intently, her pen poised above her notebook, but momentarily stilled by the depth of Clara's insight. The elderly woman's words painted a portrait of Alex not just as a subject of investigation but as a living, breathing embodiment of the precarious balance between light and darkness that resides within us all.

As Clara's narrative ventured into this uncharted territory, the detective realized that the investigation into Alex Bennett was more than a mere pursuit of facts and evidence. It was an exploration into the very essence of identity, of potentiality, and the myriad paths that a life could take, shadowed by the choices made and those left unchosen.

The room, now dim with the evening's advance, seemed to shrink around them, a cocoon where the past and the future, reality and speculation, coalesced into a singular moment of shared understanding. In Clara Jenkins, Detective Henderson found not just a witness but a guide through the complexities of the human condition, illuminated by the fading light of day.

The interview with Clara Jenkins, as it neared its conclusion in the softly dimming light of her living room, left Detective Laura Henderson in a contemplative state. The room, filled with the accumulated relics of Clara's long life, had served as a backdrop to a narrative that was as revealing as it was enigmatic. Detective Henderson, her notebook now brimming with Clara's observations, found herself deeply engrossed in thought, her professional skepticism gently eroded by the elderly woman's lucid and nuanced understanding of their enigmatic subject, Alex Bennett.

Clara's narrative had not been a straightforward recounting of events; it was more akin to a tapestry, richly woven from the disparate threads of direct encounters, overheard fragments, and intuitive leaps. This tapestry, with its intricate patterns of speculation and insight, provided Detective Henderson with a unique perspective on Alex, one that transcended the mere facts of the case to touch upon the complexities of human nature and the fluidity of time itself.

As Clara spoke, her words had traversed the realms of past interactions with Alex, reflections on his current state, and even ventured into predictions of what might lie ahead. This ability to navigate through time, to see the echoes of the past in the present and to anticipate the shadows of the future, struck a chord with Detective Henderson. It was a reflection, albeit from a vastly different vantage point, of the disjointed temporal experience that seemed to afflict Alex himself.

Detective Henderson's ruminations were not just on the content of Clara's observations but on their form and substance. The elderly woman's account was marked by a depth of perception and an empathy that cut through the surface to hint at the turbulent depths beneath Alex's outward behavior. Clara's words suggested a man caught in the throes of an internal struggle, his actions and reactions not merely his own but the manifestations of a deeper, perhaps unresolved, turmoil.

As Detective Henderson prepared to leave, stepping from the warm, lived-in ambiance of Clara's apartment into the stark reality of the investigation that awaited her, she carried with her more than just notes and recorded statements. She bore the weight of a newfound understanding, a recognition of the complex web of factors that shaped Alex Bennett's existence. Clara's insights, grounded in decades of observance and the wisdom of age, had opened new avenues of inquiry, not just into the actions of a potential suspect but into the essence of his being.

The detective's departure marked not an end but a beginning, a fresh chapter in the investigation that would now have to account for the intricate layers of personality, memory, and time. Clara Jenkins, with her unassuming acumen, had provided Detective Henderson with a key to unlock the deeper mysteries of Alex Bennett's psyche, setting the stage for an exploration that promised to be as challenging as it was necessary. The journey ahead, illuminated by Clara's reflective insights, promised to delve into realms where the boundaries between past, present, and future blurred, offering a glimpse into the heart of a man trapped by his own fragmented perception of time.

The grim shadow cast by the Dawson family tragedy had, in many ways, transformed the fabric of the community, pulling tightly woven threads into a complex, tangled skein of suspicion, curiosity, and fear. This intricate web, now ensnaring both the observer and the observed, posed profound questions about the nature of truth and the reliability of perception. Detective Laura Henderson found herself at the nexus of these converging narratives, each step forward in her investigation revealing more layers of complexity than resolution.

Alex Bennett, around whom the vortex of inquiry increasingly swirled, stood at the center of this unfolding drama—a figure both enigmatic and tragically familiar. To Henderson, the challenge was not merely to piece together the events leading to the Dawsons' untimely deaths but to navigate the murky waters of a mind that seemed as fragmented as the story it was suspected of authoring. Was Alex merely a casualty of his own inner demons, ensnared by a mind that danced precariously on the edge of sanity? Or did his disturbances mask a more sinister role in the darkness that had befallen the Dawson household?

As Detective Henderson pursued the threads of inquiry, weaving through the testimonies and evidence with a meticulousness borne of experience, she was acutely aware of the shifting ground beneath her feet. The nature of truth, often thought to be solid and immutable, now appeared fluid, its contours shaped by the lens through which it was viewed. The investigation, therefore, was not just a quest for facts but an exploration of the human condition, of the shadows that lie in the heart of every individual, waiting for a moment to emerge into the light.

The deeper Detective Henderson delved, the more the distinctions between victim and perpetrator, between madness and malevolence, seemed to blur. Each piece of evidence, each snippet of overheard conversation or fragment of a troubled past, served as a puzzle piece in a picture too vast and complex to be easily comprehended. And at the center of this puzzle was Alex, a figure as compelling as he was confounding, his life a tapestry of unanswered questions and unresolved conflicts.

The investigation, like the lives it sought to dissect, had become a journey into uncharted territory, where the familiar landmarks of logic and law were obscured by the mists of human frailty and ambiguity. As Detective Henderson pressed on, she did so with the understanding that the answers she sought might not only shed light on the tragedy of the Dawson family but also offer insights into the enigma of existence itself—the eternal interplay of light and darkness, truth and perception, that defines human experience.

Chapter 9: The Unseen Hand

In the suffocating silence of his cramped apartment, Alex found himself again ensnared in a cocoon of darkness, punctuated only by the sporadic flicker of streetlamps that fought their way through the begrimed windows, casting elongated, spectral shadows across the cluttered space. This meager light, with its hesitant dance, played across the walls, lending a macabre theater to the room that stood in stark, unsettling contrast to the tempest raging silently within Alex's psyche.

Surrounded by the remnants of his daily existence — stacks of unread books that whispered tales of forgotten lore, photographs that gazed back with eyes full of accusations and regret, and the ever-present, mocking tick of the clock that seemed to mark time in a dimension alien to his own — Alex's sanctuary felt more like a prison. The air, thick with the stagnation of unspoken words and dreams deferred, seemed to compress around him, a tangible reminder of the isolation that had become his constant companion.

As the night deepened, drawing the world into its embrace, the boundary between Alex's tormented mind and the tangible reality of his dingy apartment began to dissolve. The mundane objects around him, each a testament to a life unspooling at the seams, took on ominous significance. The shadows, animated by the flickering light, morphed into sinister forms that whispered of unseen horrors lurking just beyond perception, each flicker a portent of the impending descent into the abyss of his own creation.

This moment, suspended between the tangible world and the chasms of his inner turmoil, was the precipice on which Alex teetered. The fabric of his reality, threadbare and worn from the constant assault of his fractured thoughts, began to tear, opening fissures through which the dark, uncharted waters of his subconscious surged forth. It was in these depths, in the realm where logic and madness intertwine, that Alex's most profound fears and desires took shape, manifesting in visions that were as vivid as they were inexplicable.

The room around him, once merely a backdrop to his solitary existence, now seemed to pulse with a life of its own, each shadow a sentinel watching, waiting for the moment when the barriers would fall and the floodgates of his psyche would open. In this eerie tableau, where light and darkness played their eternal game of chess, Alex sat motionless, a solitary figure caught in the eye of an unseen storm, bracing for the descent into realms where the fabrications of his mind held dominion over the ruins of his reality.

Suddenly, the familiar confines of his apartment dissolved into the ether, replaced by an environment both foreign and alarmingly detailed. Alex was thrust into the heart of a dimly lit chamber, a place that felt both timeless and suspended in despair. The air was thick, choked with the scent of decay and the kind of fear that clings to the soul, a tangible manifestation of neglect that permeated every corner of this nightmarish setting.

In the center of this macabre tableau stood a figure, their form obscured and bound, a prisoner to both their restraints and the enveloping darkness. The shadows around them seemed alive, undulating softly as if breathed upon by an unseen, malevolent force. These movements were illuminated by a light source as elusive as the dread that filled the room, casting grotesque silhouettes that danced along the peeling walls, their origins as mysterious as the scenario in which Alex found himself.

The figure's presence was both an accusation and a plea, their identity masked by the shifting darkness that seemed almost to swallow them whole. Despite the absence of clear features, the figure exuded a visceral sense of fear and anticipation, as if aware of the grim tableau they were part of. The air around them vibrated with a silent scream, a tension so profound that it seemed to echo off the walls of the chamber, amplifying the suffocating atmosphere of anticipation and despair.

Alex, rooted to the spot, felt an overwhelming sense of dislocation, as if he had stepped through a veil into a reality that should not exist, yet which held him in its grip with alarming clarity. The weight of the air, the oppressive scent of fear and decay, and the figure before him, all painted a scene that was as horrifying in its implications as it was inexplicable. In this moment, suspended between action and hesitation, Alex was confronted with the surreal horror of a nightmare made manifest, a scenario that defied logic yet demanded his participation.

As if ensnared in a macabre trance, Alex's hands wrapped around the handle of a dense, blunt object, its cold and unyielding surface strangely familiar under his touch. A chill of recognition crept up his spine, a premonition of the dark deed his body was poised to commit. The figure before him writhed in their bindings, their movements desperate yet futile, their muffled cries for mercy rising like a haunting refrain in the thick, charged air of the chamber. These pleas, though fervent and filled with terror, seemed to dissipate into the void, leaving no mark on the unfolding horror.

With a surreal sense of disengagement, Alex watched, aghast, as his own arm acted of its own volition, guided by an unseen force that wielded him as its instrument of violence. The motion was eerily precise, the descent of the object marked by a chilling inevitability. When it connected, the sound was sickeningly distinct—a thud that resonated with the gruesome finality of life extinguished, a sound that would haunt the silent moments of his existence henceforth.

This act, though executed by his hand, felt alien to him, as if he were a mere spectator to his own horror, trapped in a body commandeered by a will outside his own. The gravity of the moment, the stark finality of the act, seemed at odds with the numbing detachment that enveloped him, creating a rift in his psyche that threatened to swallow him whole.

As the deed was done, the figure's struggles ceased, their body slumping in an eerie tableau of despair and finality. The silence that followed was oppressive, a testament to the irreversible act that had transpired. Alex stood frozen, the instrument of violence still in his grip, a symbol of the darkness that lurked within, capable of emerging in moments of unspeakable clarity.

This moment, this act, though it felt scripted by a hand other than his own, left Alex reeling in the aftermath, a soul adrift in the tumultuous sea of his own conscience. The horror of what he had witnessed, and the part he played in it, however unwilling, etched a scar upon his very being, a mark of the darkness that now seemed an indelible part of his essence.

This deed, carried out with chilling exactitude, played out as if preordained, following the inexorable script of a sinister ritual steeped in darkness. Each motion, each moment, was etched with a morbid clarity that belied the stark, unsettling detachment that enveloped Alex, rendering him a passive spectator in the grotesque drama of his own making. This detachment, a vast chasm between action and conscience, left him adrift in the surreal dichotomy of being both the executor and the witness, bereft of any agency to alter the dreadful course of events unfolding before him.

As the grim sequence unfurled, the air itself seemed to thicken with anticipation, charged with the electricity of impending doom. The shadows in the room danced with a malevolent glee, casting their elongated figures across the walls as if celebrating the grim spectacle. The sound of the fatal blow, when it finally came, resonated with a hollow finality, echoing off the bare, unyielding surfaces of the chamber, a grim punctuation to the silence that screamed louder than any cry for mercy.

In this moment, where reality blurred with the nightmarish, Alex found himself ensnared in the ghastly paradox of feeling both intimately connected to and hopelessly separated from the violence enacted by his hands. This duality, this profound disconnection from the visceral horror of his actions, cloaked him in an eerie calm, a tranquil abyss that contrasted starkly with the brutal reality of the act he had committed.

The ritualistic precision of the act, devoid of hesitation and marked by a dreadful inevitability, suggested not chaos but a terrifying order, a sequence of events dictated by a dark impetus beyond his understanding. It was this realization, the recognition of his own body as a vessel for an unfathomable will, that instilled in Alex a bone-deep chill, a fear not just of the act itself but of the unknown depths within him from which such darkness could spring.

This disconnection, this eerie spectatorship of his own actions, underscored a chilling truth: that within the confines of his mind lurked a force capable of breaching the thin veil between thought and deed, between the ethereal and the tangible. The act, though executed by his hands, felt as if directed by an unseen hand, a shadowy conductor orchestrating a macabre symphony of violence from the dark recesses of his psyche.

Just as suddenly as it had seized him, the nightmarish vision splintered, hurling Alex back into the tangible confines of his apartment, where he sat gasping for breath, his hands trembling uncontrollably under the weak illumination cast by the distant street lamps. This jolting transition from the depths of his mind's darkest corners to the familiar, yet now eerily foreign, setting of his living space served as a stark, unnerving reminder of the fragile boundary that demarcated his inner turmoil from the external reality.

The dim glow, which only moments before had seemed soothing, now appeared ghostly, casting long, sinister shadows that seemed to mock his disorientation. The air around him, once a comforting envelope of solitude, now felt charged with an oppressive silence, each breath a labored effort against the weight of his own racing thoughts.

In the aftermath of the hallucination, the room itself seemed to pulse with a latent energy, as if the walls had borne witness to the violence of his mind and now stood in judgment. Objects in his periphery, so mundane and innocuous by the light of day, took on a menacing quality, their shadows twisted into grotesque shapes that danced mockingly at the edge of his vision.

Alex's heart pounded a frantic rhythm, a cacophony that filled the silence left by the shattered vision, echoing the lingering echoes of the blows he had delivered in his mind's eye. The starkness of the room, the sparse furnishings, and the unadorned walls, which had always offered a minimalist comfort, now felt like the backdrop to a stage upon which his psyche had performed its most disturbing act yet.

This return to reality, so abrupt and dissonant, underscored the precariousness of Alex's grasp on the boundary between the imagined and the real. The haunting vividness of the hallucination, with its sensory and emotional intensity, left a residue of dread that clung to him, a spectral reminder of the dark potential that lay dormant within. The chill that had settled over him in the wake of the vision lingered, a cold embrace that whispered of the thin, almost translucent veil that separated his world of shadows from the stark light of reality.

The aftermath of this harrowing episode cast Alex into a tumultuous sea of self-examination, where the waters of doubt and fear ran deep. Was this disturbing vision merely the product of a mind fractured by its own turmoil, a shadowy reflection of internal strife played out in the theater of his psyche? Or was it, perhaps, a more ominous revelation, a glimpse into a hidden recess of his soul where darker impulses lay in wait, biding their time before surfacing into the light of action?

As he grappled with these questions, the room around him seemed to contract, the walls inching closer, as if to contain the expanding breadth of his unease. The flickering shadows, products of the intermittent streetlight glow, appeared now as specters of his own making, each one a mocking testament to the dual nature of his existence.

In this moment of vulnerability, Alex found himself at a crossroads of self-awareness, where every shadow held the potential for both insight and illusion. The vividness of the violence he had envisioned, so tangible and yet so alien, left an indelible mark on his consciousness, a stain that no amount of rationalization could cleanse.

This internal confrontation brought forth a torrent of existential dread, a fear not just of what he might be capable of, but of the very essence of his identity. Was the capacity for such violence an inextricable part of his being, a dark thread woven into the fabric of his soul? Or was it an aberration, a distortion of self, caused by the fissures in his mental landscape?

The vision, with its unsettling clarity and emotional resonance, seemed to suggest a pattern, a recurring theme in the narrative of his psyche. It posed a chilling question: if such scenes could be conjured with such realism in his mind's eye, what did that imply about the nature of his character? Was there a corner of his psyche, untouched by the light of consciousness, where such scenarios were not just possible, but inevitable?

As the night wore on, and the shadows in his apartment grew longer, merging into a uniform darkness, Alex felt the lines between reality and the realm of his inner thoughts blur further. The distinction between potentiality and actuality, between the imagined and the real, became increasingly tenuous, leaving him adrift in a sea of uncertainty. The fear that this vision could be a harbinger of actions yet to come cast a pall over his soul, a foreboding that perhaps the most terrifying aspect of his existence was not the disorder that fractured his reality, but the darkness that might dwell within him, silent and unseen, waiting for its moment to emerge.

The shadowy figure, bound and indistinct, became a symbol of Alex's deepest fears, an avatar of the unknown that taunted him from the recesses of his mind. The ambiguity of the timeline, the inability to place this event in the continuum of his lived experience, only deepened the mystery, casting a veil of obscurity over the truth of his actions. This recurring motif of violence, surfacing with disturbing clarity in his psyche, suggested not just an isolated incident but a chilling pattern, each iteration unveiling a fragment of a more sinister narrative.

The realism of the episode, its visceral impact leaving him shaken to the core, underscored the terrifying potential of his mind to construct realities as tangible as they were horrifying. The emotions that coursed through him during these visions—fear, rage, a morbid fascination—were as real to him as the air he breathed, blurring the lines between the fabrications of his psyche and the tangible world around him.

This ability, or perhaps curse, to render such detailed and emotive scenarios within the confines of his own consciousness left Alex grappling with a profound sense of dread. The terror was not solely of the violence he might be capable of—a fear that in itself was paralyzing—but also of the underlying truth such visions might reveal about his nature. Was there a darkness inherent within him, a latent violence waiting for its moment to manifest? Or were these visions mere echoes of a troubled mind, specters without substance, born of the chaos that reigned within?

The enigmatic figure, their identity shrouded in darkness, became a mirror reflecting back at Alex not just the potential for violence, but the unresolved mysteries of his own identity. Each encounter with this shadowy other left him more unsettled, each episode a puzzle piece that, rather than offering clarity, seemed to further complicate the image of himself that he was desperately trying to understand.

As Alex pondered the implications of these violent visions, he was forced to confront the unsettling possibility that his mind, in its fragmented state, was not just a prison but a crucible, forging nightmares into experiences so real they threatened to spill over into his waking life. The line between imagination and reality, already tenuous, seemed to fray further with each episode, leaving him to wonder if the darkness he envisioned was merely a reflection of his own inner turmoil or a prophecy of a fate yet to unfold.

In the silence that followed the tempest of his vision, Alex sat, a solitary figure shrouded in the dim light that barely pierced the darkness of his apartment. The tumultuous journey of his mind left him adrift in a sea of uncertainty, the echoes of his hallucinatory violence still ringing in his ears, a stark reminder of the battle being waged within. He was caught in the liminal space between action and inaction, yearning for a beacon of guidance yet paralyzed by the fear of what such guidance might reveal about the depths of his soul.

The specter of seeking help loomed large, a beacon in the tumultuous storm of his existence, promising a semblance of salvation, a path to understanding the unfathomable recesses of his mind. Yet, this same prospect filled him with an insurmountable dread, the fear that delving into the labyrinth of his psyche would lay bare truths too harrowing to confront. The notion of uncovering a darkness so profound, a predilection for violence so innate that it could drive him to enact the horrors of his visions in the tangible world, was a specter that haunted his every thought.

This duality, this agonizing indecision, became a crucible for his torment. The invisible hand that had guided his actions in the vision—a metaphor for the forces, both seen and unseen, that shaped his thoughts and deeds—now seemed to him an emblem of his own powerlessness. It symbolized not just the loss of control over his actions but the erosion of his very will, leaving him at the mercy of currents he could neither navigate nor understand.

As Alex grappled with the implications of his vision, he found himself standing at the precipice of an abyss, peering into the darkness, not of the world around him, but of his own making. The choice before him, as stark as it was profound, offered no easy answers. To seek help was to admit to the possibility of a darkness within, to confront the demons that lurked in the shadows of his mind. Yet, to shy away from this path, to allow the fear of discovery to guide his steps, was to remain forever ensnared in the cycle of his hallucinations, each episode a further descent into the maelstrom.

The aftermath of the vision, therefore, was not merely a moment of crisis but a pivotal juncture in his journey. It demanded of Alex not just a reckoning with the forces that drove him to the edge of madness but a decision that could alter the course of his life. The path he chose, whether towards the light of understanding or further into the darkness of fear and uncertainty, would define not just his future but the very essence of his being. The phantom force, once a harbinger of violence, now became a symbol of the struggle for autonomy, a battle for the soul of a man caught in the grip of his own fractured reality.

This harrowing experience marked not just a moment of profound disorientation but a watershed in Alex's struggle with his own identity. It thrust him into the murky waters between the tangible world and the phantasmagoric realm of his innermost fears, leaving him to grapple with the unsettling ambiguity of his own nature. As he peered over the precipice, the abyss of his inner world yawned wide before him, a chasm filled with the swirling mists of doubt and the specters of possibilities both dark and darker still.

The darkness that Alex faced in the depths of his hallucination was not just a metaphorical landscape of fear; it was a crucible in which the very core of his being was tested. He was forced to question whether the capacity for violence that seemed to emanate from within him was a fundamental aspect of his character, woven into the fabric of his soul, or if it was merely the manifestation of the psychological tempest that tormented him. The stark realization that he might forever be ensnared in a dance with shadows, forever on the verge of succumbing to a narrative written in the ink of his own fears, was a thought more terrifying than any phantom conjured by his mind.

The specter of losing touch with reality loomed over him, a cloud that threatened to engulf his future in its nebulous embrace. This fear of a final, irrevocable descent into the madness that skirted the edges of his consciousness was a constant companion, whispering of a fate where the line between the world of his visions and the world of flesh and blood would forever be erased. Such a future, fraught with the echoes of actions not taken and paths not chosen, was a labyrinth of existential dread from which there seemed no escape.

In this moment of existential crisis, the very fabric of Alex's identity seemed to fray, threads of self, unraveling in the face of an inscrutable truth. The challenge before him was not merely to confront the darkness he saw reflected in the mirror of his soul but to navigate the intricate maze of his own psyche, to discern reality from illusion, truth from fabrication. It was a journey that promised no easy answers, a quest that might lead him through the shadows to the light of understanding or deeper into the night that already clouded his mind.

This episode, then, was not merely an aberration, a fleeting nightmare to be dispelled with the light of dawn. It was a signpost on the road of his life, marking the path to a crossroads where the choices he made would determine not just his fate but the essence of who he was and who he might become. The darkness at the edge of his vision, the specter of a future unmoored from the anchors of reality, stood as a testament to the battle being waged within—a battle for the soul of a man caught between the world that was and the world that might yet be, in the shadowed realm of his own making.

Chapter 10: Voices of Doubt

Alex found himself imprisoned within the suffocating quiet of his own space, a stark island amidst the relentless buzz of urban existence just beyond his walls. The ambient noise of the city, with its myriad lives in motion, infiltrated his sanctum only as a distant murmur, a faint reminder of a world he felt increasingly detached from. The apartment, once a repository of cherished memories and intellectual pursuits, now echoed with a hollow sense of entrapment. Surrounded by the tangible remnants of his past—a collection of literature that spoke to a voracious mind, photographs capturing moments of ephemeral joy, and scattered artifacts of a life once lived with fervor—Alex was confronted by their silent mockery, each item a specter of unfulfilled promises and unexplored potentials.

As darkness enveloped the world outside, a profound isolation enveloped Alex, a veil that separated him from the vibrancy of life that continued unabated beyond the confines of his self-imposed exile. Within the four walls of what had once been his refuge, the boundary that delineated the real from the imagined began to disintegrate, worn thin by the relentless assault of his inner turmoil. Each episode of his mind's rebellion against itself cast a shadow over his grasp of reality, blurring the lines with an unsettling precision that left him questioning the very fabric of his existence.

The night, with its infinite possibilities for solace or torment, became a canvas upon which his fears and doubts were magnified, projecting onto the silence a cacophony of internal conflict that found no echo in the physical world. His apartment, once a sanctuary of solitude and introspection, now mirrored the labyrinth of his psyche, each room a corridor leading deeper into the maze of his own unresolved mysteries.

This disquieting blend of isolation and introspection transformed the very essence of his dwelling into something unrecognizable, a place where the ghosts of his own making roamed freely, unchallenged by the light of reason or the warmth of human connection. The tangible silence that enveloped him became a palpable entity, a suffocating embrace that threatened to extinguish the flickering flame of his will to seek answers beyond the veil of his own perceptions.

In these hours of introspective confinement, the fragile line that once separated the real from the unreal not only frayed but seemed to vanish altogether, leaving Alex adrift in a sea of uncertainty where each fleeting shadow, each whisper of the wind, became a harbinger of truths yet uncovered, and each haunting episode a tide pulling him further from the shores of reality into the uncharted waters of his own unraveling mind.

Within the oppressive stillness of his apartment, each tick of the clock melded into a relentless march, marking not just the passage of time but the deepening of Alex's entanglement with his inner demons. The once comforting solitude of his surroundings now amplified the cacophony of his doubts, turning the darkness into a canvas where his deepest anxieties were painted in stark, unforgiving strokes.

The quiet became a breeding ground for the specters of his psyche, each doubt a shadow that loomed larger in the absence of distraction, their presence as suffocating as the tangible walls that encased him. These specters whispered insidious truths, their voices a constant murmur that filled the void left by the absence of human connection, a reminder of the isolation that both protected and imprisoned him.

The fear of madness was a relentless undercurrent, a dark river that flowed through the recesses of his mind, its waters murky with the detritus of fragmented thoughts and unbidden memories. This fear was not just of losing grip on reality but of discovering that his reality was a construct, as fragile and illusory as the visions that haunted his nights.

Violence, too, lurked in the shadows of his introspection, an uninvited guest that whispered of capabilities Alex dared not fully acknowledge. The mere possibility of harboring such darkness within himself was a weight that pressed down on him, a burden of potential that he could neither shed nor fully embrace. The boundary between the violence of his nightmares and the potential for such violence in his waking life became blurred, a fog of uncertainty that clouded his every interaction, casting a pall over his sense of self.

And then there were the depths of his own mind, vast and uncharted territories that he navigated with trepidation. Each journey inward was a descent into a labyrinth where light rarely reached, and what light there was cast long, distorted shadows. The complexity of his own psyche was a map with missing pieces, a puzzle that he was compelled to solve even as he feared what the completed picture might reveal.

This introspective spiral was a dangerous descent, each turn revealing darker corners, each echo a reminder of the vastness of the unknown within him. The doubts that assailed him were not just reflections of his fears but markers of the journey he was on—a journey that promised no easy answers, no clear path forward. Each step taken in the darkness of his mind was a step further from the safety of ignorance, a deliberate movement toward a truth that he both sought and feared.

In the silence and solitude of his apartment, with the city's muted hum as the only reminder of the world beyond, Alex stood at the crossroads of his own being, a traveler in the dark, seeking the light of understanding in a landscape shrouded in shadow. The journey was his alone to make, a solitary quest through the tangled underbrush of his psyche, where each shadow, each specter of doubt, was a guidepost on the path to discovering the true nature of the darkness that dwelled within.

Abruptly, from the tempest of his inner turmoil, a stark, vivid memory broke through the surface, casting Alex adrift into the turbulent waters of his younger years. There, amidst the echoes of a forgotten past, he stood face to face with Michael, the bonds of their childhood friendship strained to breaking by the fervor of their conflict. Though the cause of their disagreement had long since dissolved into the ether of memory, the intensity of their emotions remained undiminished, crackling through the space between them with the ferocity of a gathering storm.

Michael's expression was a mirror of Alex's own—a tumultuous mix of anger, betrayal, and an underlying current of sorrow that neither of them could quite name. Their words, sharp and reckless, flew like arrows, each one aimed with precision but blind to the potential wounds they might inflict. There was a desperation to their exchange, a sense that something more significant than either could articulate was at stake.

The air seemed to thicken with their shouted accusations and defenses, each word adding fuel to the inferno of their dispute. The world around them receded until nothing existed but the space they occupied, a bubble of intensity that neither could escape. The silence that followed their barrage of words was heavy, fraught with the weight of things unsaid, a moment suspended in time as both stood on the brink, caught in the eye of the emotional hurricane they had conjured.

Then, with a swiftness that left Alex reeling even in recollection, the delicate balance shattered. Movement blurred the lines between intention and instinct as Alex found his body lunging forward, propelled by a surge of raw emotion. His hands, acting as if of their own accord, found purchase on Michael's chest, pushing with a force that belied the turmoil roiling within him.

The fallout was immediate and irrevocable. Michael's backward stumble, a dance with gravity he was destined to lose, ended in tragedy as his head made contact with the unforgiving edge of a nearby table. The sound of the impact was a grotesque punctuation to their altercation, a final note in the cacophony of their conflict.

The aftermath of the incident lay before Alex like a tableau of despair, Michael's prone form a stark reminder of the razor-thin line between anger and calamity. The sight of his friend, so still, so suddenly vulnerable, was a visceral blow to Alex, a stark realization of the destructive potential that lay within him, a force he had unwittingly unleashed.

This memory, resurfacing with the clarity of a bell in the stillness of his dark apartment, was a specter from the past that Alex could neither banish nor fully comprehend. It stood as both a warning and a marker, a point on the map of his life that he could never return to, yet could never quite leave behind. The unresolved echoes of that day, the what-ifs and the might-have-beens, wove themselves into the fabric of his current turmoil, a thread of darkness that colored his perceptions and fueled his fears.

In the quiet aftermath of this recollection, Alex found himself grappling with the duality of his nature, the delicate balance between the person he believed himself to be and the person that moment had revealed. The memory of Michael, and the incident that had so irrevocably altered the course of their friendship, was a shadow that trailed Alex, a constant reminder of the fragility of human connections and the perilous depth of his own capacity for harm.

Michael's visage was a storm of emotion, mirroring the tempest that raged within Alex. The air crackled with their mutual animosity, each word they hurled at each other was a missile, aimed not just to strike but to scar. The hostility that simmered between them was palpable, a tangible force that seemed to distort the very air around them. Their faces, mere inches apart, were maps of the tumult that wracked them both—veins standing out, eyes alight with the fire of confrontation.

Their conversation, if it could be called such, was a dance of aggression, a verbal sparring match where each phrase was sharpened on the whetstone of their shared history, designed to cut deep and leave lasting marks. The space between words was filled with the unspoken, the history, and the hurts that had accumulated like sediment in the riverbed of their friendship.

Then, in a heartbeat, the world seemed to hold its breath—the moment elongated, stretching taut the thin veneer of civility that had restrained their baser impulses. This pause was electric, charged with the potential for destruction, a precariously balanced scale waiting for the slightest nudge to tip it into calamity.

It was a silence that spoke louder than any of their shouted accusations, a pregnant void where the unsaid gathered force. The air was thick with the weight of impending rupture, the tension of a string drawn too tight and ready to snap. In this moment, suspended outside of time, the inevitability of their collision course became painfully clear. The fragile barrier that had held back the floodwaters of their pent-up frustrations and long-buried grievances was about to break, and the ensuing deluge promised to sweep away the remnants of their frayed bond.

In an instant, the room transformed from a battlefield of words to a theater of physical aggression. The transition was abrupt, as if a line had been crossed into territory from which there could be no retreat. Alex, propelled by a surge of unbridled rage that seemed to originate from a place deep within him, became both actor and observer in the unfolding tragedy. He watched, as though from outside himself, his hands extending with a force that felt both foreign and inevitable, making contact with Michael's chest in a push that was as decisive as it was reckless.

Michael's response was a dance of imbalance, his body recoiling from the force of Alex's anger. The backward stagger, a desperate attempt to regain equilibrium, was thwarted by an unseen obstacle that lay in wait like a predator. His foot ensnared, the moment stretched into eternity as Michael teetered on the precipice of disaster. Then, gravity, indifferent to the human dramas that played out within its laws, claimed its due. Michael's descent was a study in helplessness, a fall from grace that was both literal and metaphorical.

The sound that followed—the sickening crack of bone meeting the hard, unyielding edge of the table—was a punctuation mark in the silence that enveloped the room. It was a sound that would echo in the recesses of Alex's memory, a grim reminder of the fragility of human life and the destructive power of human emotion. The aftermath of the fall was a tableau of horror, Michael's body a crumpled testament to the tragic endpoint of their confrontation.

This moment of impact, where the consequences of Alex's actions were laid bare in the most brutal fashion, marked a turning point. The realization of what he had done, the gravity of the violence he had unleashed, descended upon him with the weight of a thousand stones. Michael, his lifelong friend, now lay motionless, a silent rebuke to the fury that had driven Alex to this unforgivable act.

As the reality of the situation set in, Alex was consumed by a vortex of shock and disbelief. The transition from heated argument to physical violence had been alarmingly swift, a slip from the precipice into the abyss that lay beyond the edge of reason. The physical space between them, once charged with the electricity of their verbal spar, was now a chasm of consequence, a gap bridged by an act of aggression that could not be undone.

This moment, frozen in time, was a mirror reflecting the darkest aspects of Alex's nature. The horror of witnessing Michael's fall, the sound of the impact, and the sight of his friend's inert form were imprints that would etch themselves indelibly onto his psyche. The realization that he was capable of causing such harm, that his anger could manifest in such a devastatingly tangible way, was a revelation that would haunt him, shaping the contours of his guilt and the landscape of his remorse in the years to come.

That moment of catastrophe became a nexus of Alex's deepest fears and insecurities, a point at which the darker facets of his character were laid bare against the backdrop of tragedy. Michael's inert form, sprawled in a grotesque stillness, became the embodiment of Alex's worst apprehensions about himself—a tangible representation of the thin line between anger and violence that he might unwittingly cross. This incident, etched into the fabric of his memory with stark clarity, served as a constant, haunting reminder of the fragility of human connections and the devastating impact of momentary lapses in control.

The echoes of that day reverberated through Alex's mind, a relentless tide of self-reproach and existential dread. The whispers of doubt, those insidious tendrils of thought that sought to undermine his grasp on reality, found fertile ground in the soil of this memory. They grew in strength and number, weaving a narrative that suggested this violent outburst was not merely an aberration, but rather a glimpse into the abyss of his own potential for harm. These voices, imbued with the venom of his worst fears, suggested that the capacity for such violence was not an external force, but an integral part of his being, a shadow self that lurked just beneath the surface of his conscious mind, waiting for an opportunity to emerge.

This perception of himself as a vessel capable of harboring such darkness was a burden that Alex carried with him, a specter that colored his interactions with the world around him. The memory of Michael's fall became a prism through which he viewed his actions and motivations, casting a pall of suspicion and doubt over even his most benign intentions. The fear that he could, under certain circumstances, become an agent of harm once again, that he could inflict pain and suffering on those around him, became a cage of paranoia and self-imposed isolation.

The incident with Michael, therefore, transcended its status as a mere recollection of a past event; it evolved into a symbol of Alex's internal struggle with his own nature. It served as a stark reminder that within the heart of every person lies the capacity for both great kindness and devastating cruelty, and that the line dividing these two extremes is perilously thin and easily crossed. For Alex, the journey forward was one fraught with the challenge of reconciling this aspect of his character with his desire for redemption and the yearning to believe in the inherent goodness within himself.

As dawn's first light began to seep through the curtains, casting a gentle illumination that contrasted sharply with the darkness of his ruminations, Alex was left to ponder the complex tapestry of his own psyche. The path to understanding the true nature of the events that shaped him, and by extension, the essence of his own identity, was obscured by shadows and doubts. In this quest for clarity, the memory of that fateful day with Michael stood as a beacon of uncertainty, a question mark that loomed large over his efforts to navigate the murky waters of his past and the uncertain seas of his future.

As the first rays of dawn breached the confines of Alex's apartment, illuminating the clutter of his existence with a soft, forgiving light, the stark contrast between the day's promise and the night's turmoil became painfully apparent. There, amidst the silence of a new day, Alex found himself at the mercy of a torrent of introspection, a solitary figure grappling with the shadows of a past that refused to remain buried. The resurgence of this memory, so vivid and fraught with unresolved emotion, acted as a catalyst for a deep, existential crisis.

The delineation between what was an accident born of heated moments and what could be construed as an underlying propensity for violence blurred into obscurity. This ambiguity, this inability to define the nature of his actions, thrust Alex into a vortex of introspection that questioned the very foundations of his moral compass. The incident with Michael, once a mere specter of regret tucked away in the recesses of his mind, now loomed as a monolith of doubt, casting its long, dark shadow across every facet of Alex's self-perception.

This flashback did not merely serve as a window to a moment best forgotten; it transformed into a mirror reflecting a version of himself Alex struggled to recognize. The potential for darkness, for causing harm—whether by design or accident—introduced a fissure in his identity that could not easily be mended. His interactions, once navigated with a measure of confidence, now teetered on the edge of paranoia, each engagement with the world around him colored by the fear of what might lie dormant within.

Alex's solitude deepened, not just as a physical reality of his existence, but as a chasm within his soul. The knowledge—or the suspicion—of his capacity for violence became a barrier between him and the rest of humanity, a divide that seemed insurmountable. Each social interaction, each moment of connection, was now fraught with an undercurrent of fear, a silent question of what he was capable of under the wrong set of circumstances.

The dawn's light, rather than heralding a new beginning, served only to illuminate the complexity of Alex's struggle. The clarity it brought was not one of understanding, but of recognition—the recognition of the labyrinthine nature of his own psyche, and the realization that the path to reconciliation with himself was obscured by more than just the shadows of night. In this moment, caught between the fading darkness and the burgeoning light, Alex stood on the precipice of self-discovery, a journey into the heart of his own darkness in search of a light that seemed, at once, both tantalizingly close and infinitely out of reach.

Within the confines of his mind, Alex navigated the tumultuous waters of his conscience, a lone voyager seeking clarity amidst the storm. The memory of the altercation with Michael—a scene fraught with raw emotion and tragic consequence—loomed like a specter, challenging his perception of self. This internal strife set him adrift on a sea of introspection, where the echoes of doubt reverberated against the walls of his psyche, each resonance a reminder of the darkness he might harbor within.

The crossroads at which Alex found himself was marked by two distinct paths: one of denial, where the memory could be relegated to the realm of distorted recollection, a mere byproduct of his fractured state of mind; the other, a path of acceptance, acknowledging that the capacity for violence, however dormant, resided within him, woven into the very fabric of his identity.

This duality of thought ensnared him in a paradoxical struggle, the decision between dismissing the past and confronting it head-on a pendulum swinging with relentless momentum. The incessant whispers of doubt, once mere murmurs in the back of his mind, now crescendoed into a deafening cacophony, each voice a harbinger of the fear that the violence witnessed in his flashback was not an aberration but an integral part of his essence.

The haunting possibility that the darkness he recoiled from was not lurking in the shadows of the world but nested within the recesses of his own soul became a source of existential dread. This realization—that the danger he sought to understand and contain might emanate from within—cast a long shadow over his quest for self-discovery, turning his introspective journey into a labyrinthine ordeal.

Alex's struggle at this juncture was emblematic of a larger battle, one that transcended the specifics of his memory with Michael. It was a battle for self-awareness, waged on the battleground of his own conscience, where the stakes were nothing less than his sense of humanity. The choice before him, whether to view the memory as an isolated incident or as evidence of a deeper, darker predisposition, was not merely about reconciling with his past but about defining who he was in the present and who he wished to be in the future.

In the silence of his apartment, as the dawn crept ever closer, casting its impartial light on the world outside, Alex stood at the precipice of understanding. The decision to explore the depths of his psyche, to confront the darkness within and seek the light of truth, was his alone to make. The journey would be fraught with challenges, each step forward a test of his resolve, but it was a path he recognized he must embark upon, for the echoes of doubt would find no silence until he faced the storm within.

The burgeoning light of daybreak, as it filtered through the curtains, cast a soft yet unforgiving illumination over Alex's world, both physical and mental. This new dawn did not bring the clarity Alex so desperately sought but instead highlighted the complexity of his predicament. The demarcation between the tangible world and the specters of his mind had blurred to such an extent that discerning one from the other had become an exercise in futility. Each memory, each flash of insight that surged forth in his quest for understanding, was

akin to a piece of an enigmatic jigsaw puzzle—
seemingly significant yet obstinately resistant to
integration into a coherent whole.

In this liminal space between night and day, Alex
found himself wrestling with a dual reality: the
physical one, where his apartment served as both
sanctuary and prison, and the internal one, where
his thoughts and memories danced a delicate ballet
on the edge of comprehension. The whispers of
doubt that accompanied his introspection were not
just background noise but active participants in this
dance, each one a reflection of the fears that had
taken root in the depths of his being. These fears—of
madness, of inherent violence, of the unknown
recesses of his own mind—were not entities that
could be easily confronted or dismissed. They were
integral to his psyche, woven into the very fabric of
his self-perception.

His search for clarity, a quest that had once seemed
a straightforward path to self-discovery, now
resembled a journey through a dense fog, where
every step forward seemed to only deepen the
enigma. The more he sought to untangle the web of
his thoughts and memories, the more entangled he
became, caught in a cycle of introspection that
offered no escape, no respite from the incessant
questioning of his own nature.

The whispers of doubt, once mere whispers in the darkness, had grown into a cacophony by dawn's light, a chorus that seemed to echo off the walls of his apartment, magnifying his isolation. This chorus did not offer guidance; instead, it presented a litany of fears, each more daunting than the last, leaving Alex to navigate a sea of uncertainty with no compass to guide him. The longing for a beacon of truth—a signpost pointing the way out of the darkness—was palpable, yet seemingly beyond reach, obscured by the very doubts that plagued him.

As the day broke fully, casting its indifferent light upon the world outside, Alex remained ensconced in his apartment, a figure both literally and metaphorically overshadowed by the complexity of his predicament. The dawn, rather than heralding a new beginning, served only to underscore the uncertainty that enveloped him, a reminder of the journey he had yet to undertake. This journey, fraught with challenges and devoid of clear markers, promised no easy solutions, no definitive answers. Instead, it offered the prospect of a deeper exploration into the labyrinth of his own psyche, a venture into the unknown that required not just courage but a willingness to confront the very essence of his being.

In this moment, at the threshold of day, Alex stood not just on the cusp of a new day but at the precipice of understanding, gazing into the abyss of his own soul, searching for the light of truth amid the shadows of doubt. The path forward was obscured, the destination uncertain, but the quest for clarity, however daunting, remained the only beacon in the darkness, a flicker of hope in the enveloping gloom.

Chapter 11: The Illusion of Progress

Beneath the unyielding luminescence that bathed the city's expanse—a city that pulsed with life, indifferent to the passage of hours—Detective Laura Henderson found herself ensnared in the depths of contemplation. The precinct, encased within walls that bore witness to countless tales of human frailty and resilience, resonated with the quiet intensity of purpose and the specter of challenges unmet. Here, amidst the undercurrent of activity that never quite stilled, even as the night deepened, Alex emerged not merely as a subject of inquiry but as the embodiment of the riddle itself. His narratives, a rich tapestry of interwoven realities and imagined planes, danced tantalizingly on the edge of comprehension, casting him in the dual light of suspect and sage, his very essence a question mark that challenged the boundaries of conventional investigation.

The precinct, that bastion of resolve in the face of the city's relentless beat, served as both haven and battlefield for Henderson and her peers. Within its confines, the steady drone of diligence and the undercurrent of frustration mingled, creating a backdrop against which Alex's story unfolded—a narrative so labyrinthine it seemed to defy the laws of time and space themselves. This place, steeped in the pursuit of truth, became the staging ground for a quest that ventured beyond the mere facts of crime and into the realm of existential inquiry. Alex, with his aura of mystery and the uncanny depth of his insights, stood at the heart of this chaotic storm, his accounts a challenge to the detectives' understanding of reality, urging them to look beyond the veil of the tangible, to question the very nature of truth and deception.

As the clock's hands marched inexorably toward the witching hour, the precinct—a microcosm of the city's broader canvas of light and shadow—echoed with the silent resolve of those within. Henderson, her mind a whirlwind of theories and conjectures, faced the enigma of Alex with a resolve forged in the countless hours of sifting through the chaff of misinformation for the kernels of truth. In this nocturnal vigil, the detective found herself at the precipice of the known world, peering into the abyss of the unknown, where Alex's stories suggested realms untold and realities unseen.

This was the crucible within which their investigation simmered—a place where the quest for justice met the mysteries of the human psyche, where the search for answers became a journey into the heart of darkness and light. The precinct, alive with the muted sounds of a city that never truly sleeps, stood as a lighthouse against the night, a symbol of the search for clarity in a world mired in shades of grey. And at the center of this swirling nexus of doubt and determination, Alex remained the most perplexing puzzle, a beacon of enigmas that beckoned Henderson and her colleagues deeper into the uncharted waters of their investigation, where the line between shadow and revelation was as thin as the veil between day and night.

Within the confines of Alex's domain, amidst the remnants of his solitary existence, lay artifacts imbued with the essence of mysteries both ancient and undivulged. An age-worn key, its metal kissed by the patina of time, seemed to hum with the promise of doorways shrouded in the annals of history, each turn of its bow a silent testament to the countless thresholds it might once have opened. These doorways, hidden in the creases of the world as we know it, beckoned with the allure of secrets that danced tantalizingly on the edge of the tangible, inviting those brave enough to step beyond the known and into the realms of the ethereal.

The diagrams, intricate labyrinths of lines and circles, spoke in the language of the esoteric, each stroke a verse in the hymn of hidden wisdom. Their complex arrays suggested a map to the intangible, a guide through the celestial mechanics of knowledge forbidden to mere mortals. These symbols, intertwined in a dance of cosmic and earthly energies, offered glimpses into rites long forgotten, into sciences that blurred the lines between magic and reality, hinting at powers and principles that lay buried under layers of time and skepticism.

Encoded messages, their alphabets a cipher of shadows, held conversations frozen in secrecy, their narratives encrypted within the confines of a script that defied easy unraveling. These writings, a patchwork quilt of historical whispers and contemporary enigmas, spoke of a world parallel to our own, where truths were guardians of their own mysteries, and understanding was the prize awarded to those who could decipher the language of the veiled.

For Detective Henderson, these artifacts transformed from curiosities into beacons, their enigmatic nature no longer a barrier but a bridge to understanding the labyrinth that was Alex's mind and the tragedy that had befallen the Dawson family. Each item, a fragment of a larger puzzle, became a source of illumination, casting light on the shadows that had thus far cloaked the investigation in darkness. The ancient key suggested not just literal doorways but the unlocking of mysteries ensconced within the human psyche; the diagrams, more than mere drawings, emerged as blueprints to understanding the arcane forces that Alex believed shaped their fates; the coded messages, once indecipherable, now hinted at a narrative far more complex and intertwined with the fabric of reality than previously imagined.

These relics, standing at the confluence of the mystical and the mundane, guided Henderson and her team through the fog of uncertainty that had enshrouded the Dawson case. In their silent eloquence, these objects whispered of pathways yet to be explored, of doors yet to be opened, and of truths yet to be unveiled. They served as the compass by which the detectives navigated the murky waters of the investigation, each clue a step closer to unraveling the mystery that lay at the heart of the tragedy, and perhaps, to understanding the enigmatic figure of Alex himself, who stood as both the map and the territory in the search for answers.

As days melded into weeks with no clear breakthrough, the atmosphere within the precinct grew heavy, each tick of the clock a resonant reminder of the urgency and gravity that the Dawson case commanded. The air seemed thick with the weight of expectation, each new sunrise not a herald of hope but a marker of the persistent shadow of uncertainty that loomed over the investigation. This shadow was not merely a metaphorical presence but a palpable force, felt by all who ventured too close to the heart of the mystery, a dark cloud that obscured the path to clarity and truth.

For the Dawson family, the passage of time was a cruel adversary, each moment a chasm that widened the gap between their present agony and the memories of a past untainted by sorrow. Their grief was a constant echo in the corridors of the precinct, a sorrowful melody that underscored the silence of unanswered questions. It was a grief that transcended the personal, becoming a mournful symphony for what was lost, a harmony of hope and despair that resonated within the walls of their broken home. Their quest for closure, for some semblance of understanding in the wake of devastation, was a beacon that guided the investigation, a reminder of the human cost at the heart of the procedural and the analytical.

The community's vigil, a collective state of suspended hope, mirrored the tension that gripped the detectives tasked with piercing the veil of mystery that surrounded Alex's involvement. This watchful anticipation, a blend of fear and longing for resolution, cast a long shadow over the precinct's efforts, a silent jury to the painstaking process of justice in motion. The gaze of the public, fraught with the need for reassurance, for a return to a semblance of normalcy, was a constant pressure, a demand for answers that the detectives felt keenly. This communal yearning for closure, for the peace that comes with understanding, was both a motivator and a burden, fueling the drive to delve deeper into the complexities of the case while also serving as a stark reminder of the high stakes for which they toiled.

In this landscape of collective anticipation and private despair, the investigation pressed on, each new piece of evidence, each revisited interview, and each day's end marked by the setting of the sun, a cycle of effort and hope against the backdrop of a community in waiting. The detectives, bearers of the community's trust and the family's hopes, navigated this terrain with a mixture of determination and the heavy knowledge that the resolution, when it came, would carry the weight of all that was lost and might yet be found. In the quest for answers, the weight of the investigation was a constant companion, a reminder of the delicate balance between the pursuit of truth and the human cost of the tragedy at its heart.

Detective Jameson, with his feet firmly planted in the realm of logic and evidence, served as the perfect foil to Henderson's more intuitive approach. His skepticism was not born of cynicism but of a deep-seated belief in the sanctity of facts and the tangible. "Navigating through this morass of uncertainties and half-truths requires more than just intuition," he often remarked, his tone imbued with the gravitas of experience. "It demands a relentless pursuit of verifiable facts, a commitment to sift through the chaff to find the kernels of truth buried within." His perspective, rooted in the pragmatic, offered a crucial balance to the investigation, ensuring that every hypothesis was meticulously vetted, every lead pursued with rigor.

"The terrain we navigate is shadowed, Laura, dense with the fog of Alex's convoluted narratives," Jameson continued, his gaze steady and unwavering. "But amidst this obscurity, if there lies even a filament of truth, it is incumbent upon us to seek it out, to trace its winding path back to its source." His resolve was palpable, a testament to his dedication to the principles of justice and truth. "Our duty transcends the mere assembly of facts; it is a quest to piece together a mosaic of reality from fragments of possibility, to shine a light into the darkest corners of this case and reveal the truth that lies hidden."

This dynamic between Henderson and Jameson, the interplay of instinct and analysis, became the foundation upon which their investigation stood. Jameson's cautionary stance served as a necessary counterbalance to Henderson's more exploratory methods, a reminder of the need to anchor their inquiry in the bedrock of evidence and reason. "We are explorers in a landscape devoid of maps, tasked with charting a course through unmarked territory," he mused thoughtfully. "The challenge before us is formidable, yet it is through this very process of search and discovery that the essence of our investigation will emerge."

Together, they embarked on this journey through the intricate maze constructed by Alex's disclosures, each step forward a foray into the unknown.

Jameson's skepticism, far from being a hindrance, became a vital component of their methodology, a sieve through which every theory was strained, ensuring that only the most credible of insights were pursued. "The shadows we navigate are deep and disorienting," he acknowledged, his voice a beacon of resolve in the enveloping uncertainty. "But it is within these shadows that the truth resides, obscured yet not unreachable. Our task is to pierce through this veil of obscurity, to trace the labyrinthine pathways of Alex's narrative to their core and unearth the truths concealed within."

In this shared mission, Henderson and Jameson found a common ground, a mutual understanding that, though their approaches differed, their objective remained singular: to unravel the Gordian knot at the heart of the Dawson family tragedy and to bring the light of understanding to the darkened corners of this most perplexing case.

In the quietude of her introspection, amidst the precinct's nocturnal stillness, Detective Henderson found herself at the precipice of a profound realization. The world outside, with its incessant hum and hustle, receded into the background, granting her the serenity to navigate the labyrinth of Alex's narratives. What once appeared as mere ramblings, a disjointed collection of fantastical claims and paranoid delusions, now hinted at a deeper, more structured form of expression. Alex's frequent references to the "watcher" — previously dismissed as the product of a deluded mind — began to resonate with Henderson as a profound symbol, a representation of the invisible hands that mold our destinies, unseen yet omnipresent.

This "watcher," as Henderson now contemplated, was not merely a character in Alex's personal drama but a universal archetype, emblematic of the forces that operate beyond our immediate perception, shaping the course of events in ways subtle and overt. It was a concept that transcended the individual, touching upon the collective experience of humanity, the idea that we are all under the surveillance of entities or forces beyond our understanding, be they societal, psychological, or even metaphysical.

Henderson's mind raced as she considered the implications of this newfound perspective. Alex's fixation on the idea of being observed, influenced, and directed by an unseen "watcher" could be interpreted as an acute awareness of the complex interplay between individual agency and external control. It was a narrative thread that, when pulled, unraveled a tapestry of interconnected themes — free will versus determinism, the individual versus the collective, the seen versus the unseen.

In this moment of clarity, Henderson recognized the potential value in Alex's narratives, not as literal accounts of his experiences, but as allegorical expressions of a more universal human condition. The stories he spun, imbued with the essence of myth and legend, were not merely escapist fantasies but a reflection of the deep-seated human need to make sense of the forces that shape our lives, to name and thus gain some semblance of control over the unknowable.

Emboldened by this insight, Henderson resolved to delve deeper into the symbolism and metaphor inherent in Alex's accounts. The "watcher" would serve as her guide, a conceptual key to unlocking the broader meanings hidden within the ostensibly chaotic weave of his testimony. This approach, while unconventional, offered a new avenue of inquiry, a way to explore the underlying truths that might lead them closer to resolving the mystery at hand.

As she prepared to revisit the case with this fresh perspective, Henderson felt a surge of optimism. The path forward was still shrouded in uncertainty, but the lens through which she now viewed Alex's narrative promised to illuminate the investigation in ways previously unimagined. The "watcher," once a source of bafflement, had become a beacon, shedding light on the darkened pathways of human experience and guiding her toward the elusive truths that lay waiting to be discovered.

Embarking on this unconventional journey, Detective Henderson and her partner Jameson found themselves navigating through a metaphysical landscape, where each clue unearthed from Alex's trove of mysteries served as a beacon, guiding them deeper into the uncharted territories of the human psyche and the hidden realms of the cosmos. Their quest for understanding led them to the doorsteps of those who dwelt in the liminal spaces between the empirical and the esoteric — historians of the arcane, cryptographers versed in the art of hidden languages, and scholars of myth who spoke of truths veiled in allegory.

This eclectic assembly of experts became their allies in the quest to decode the labyrinthine narrative spun by Alex. With each meeting, the detectives wove together strands of knowledge, piecing together a mosaic that was as breathtaking in its complexity as it was enigmatic in its significance. The old keys collected from Alex's apartment, once enigmatic relics, were now seen as symbols of thresholds yet to be crossed, of doors to realities that lay just beyond the grasp of conventional understanding. The diagrams, intricate in their design, were deciphered as maps charting the intersections of time and space, or perhaps, as schematics for navigating the layers of consciousness that separate the tangible from the transcendental.

Encoded messages that had once confounded them were now painstakingly translated, revealing narratives that spoke of the cyclical nature of history, of wars waged in the shadows, and of societies that thrived beyond the veil of the ordinary. Each discovery was a revelation, a glimpse into a world that was at once terrifying and awe-inspiring, a reminder of the vastness of the universe and the myriad mysteries that it harbored.

The investigation, now a quest in the truest sense, challenged Henderson and Jameson's perceptions of reality. They found themselves questioning the boundaries of their own beliefs, confronted with evidence that suggested the existence of phenomena that defied logical explanation. Yet, despite the existential vertigo that accompanied these revelations, they pressed forward, driven by a relentless desire to uncover the truth behind the Dawson tragedy.

As they delved deeper into the esoteric, the detectives realized that the key to solving the case lay not in the material evidence they gathered but in understanding the symbolic language through which Alex communicated his experiences. It was a language of archetypes and symbols, a dialect of the deep subconscious that transcended words and ventured into the realm of the universal truths that bind humanity across the ages.

This realization marked a turning point in the investigation. Henderson and Jameson, once adherents to the strict regimen of empirical evidence and logical deduction, now embraced a broader view of inquiry, one that acknowledged the power of myth and symbolism as conduits to understanding the human condition. Their journey through the shadows had illuminated not only the mysteries surrounding the Dawson case but also the endless potential for wonder and discovery that lies at the heart of the detective's craft.

In this new light, the Dawson family tragedy was no longer a mere crime to be solved but a saga woven into the tapestry of human experience, a narrative rich with the themes of loss, redemption, and the eternal quest for meaning in a world replete with mysteries. Henderson and Jameson, transformed by their odyssey, stood at the threshold of revelation, ready to confront the truths that awaited them, armed with the knowledge that the most profound mysteries are those that dwell within the soul of man.

As Henderson and Jameson delved deeper into the intricacies of the case, they uncovered a narrative that transcended the bounds of conventional detective work, weaving through the annals of forgotten history and the shadowy corners of arcane knowledge. The Dawson family tragedy, once a singular point of focus, now appeared as a node in a vast network of interconnected mysteries that spanned epochs and cultures, suggesting a pattern of events influenced by forces both ancient and elusive.

The detectives' journey through this labyrinth of secrets led them to uncover connections between the Dawsons and a series of historical events that seemed, at first glance, entirely unrelated. They stumbled upon cryptic references to the Dawsons in medieval texts, tales of a family blessed — or cursed — with knowledge that skirted the edge of heresy. There were whispers of ancestors who had dabbled in alchemy, seeking the elixir of life, and others who had consorted with mystics, delving into the mysteries of the cosmos beyond the reach of the church's condemning gaze.

Each discovery peeled back layers of history, revealing a lineage touched by the divine and the demonic in equal measure, a lineage that had danced on the knife-edge of the world's hidden wonders and terrors. The Dawson family's legacy, Henderson and Jameson learned, was intertwined with a clandestine society known as the "Order of the Luminous Veil," a group that had sought to understand and harness the powers that lay at the fringe of human comprehension.

This society, shrouded in secrecy, had operated in the shadows of history, influencing events from behind the scenes, guiding humanity's evolution according to a grand, enigmatic design. The Dawson tragedy, the detectives realized, was not an isolated incident but a pivotal event in the ongoing saga of the Order's machinations, a saga in which Alex, with his cryptic tales and esoteric knowledge, played a crucial role.

The revelation that the Dawson family was entangled in a narrative of cosmic significance, a narrative that challenged the very limits of human understanding, was both exhilarating and daunting. Henderson and Jameson found themselves grappling with questions that defied logic, confronted with a truth that was as magnificent as it was terrifying. The investigation had become a voyage into the unknown, a quest to uncover secrets that had been guarded for centuries by those who walked the line between light and shadow.

As they stood on the brink of this unprecedented discovery, the detectives realized that the key to solving the Dawson case lay in understanding the ancient wisdom and hidden truths that Alex, unwittingly or not, had brought to light. It was a realization that propelled them forward, driving them to unravel the final mysteries of the case, to decode the symbols and signs that pointed the way to the heart of the darkness that had claimed the Dawson family.

Their journey through the realms of the unknown had transformed them, imbuing them with a sense of purpose that transcended the confines of their previous worldview. They were no longer mere detectives; they had become seekers of truth in a world where truth was layered with myth, where reality was interwoven with the fabric of dreams and nightmares. The path ahead was fraught with peril, but Henderson and Jameson pressed on, guided by the conviction that the illumination of truth, no matter how concealed by the shadows of the past, was within their grasp.

In their relentless search, Detectives Laura Henderson and Jameson moved through a mix of old stories and mysterious clues that Alex shared. Each step they took was like stepping into unknown territory, blurring the lines between what's real and what's not. Their investigation became more than just looking for clues; it turned into an adventure that questioned everything they knew about the world.

They weren't just chasing after a criminal anymore; they were exploring a whole new world of ancient stories and secrets. The pieces of evidence they found, like the old key and strange drawings, started to make sense as they put them together. These clues pointed them toward a bigger mystery, one that connected the Dawson family's tragedy to stories and beliefs that were much older and deeper than they ever imagined.

As they dug deeper, Henderson and Jameson felt like they were part of a bigger story, one where good and bad forces have always been fighting. They began to see the clues not just as random objects but as signs that guided them closer to understanding the true nature of the case. Their search took them to places and ideas far beyond the usual detective work, talking to experts in old legends and hidden knowledge to shed light on the Dawson mystery.

The deeper they went, the more they realized how big and complicated the mystery was. It was like uncovering a giant puzzle that stretched across history, filled with secrets and battles between light and dark. But Henderson and Jameson kept going, driven by the hope that solving the Dawson case would help them understand not just one tragedy but the larger battle between understanding and mystery that has always been part of human history.

Their determination to find the truth, no matter how strange or difficult the path, showed their deep commitment to solving the case. They were ready to face any challenge, using every clue to reveal the truth hidden in the shadows. As they moved forward, guided by the faint light of hope, they were determined to uncover the hidden truths that lay just beyond their reach, proving that even in the darkest moments, the search for truth can lead the way.

Chapter 12: Shadows of the Mind

Alex's adventure went beyond just moving through time. It felt like he was diving into a mysterious maze where past, present, and future all blended together into one big scene. This wasn't just happening by chance. It seemed like fate itself was guiding him through the hidden parts of his mind. Every vision he had was like a colorful painting that showed his biggest worries and deepest hopes, revealing parts of him that he didn't usually think about.

These visions weren't just made-up fantasies. They showed the complex nature of life. Every time Alex saw a new scene in his mind, he found himself in situations that made him rethink who he was and what reality meant. These visions were filled with symbols and emotions, acting like a mirror that showed life's complicated pattern, where facing a fear or recognizing a wish helped shape who he is.

As Alex moved through this dream-like world, the line between the real world and the world of what could be started to fade. Time wasn't just a straight line from beginning to end anymore. It opened up, letting him revisit moments, see possible futures, and even think about changing what happens next. This was exciting but also scary for Alex because it made him feel like he had some control over his destiny, while also showing him how complex making choices can be.

During this journey with things that can't be touched or easily explained, Alex started to see that these visions weren't just confusing or scary experiences. They were actually helping him uncover deep truths about himself, guiding him as he tried to figure out who he really is. By looking at the mix of fears and hopes each vision brought up, Alex was learning how to find his way through the complicated world inside him, a place as big and mysterious as anything outside.

Alex's trip through time and his own thoughts was really a deep dive into who he is, filled with chances to learn and moments that could make him feel lost. But he had to go through it because hidden in these visions were the answers he'd been looking for and the secrets of his heart ready to be found. By following this path laid out by fate, Alex wasn't just facing what might happen in the future; he was fully understanding himself, getting ready to step into a new level of awareness at the end of his journey.

In the oppressive silence of the courtroom, Alex found himself isolated, enveloped by a multitude of expectant eyes that bore into him, each gaze laden with judgment and anticipation. The atmosphere was electric, charged with the tension of unvoiced thoughts and the collective anticipation of those present, all awaiting the momentous verdict. When the judge's gavel descended with finality, the word "Guilty" cut through the stillness, reverberating throughout the room as though it were a death knell. This pronouncement was more than a verdict; it was an existential condemnation, branding Alex with an indelible mark of culpability that seemed to transcend the specifics of the crime in question.

This moment of judgment was fraught with contradiction. The label of guilt imposed upon him was a mantle Alex felt draped over his shoulders, a burden both foreign and intimately familiar. His hands, outwardly unblemished, became emblematic of the turmoil that churned within his soul. They were a stark representation of the dichotomy he faced: the palpable sense of innocence that anchored his identity, now at odds with the guilt attributed to him by the judgment of those who looked on. This internal conflict was not merely about the truth of his actions but touched upon the deeper essence of who Alex believed himself to be versus how he was perceived by the world around him.

The courtroom, with its imposing walls and the solemnity of its proceedings, transformed into an arena where Alex's very self was laid bare, scrutinized under the unforgiving lens of societal judgment. The verdict, while ostensibly a legal determination, morphed into a profound statement on Alex's character, challenging his sense of self and casting him adrift in a sea of existential doubt. In this pivotal moment, the battle lines were drawn not just between innocence and guilt in the legal sense but between Alex's understanding of his own integrity and the external imposition of shame and culpability by the collective other.

As the grim setting of the courtroom dissolved into the embrace of daylight, Alex found himself under the open sky, the sun's rays banishing the specters of doubt and despair that had long haunted him. This unexpected freedom, as sudden as a storm's clearing, felt almost otherworldly, a gift bestowed by an unseen hand, yet it carried with it the weight of the past, a silent testament to the battles fought and the time irretrievably lost to the depths of accusation and suspicion.

Standing at the threshold of a new beginning, Alex breathed in the liberation that surrounded him, a sensation as intoxicating as it was bewildering. The world, once narrowed to the confines of judgment and retribution, now lay expansive and uncharted before him. Yet, this liberty was not without its scars; it bore the indelible marks of the ordeal he had endured. Every glance of passersby, every whisper of the wind seemed to echo the words of condemnation that had once defined his existence. The exoneration, though legally absolving, could not fully cleanse the stain of public scrutiny, leaving Alex to navigate a landscape altered not by his actions, but by the perceptions of those around him.

The juxtaposition of freedom and the lingering aftereffects of his trial painted Alex's world in shades of complexity he had never anticipated. The joy of liberation was tempered by the realization that the shadows cast by his ordeal stretched far into the landscape of his future, a reminder that though he had stepped out of the darkness, its tendrils could still brush against the contours of his life. With each step away from the courthouse, Alex ventured not just into the physical realm of the free but into a personal odyssey, a journey to reclaim his identity from the clutches of a narrative he had never authored.

This liberation, as profound as it was precarious, offered Alex a paradoxical sense of existence. On one hand, he reveled in the possibilities that now sprawled before him, a canvas awaiting the brushstrokes of his choices and desires. On the other, he grappled with the specters of his past, the echoes of guilt and innocence that mingled in the air around him, crafting a melody of redemption and regret. The sunlight, though warm, cast long shadows, a constant reminder of the duality of his circumstance—free yet bound, exonerated yet never entirely absolved in the eyes of an ever-watchful world.

In this moment of liberation, Alex stood at the crossroads of his life, the path behind him etched with the trials of his past, the road ahead shrouded in the mists of uncertainty. Yet, within him burned a resolve, a determination to forge ahead, to redefine the contours of his destiny with the knowledge that freedom, in all its complexity, was his to shape. The journey forward was his to chart, a passage through light and shadow towards a horizon that promised not just renewal, but the chance to transcend the dichotomies that had once threatened to define him.

The liberating daylight that had heralded Alex's newfound freedom soon took on a sinister hue as the specter of pursuit cast its long shadow over his steps. The once welcoming streets morphed into a labyrinth of paranoia, where every corner concealed potential threats and every rustling leaf seemed a harbinger of imminent danger. The sound of footsteps trailing just behind him became the metronome to his life, a constant, unnerving rhythm that underscored the precariousness of his situation. These footsteps, though never materializing into a physical form, were as real to Alex as the ground beneath his feet, their presence a tangible expression of the psychological torment that haunted his every move.

The nature of his pursuer remained elusive, a phantom that defied identification, shifting forms with the adeptness of a shadow sliding across varied terrains. At times, it seemed a mere extension of Alex's own psyche, a dark reflection birthed from the depths of his subconscious. At others, it appeared as a tangible embodiment of his deepest fears, a creature forged from the collective anxieties that had accumulated over years of turmoil and uncertainty. This chase, a grim dance between prey and predator, transcended the physical realm, delving into the metaphysical, where the concepts of hunter and hunted blurred into a cyclical dance of existential dread.

This pursuit was more than a mere echo of past nightmares; it was an allegory for the human condition, a representation of the relentless struggle against the darker facets of our nature. Alex found himself caught in an eternal flight not from a physical adversary but from the manifestations of his own inner turmoil, from the doubts and fears that clung to him more persistently than any external foe could. The constant vigilance, the perpetual motion, was exhausting, a draining endeavor that left little room for peace or reflection.

Yet, within this relentless pursuit lay a deeper truth, a realization that the chase itself was a journey towards understanding. Each step taken in flight, each moment spent evading the formless dread that pursued him, was a step towards confronting the demons that resided within. This realization brought with it a paradoxical sense of empowerment; though he ran, it was not merely away from danger but towards a confrontation with the very essence of his fears.

In the dance of pursuit, where shadows played as much a part as the light that cast them, Alex discovered a resilience he had not known he possessed. The relentless chase, while a source of perpetual anxiety, also served as a forge for his spirit, tempering his resolve and sharpening his will. The path ahead remained shrouded in uncertainty, the identity of his pursuer an enigma wrapped in the mists of his own psyche. Yet, armed with the knowledge that the pursuit was as much about the journey inward as it was about the flight from external threats, Alex moved forward, a solitary figure navigating the twilight that lay between fear and understanding, darkness and light.

The aftermath of these prophetic dreams found Alex adrift, suspended in the vast, uncharted waters of his own consciousness, where the currents of time played tricks on his sense of reality. The vividness of each vision, with its stark emotions and complex scenarios, left a deep imprint on his psyche, blurring the lines between the tangible world and the ethereal realm of what might be. These glimpses into potential futures, each as real to Alex as his memories of the past, wove a complex tapestry of fate, suggesting not a predetermined path but a labyrinth of branching possibilities, each turn dictated by the interplay of his deepest fears, most fervent hopes, and the indomitable force of human agency.

In this state of liminality, Alex found himself questioning the very nature of destiny. Was the future a rigid construct, a book whose pages were already written, or was it a fluid, ever-changing stream, shaped by the choices we make and the dreams we dare to chase? The possibilities that stretched out before him, myriad and multifaceted, seemed to suggest the latter—a universe in which fate was not a jailer but a dance partner, leading him through the steps of what could be, guided by the hands of aspiration and trepidation.

This realization was both a burden and a liberation. On the one hand, it placed the weight of the future squarely on Alex's shoulders, imbuing every decision with the gravity of potential consequences, turning each crossroad into a moment of profound significance. On the other, it offered him a canvas, wide and waiting, upon which he could paint the story of his life in the hues of his own choosing, free from the constraints of a destiny carved in stone.

Amidst this tumult of thought and emotion, Alex began to see his visions not as chains binding him to certain outcomes but as beacons, illuminating the path through the darkness of uncertainty. Each vision, with its echoes of joy and shadows of despair, became a lesson, teaching him about the resilience of the human spirit, the power of hope to transcend the bleakest of circumstances, and the capacity of fear to shape, but not define, the journey of life.

As he navigated this sea of possibilities, Alex's resolve hardened. He understood that while the future might be influenced by forces beyond his comprehension, the essence of his destiny lay in his own hands. Armed with this knowledge, he set his sights on the horizon, where the storm clouds of doubt were breaking, giving way to the promise of a dawn painted with the colors of his own making—a future not foretold but forged in the crucible of his will, a testament to the enduring power of hope to sculpt the shape of what is yet to come.

In the quiet aftermath of these spectral visitations, Alex found himself at a crossroads, enveloped in the deep solace of introspection. This was a time unbound by the strictures of the ticking clock, a liminal space that hovered delicately between the resonant echoes of a past fraught with turmoil and the hushed, yet vibrant, anticipation of futures untold. The visions, fleeting as they were, unfolded before him like ethereal tapestries, each thread woven with the intricate patterns of possibilities and perils that lay ahead on his journey.

This path, illuminated by the ghostly light of what had been and what could be, was lined with the phantoms of memory and aspiration. Here, the specters of bygone days mingled freely with the specters of tomorrows yet to dawn, their presence a constant reminder of the dual nature of existence, where every joy is shadowed by sorrow, and every defeat may herald an unseen victory.

For Alex, each step forward on this path was akin to a dance, a delicate ballet performed with the shadows that skulked in the hidden alcoves of his psyche. These were not just figments of imagination or remnants of dreams but were, in truth, facets of his very self—whispers of doubt, flares of hope, and the myriad shades of emotion that painted the canvas of his soul.

This period of introspection was more than a mere pause in the narrative of his life; it was a crucible, a place of transformation where the alchemy of introspection transmuted the leaden weight of uncertainty into the golden light of understanding. The visions, once cryptic and disquieting, now revealed themselves as guideposts, each one a beacon that shed light on the labyrinthine corridors of his inner world, offering glimpses of the lessons to be learned and the battles to be waged within the arena of his own heart and mind.

As Alex traversed this introspective landscape, he grappled with the duality of his nature, the perpetual conflict between the darkness that sought to ensnare him and the light of his higher aspirations. This journey through the shadowed valleys of his own consciousness was a pilgrimage, a quest for the sacred grail of self-awareness that lay buried beneath layers of fear, regret, and longing.

The aftermath of his visions became a fertile ground for growth, a garden in which the seeds of future potential were sown. Each echo of the past, each whisper of the future, nurtured these seeds, watering them with the dew of reflection and the light of newfound wisdom. In this sacred space, Alex came to realize that the journey ahead, though fraught with the specters of past and future, was also adorned with the possibility of redemption, of transformation, and of the eventual triumph of light over the shadows that danced in the recesses of his own mind.

In the subdued light of his inner contemplation, Alex mulled over the profound teachings imparted by his visions. The experiences of conviction and liberation, starkly contrasting as they were, emerged as dual beacons of possible futures that lay on his life's horizon. Each painted a vivid tableau of the myriad paths fate might weave, suggesting that destiny is not a single thread but a complex tapestry of intertwined possibilities. Yet, it was the vision of pursuit that resonated with him most deeply, offering a poignant reflection on the eternal struggle that defines the human condition.

This relentless chase, with its nebulous threat forever at his heels, was emblematic of a universal truth that transcended the specifics of his situation. It was a powerful allegory for the human journey itself, a representation of the ceaseless battle against the darker aspects of our nature. This vision illuminated the reality that true liberation is not found in the mere evasion of external constraints but in the bravery required to confront one's deepest fears and darkest inclinations. It was a call to arms, challenging him to stand firm in the face of the internal specters that sought to undermine his resolve.

Alex recognized in this pursuit a reflection of life's inherent duality—the perpetual interplay between light and shadow that each person must navigate. The vision underscored the importance of vigilance and fortitude, reminding him that the path to enlightenment is paved with the acknowledgment and acceptance of one's own imperfections. It was a lesson in the art of self-confrontation, an admonition that the journey toward self-discovery and true freedom demands an unflinching examination of the soul's darkest corners.

This metaphor of pursuit, then, was not just a harbinger of a potential future but a microcosm of the human experience. It encapsulated the odyssey of growth and evolution that lies at the heart of existence, highlighting the fact that each individual's quest for peace and self-realization is inextricably linked to their willingness to engage with their internal adversities.

In the quiet of this twilight introspection, Alex found a renewed sense of purpose. The lessons of the visions, particularly the symbolism of the pursuit, galvanized him, instilling a newfound determination to embrace the complexities of his being. He understood now that the fabric of his destiny was woven from both the light of his aspirations and the darkness of his fears. The pursuit was not a curse to be evaded but a challenge to be met, an opportunity to forge strength from vulnerability and wisdom from the acknowledgment of one's own frailties.

This realization marked a pivotal moment in Alex's journey, a turning point where he began to see his visions not as ominous portents but as guiding lights on the path to deeper self-awareness. In embracing the metaphor of the pursuit, Alex stepped into a broader understanding of freedom — one that acknowledged the necessity of facing the shadows head-on, armed with the courage to transform and transcend them.

Emerging from the profound depths of his contemplation, Alex found himself once again attuned to the tangible world that enveloped him. The clarity of his surroundings contrasted sharply with the lingering shadows that danced at the periphery of his consciousness, serving as a mute reminder of the journey he had just undertaken within the vast landscapes of his mind. These shadows, though no longer commanding his immediate focus, persisted as enduring symbols of the myriad mysteries and complexities that define the human experience.

The external world, with its vivid colors and distinct forms, seemed momentarily more vibrant, imbued with a newfound depth by the introspective voyage Alex had navigated. Yet, this enhanced perception did not dispel the shadows; instead, it lent them a certain gravity, a recognition of their integral role in shaping the contours of his inner world. These shadows, the remnants of his visionary odyssey, stood as guardians of the threshold between the known and the unknown, the articulate and the ineffable.

In this moment of transition, Alex perceived the world with a duality of vision, seeing not only the physical reality that surrounded him but also the ethereal echoes of his visions, each casting its own light and darkness. The shadows of the mind, once sources of fear and confusion, now assumed a new character, embodying the rich tapestry of thoughts, emotions, and potentialities that comprised his deeper self. They were not entities to be feared or eradicated but acknowledged and understood, signifiers of the vast, uncharted territories of the psyche that awaited exploration.

The persistence of these shadows, even in the wake of his return to consciousness, underscored the indelible impact of the visions on Alex's perception of reality. They reminded him that beneath the surface of everyday existence lies a profound depth of meaning and mystery, accessible only to those willing to delve into the darkness and embrace the full spectrum of their being. The shadows, therefore, were not mere remnants of his visions but vital aspects of his psyche, encapsulating the essence of the unseen forces that influence and inform the human journey.

As Alex stepped forward into the continuum of his life, the shadows of the mind accompanied him, not as specters of past fears but as companions in his ongoing quest for understanding and self-discovery. They served as a constant reminder of the delicate balance between light and shadow, the seen and the unseen, that defines our existence. In acknowledging and integrating these shadows, Alex embarked on a path of greater awareness and acceptance, recognizing that the true depth of one's character is measured not by the absence of darkness but by the ability to navigate and illuminate its depths.

Chapter 13: A Break in the Case

The investigation into the Dawson family tragedy, long mired in the quagmire of stagnation and dead ends, suddenly surged forward with the emergence of an unexpected witness. Eric Nolan, a seemingly unremarkable local shopkeeper, came forward with testimony that could potentially unravel the complex web of mysteries that had baffled Detective Laura Henderson and her team for months. Nolan's account of seeing Alex under suspicious circumstances on the night of the tragedy offered a ray of hope, a glimmer of possibility that the case might finally break open.

This new development rekindled the flames of determination within the investigative team. It was as though Nolan's testimony was the missing piece they had been desperately seeking, the key that could unlock the door behind which the truth lay hidden. The potential breakthrough came at a time when morale was at its lowest, when the path forward seemed obscured by an impenetrable fog of doubts and uncertainties.

Detective Henderson, ever the pragmatist, tempered her optimism with caution. The journey thus far had taught her that in cases like this, where shadows obscured the lines between truth and deception, nothing could be taken at face value. Yet, Nolan's emergence in the narrative of the Dawson family tragedy was an undeniable beacon of hope. It promised to illuminate the darkened corridors of the case, to reveal the contours of a reality that had remained just out of reach.

The investigative team, rejuvenated by this unexpected turn of events, rallied around the new lead with renewed vigor. They were acutely aware that Nolan's testimony, while potentially pivotal, was but a single thread in the intricate tapestry of the Dawson tragedy. Pulling on this thread could either unravel the mystery or further complicate the already convoluted narrative.

Yet, the possibility that this could be the moment of breakthrough they had been striving for infused them with a sense of purpose. The fog of uncertainties that had enshrouded their path began to dissipate, giving way to the clarity of focused investigation. Detective Henderson and her team, guided by the light of Nolan's testimony, ventured deeper into the maze of the Dawson family tragedy, their steps buoyed by the cautious optimism that this time, they might finally find their way through to the truth.

In the dim light of the interrogation room, Eric Nolan sat across from Detective Laura Henderson, his demeanor a mix of solemnity and unease as he delved into his recollection of the events that had transpired on that pivotal night. With each word, he sought to reconstruct the scene, his testimony serving as a window into the moments that had caught Alex in a web of suspicion.

According to Nolan, the night air was thick with an unspoken tension, the kind that whispered of secrets lurking just beneath the veneer of normalcy. It was against this backdrop that Alex appeared, emerging like a specter from the shadowed confines of the Dawson residence. Nolan's eyes, he claimed, had been drawn almost magnetically to the figure that stumbled into the wan illumination cast by the lone streetlamp that stood sentinel on the otherwise darkened street.

There, under the lamp's pallid light, Alex's figure was momentarily etched in stark relief against the darkness. Nolan described him as a man on the edge, his movements erratic and imbued with a desperation that spoke volumes. The dishevelment of his clothes, the wildness in his eyes, and the way his gaze darted to and fro, scanning the darkened corners of the street as if expecting pursuit at any moment, painted a picture of a soul in turmoil.

For a fleeting instant, as Alex paused beneath the streetlamp's glow, Nolan recounted the palpable sense of apprehension that seemed to radiate from him. It was as if Alex was caught in an internal struggle, a battle between the urge to flee and the necessity of caution. Then, as quickly as he had appeared, Alex seemed to make his decision, casting one last, lingering look into the darkness before vanishing into the night from which he had emerged.

Nolan's account, delivered with a gravity that suggested the weight of what he had witnessed, offered a vivid snapshot of a man ensnared by circumstances beyond his control. Yet, as Detective Henderson listened, her experienced mind sifted through Nolan's words, searching for the threads of truth amid the tapestry of human perception and memory. Nolan's narrative, while compelling, was but a single piece in the complex puzzle of the Dawson family tragedy, a puzzle that Detective Henderson was determined to solve.

Detective Henderson, seasoned in the nuances of human memory and the often deceptive clarity of eyewitness accounts, found herself navigating through the murky waters of Eric Nolan's testimony with a mixture of skepticism and intrigue. Each iteration of his story seemed to warp subtly, like a reflection in rippling water, altering details that should have been anchored in certainty.

Nolan's initial certainty about the time he claimed to have seen Alex—a critical anchor point in the timeline of the Dawson family's tragedy—gradually became a slippery notion, shifting forward and backward as if untethered by reality. What was once stated with conviction now seemed hedged with qualifiers, "around" and "maybe" becoming the scaffolding of his narrative.

Moreover, the physical details Nolan provided, crucial in painting a believable picture of Alex's alleged post-crime appearance, began to unravel under Detective Henderson's methodical questioning. The bloodstains Nolan described with vivid detail in his first recounting became less definitive, their existence more suggested than assured. The supposed argument, a piece of his testimony that had initially seemed like a concrete clue, now felt more like a ghost of a memory, its reality questionable given Nolan's admitted distance from the scene.

Detective Henderson, with a practiced eye, recognized these fluctuations not as the deliberate obfuscations of a man with something to hide but as the hallmarks of human memory's inherent frailty. Nolan, like all witnesses, was subject to the distortions of time and the influence of subsequent information, his recollections a blend of what he had seen, what he had heard, and what he had come to believe.

This realization brought Detective Henderson to a critical juncture in the investigation. The inconsistencies in Nolan's testimony, while frustrating, mirrored the complex web of truths and half-truths that characterized the entire case. They served as a stark reminder of the challenges inherent in distinguishing between reality and perception, between what was witnessed and what was imagined or inferred.

As she continued to probe the depths of Nolan's account, Detective Henderson remained acutely aware of the delicate balance required to navigate this terrain. The quest for the truth in the Dawson case—a truth that seemed increasingly elusive—demanded not only a meticulous examination of the facts but also an understanding of the subjective nature of human memory and perception. Nolan's testimony, fraught with contradictions though it might be, was a piece of the puzzle that could not be disregarded but instead needed to be weighed and woven into the larger tapestry of the investigation with care and discernment.

Detective Henderson found herself particularly perplexed by Eric Nolan's description of Alex on the night of the murder. Nolan's account, which vividly depicted Alex as bearing the physical evidence of a violent encounter, contradicted the absence of such details in the physical evidence collected from the scene and from Alex himself in the immediate aftermath. The "sanguine marks" Nolan insisted he saw on Alex's clothing were nowhere to be documented in the case file, raising questions about the accuracy of his observation or the possibility of misinformation.

Furthermore, Nolan's claim of overhearing a heated argument between Alex and an unidentified party posed yet another conundrum. Given his stated location at the time—inside his shop, some distance away from the Dawson's apartment—such auditory details seemed implausible, if not impossible. The specificity with which Nolan described the supposed altercation, down to the tone and intensity of the voices, suggested a level of detail that his physical proximity to the event could not possibly support.

These discrepancies in Nolan's testimony added layers of complexity to an already intricate case. For Detective Henderson, the challenge was not merely in assessing the credibility of Nolan's account but in understanding how these seemingly incongruent pieces fit into the broader narrative of the night in question. The absence of corroborative evidence to support Nolan's vivid descriptions raised critical questions about the source of his information. Was it a case of mistaken identity, a genuine but flawed attempt to recall the events of that night, or were there other, unseen factors at play that influenced his recollection?

Detective Henderson considered the possibility that Nolan's account was colored by the subsequent public discourse surrounding the case. The human tendency to conflate hearsay and media reports with personal memory could not be overlooked, and

Nolan's testimony might well be a mosaic of factual observation and externally influenced fabrication. This phenomenon, known in psychological circles as the misinformation effect, could explain the vividness of Nolan's recollections despite their lack of alignment with the factual evidence.

As she delved deeper into the inconsistencies of Nolan's account, Detective Henderson remained vigilant to the dual challenge it presented. On one hand, it was a potential lead that could not be summarily dismissed without thorough investigation. On the other, it was a stark reminder of the pitfalls that lay in relying too heavily on eyewitness testimony, especially when such testimony stood in stark contrast to the physical evidence and lacked independent verification.

The task before Detective Henderson and her team was to navigate these murky waters with a critical eye, weighing the value of Nolan's testimony against the potential for it to mislead or detract from the pursuit of tangible leads. In the complex puzzle of the Dawson family tragedy, Nolan's account was both a piece to be considered and a cautionary tale in the limitations and vulnerabilities of human perception and memory.

Detective Henderson found herself at a crossroads, the testimonies of Nolan and Alex laying before her like two diverging paths shrouded in mist. Each account, fragmented and laced with contradictions, seemed to challenge the very foundations of the investigation, suggesting a reality far more complex and elusive than the straightforward narrative she had hoped to uncover. It was as if the case had become a mirror, reflecting the inherent ambiguity of human experience and the fluidity of truth itself.

This reflection led Henderson to ponder the fragile nature of memory and the role of perception in shaping our understanding of events. The more she delved into the accounts of Nolan and Alex, the more she recognized the impact of subjective interpretation on what was believed to be objective reality. It was a realization that thrust her into the murky waters of epistemological inquiry, where the line between fact and fiction, witness and narrator, blurred into obscurity.

The investigation had thus transformed from a mere collection of evidence and statements into a philosophical journey into the nature of truth. Henderson was forced to confront the possibility that the "reality" of the Dawson family tragedy might not be a singular, immutable construct, but rather a tapestry woven from the diverse perspectives and memories of those involved. This notion, unsettling as it was, opened up new avenues of thought and inquiry, compelling her to approach the case with a heightened awareness of the complexities involved.

The challenge now was not only to ascertain the facts of the case but also to navigate the subjective landscapes of human memory and perception. Henderson recognized that in doing so, she was engaging in a delicate balancing act, weighing the credibility of each account against the backdrop of psychological and cognitive biases that could influence recollection and interpretation.

This introspective turn in the investigation underscored the multidimensional nature of the task at hand. Henderson was no longer merely a detective seeking to solve a crime; she had become a seeker of truth in a realm where truth was as fluid and evasive as the morning fog. The testimonies of Nolan and Alex, with their inherent contradictions and complexities, served as a poignant reminder of the limitations of human cognition and the subjective lens through which we all view the world.

In this new light, Henderson approached the investigation with a renewed sense of purpose and caution. She understood that to unravel the mystery of the Dawson family tragedy, she must tread carefully through the labyrinth of human memory, guided by the faint light of empirical evidence but always mindful of the shadows cast by perception and prejudice. The journey ahead promised no easy answers, but Henderson was prepared to confront the challenge, armed with a deeper understanding of the elusive interplay between memory, perception, and truth.

The introduction of Nolan's account into the heart of the investigation shed light on the profound complexities that lay beneath the surface of the Dawson case. Detective Henderson, faced with the intricacies of Nolan's inconsistent and sometimes contradictory testimony, realized that the quest for truth was ensnared by more than the mere silences and lies of those involved. It was a struggle against the ever-shifting sands of human memory, against the distortions wrought by time and subjectivity on the fragile tapestry of recollection.

This insight cast the investigation in a new, more challenging light. The variability of human perception, with its capacity to reshape and color past events, emerged as a formidable adversary, one that could obscure the path to clarity with shadows of doubt and ambiguity. Henderson understood that each witness's account, including Nolan's, was not a mere recounting of facts but a narrative reconstructed from the fragments of memory, each piece colored by emotion, bias, and personal interpretation.

The realization that memory could be both ally and foe in the quest for justice compelled Henderson to navigate the investigation with a heightened sense of caution and discernment. It was a stark reminder that the "truth" sought after was not a monolith but a mosaic, composed of myriad pieces, each shaped by the individual lenses through which the witnesses viewed the world.

The challenges posed by the inherent variability of human cognition underscored the need for a nuanced approach to the investigation. Henderson was now tasked with not only piecing together the factual elements of the case but also understanding the psychological underpinnings of each witness's account. It was an endeavor that required not just the skills of a detective but the insight of a psychologist, discerning the kernels of truth that lay hidden beneath layers of subjective experience and cognitive bias.

This revelation transformed the investigation into a more complex but potentially enriching journey. As Henderson delved deeper into the murky waters of human memory and perception, she became acutely aware of the delicate balance between skepticism and empathy, between the need to question and the need to understand. The pursuit of truth in the Dawson case had evolved into an exploration of the human condition itself, a quest not just for justice but for a deeper comprehension of the enigmatic nature of memory, perception, and truth.

In navigating these challenges, Henderson found herself at the forefront of a battle that was as much

intellectual as it was investigative. The revelation of
Nolan's testimony, with all its inherent complexities,
served as a crucial turning point, a moment that
underscored the multidimensional nature of the
quest for truth. It was a journey fraught with
obstacles but illuminated by the possibility of
uncovering not just the facts of the Dawson tragedy
but also insights into the intricate workings of the
human mind.

Nolan's testimony, emerging like a beacon through
the dense fog of uncertainty that had enveloped the
Dawson family tragedy, heralded a pivotal moment
in the investigation. It promised a new direction, a
thread that, if carefully unraveled, could lead
Detective Henderson and her team out of the mire of
confusion that had thwarted their progress. This
glimmer of potential breakthrough, however, was
not without its own shadows, casting a complex
array of challenges that mirrored the very essence of
the case they were trying to solve.

The pathway opened by Nolan's revelations was
fraught with the inherent ambiguities of human
perception. As Detective Henderson delved into the
depths of this new lead, she found herself
navigating a terrain where the boundaries between
objective reality and subjective experience were
blurred, where the solid ground of factual evidence
gave way to the quagmire of personal interpretation
and flawed memory. It was a realm where truth was

not a static entity to be unearthed but a fluid concept, constantly reshaped by the lenses through which it was viewed.

This realization underscored the delicate nature of the investigative process. The detective's quest for clarity had become a dance with shadows, an intricate ballet performed on the stage of human cognition, where each step forward was matched with the realization of the complexity of the journey ahead. Nolan's account, while a critical piece of the puzzle, was also a reflection of the convoluted interplay between memory and reality, a microcosm of the broader challenges that faced the investigation.

The breakthrough, therefore, was not just a step closer to solving the mystery of the Dawson tragedy but also a deeper dive into the complexities of the human psyche. It served as a poignant reminder that the pursuit of justice was inextricably linked to the understanding of the nuanced ways in which individuals perceive and recall their experiences. The investigation, in essence, had transcended the mere accumulation of evidence to become a probing inquiry into the nature of truth itself, exploring how it is shaped, distorted, and ultimately understood within the confines of the human mind.

As Detective Henderson and her team ventured further along this newly illuminated path, they were acutely aware of the dual nature of their quest. The revelations brought forth by Nolan's testimony provided a map through which they could navigate the labyrinth of the Dawson case, offering clues and directions that had previously eluded them. Yet, this map was drawn not in the definitive lines of incontrovertible fact but in the shifting contours of perception and memory, requiring a careful and discerning eye to interpret its meanings.

The investigation, enriched by the complexity of its challenges, had evolved into a profound exploration of the interplay between reality and perception. The breakthrough represented by Nolan's account, with its blend of enlightenment and complication, underscored the multifaceted nature of the quest for truth. It was a journey that promised not only the possibility of resolving the tragedy of the Dawson family but also deeper insights into the elusive dynamics of human cognition and the ever-changing landscape of reality as it is perceived and remembered.

As Detective Laura Henderson delved deeper into the complexities unveiled by Eric Nolan's testimony, the investigation into the Dawson family tragedy transformed into an expedition through a landscape shrouded in ambiguity. Each step forward, guided by the enigmatic clues provided by Nolan, seemed to reveal further layers of mystery, challenging the team's understanding of what was truly real versus what was merely perceived. This quest for justice became a testament to their unwavering commitment, a search for clarity amidst a sea of uncertainty where facts and illusions intertwined indistinguishably.

Henderson's approach to Nolan's contradictory statements required a navigation of the intricate interplay between objective evidence and subjective experience. The investigation, therefore, transcended the conventional boundaries of detective work, morphing into an exploration of the human condition itself. The testimonies, once considered mere data points in the accumulation of evidence, were now seen as windows into the complex fabric of human memory and perception.

The detective and her team found themselves charting a course through uncharted waters, where the lighthouse of truth flickered intermittently through the fog of conjecture and speculation. Nolan's account, while initially seen as a beacon of hope, had complicated the narrative, introducing a myriad of potential paths to follow, each obscured by the mists of human fallibility.

This relentless pursuit of clarity in a realm where certainty seemed as elusive as a mirage underscored the resilience and dedication of Henderson and her team. They recognized that justice for the Dawson family hinged not only on the uncovering of factual evidence but also on the understanding of the deeper, more abstract elements of human psychology and perception.

As the investigation progressed, Henderson's strategy evolved to accommodate the fluid nature of the evidence before her. She employed a blend of meticulous analysis and intuitive insight, piecing together the fragmented puzzle of Nolan's testimony with the broader tapestry of the case. This methodical yet adaptive approach reflected the unique challenges posed by the investigation, where the journey towards resolution was as much about understanding the nuances of human memory as it was about solving a crime.

The quest for justice for the Dawson family, therefore, became a symbolic journey through the labyrinth of the human psyche, a voyage that tested the limits of the investigative team's resolve. It was a journey that promised no easy answers but offered the potential for profound insights into the nature of truth, memory, and perception. As Detective Henderson ventured further into this realm of shadows and light, she remained steadfast in her conviction that somewhere within the elusive interplay of reality and perception lay the key to unlocking the mystery of the Dawson tragedy, a truth waiting to be discovered in the space where the tangible and the intangible converge.

Chapter 14: The World Through Distorted Glass

As the first rays of dawn sliced through the blinds, casting long shadows across the chaos that filled Alex's small, cluttered apartment, it was as if the room itself bore witness to a battle waged through the night. Amidst this disarray, Alex sat, a solitary figure surrounded by the detritus of his fevered quest for clarity. His hands, once steady and purposeful as they moved from one piece of evidence to the next, now lay still, weighed down by a fatigue that was more mental than physical. The maps, once hopeful beacons guiding him toward enlightenment, sprawled across the floor in a disorganized sprawl, their routes and landmarks mocking him with their promise of answers just beyond reach.

The newspaper clippings, which had fluttered like whispers of possibility under the scrutiny of his late-night vigils, were now silent, their headlines and stories blending into a cacophony of information that no longer seemed to hold the key he so desperately sought. In the dim morning light, these artifacts of his investigation transformed from potential guides to relics of his isolation, each one a reminder of the distance between the world they depicted and the inner turmoil that consumed him.

Alex's gaze, once sharp and searching, had dulled, the focus blurred by hours spent poring over the ephemeral connections he hoped to find within the paper maze that surrounded him. The redness of his eyes spoke not just to the physical toll of his sleepless night but to the emotional exhaustion of confronting, again and again, the walls of his self-imposed labyrinth. The resolve that had fueled his night-long endeavor had ebbed, leaving behind a palpable sense of defeat, a feeling that for all his efforts, he was no closer to understanding the reality of the Dawson family tragedy or his place within it.

This moment of quiet, in the stark contrast to the frenetic activity that had preceded it, offered Alex a mirror to his own state of mind. The apartment, with its scattered maps and clippings, mirrored the disarray of his thoughts, each piece a fragment of a larger puzzle he could not complete. The search for patterns and connections had led not to discovery but to a deeper entrenchment within the maze of his own creation, a realization that dawned on him with the clarity of the morning light.

As he sat amidst the remnants of his night's work, the truth of his situation settled over him with the weight of the morning air—thick and immovable. The path to understanding, he now saw, was not to be found in the external trappings of maps and newspapers but within the more daunting, uncharted territory of his own mind. The realization was a pivot, a moment of profound introspection that marked the end of one journey and the beginning of another, more introspective quest for truth.

Alex found himself at the edge of understanding, peering into the void that separated the world within from the world without. The maps sprawled across his apartment floor, once meticulously arranged in a semblance of order, had become a jumbled mess of paper and ink, each one a testament to his failed attempts to anchor his fragmented memories to the solid reality of geography and events. These cartographic fragments, intended to be guides through the fog of confusion, had instead become symbols of his disorientation, their routes and boundaries a mocking reminder of the elusive nature of truth in the maze of his mind.

The once-clear lines on these maps, representing streets and landmarks, now seemed to twist and turn upon themselves, creating a nonsensical pattern that mirrored the turmoil within Alex. Each attempt to trace a path from his disjointed flashbacks to the physical location of the Dawson family's murder had only served to deepen the chasm between his internal experience and the external world. The harder he tried to make sense of the overlapping landscapes of memory and reality, the more apparent it became that the true path to understanding lay not in the external world of concrete and stone but in the murky depths of his own psyche.

As dawn illuminated his futile efforts, the maps and clippings that surrounded him no longer represented a potential route to clarity but a stark illustration of his isolation within a self-constructed labyrinth of confusion. The geography they depicted, once full of possibility, now seemed alien and unreachable, a foreign land separated from him by an insurmountable gulf of misunderstanding and mis-recollection.

This realization struck Alex with the force of revelation, the understanding that his search for connections in the physical realm was a reflection of a deeper disconnection within. The tangible geography of the city, with its streets and buildings, had become an inadequate proxy for the intricate topography of his thoughts and memories, where truth and fiction intersected in unpredictable ways. The real challenge, he saw, was not to map his experience onto the world outside but to navigate the inner landscape of his own mind, to bridge the chasm between perception and reality from within.

In this moment of clarity, Alex understood that the true journey ahead was one of introspection and self-exploration, a voyage into the heart of his own memories and fears. The scattered maps and clippings, once tools in his quest for external validation of his fragmented recollections, now served as a poignant reminder of the necessity to turn his gaze inward, to confront the distorted reflections of his own mind and seek the truth that lay buried beneath layers of confusion and doubt.

The articles, once thought to be lanterns illuminating the shadowy corridors of Alex's quest, now seemed to mock him with their ambiguity. Each story, each headline that had promised a glimmer of insight, now wove a tapestry of enigma that cloaked rather than clarified the truth he sought. As he pored over them, the words blurred into an aberrant whirl of information, a cacophony of global tragedies, local scandals, and political intrigue that resonated with the turmoil within him but offered no clear path forward.

With every article that Alex scrutinized, the hope of finding a nexus to his disjointed memories and the harrowing night of the Dawson tragedy dimmed. What had once seemed like potential revelations now appeared as cryptic puzzles, each piece infused with meaning yet obfuscated by the complex language of coincidence and conjecture. The secrets they held seemed to flicker in and out of clarity, like phantoms in the periphery of his vision, suggesting connections that vanished upon closer inspection.

This dance of comprehension and elusion was maddening. The articles, in their silent watch over his growing despair, became not just fragments of a world beyond his confines but symbols of the elusive nature of truth itself. They were the bearers of stories untold, of lives intersected by fate and circumstance, resonating with the echoes of his own fragmented narrative yet refusing to yield the coherence he so desperately sought.

In this maze of paper and ink, Alex found himself chasing after the specters of meaning, each article a tantalizing mirage that promised answers but delivered only more questions. The secrets they whispered in the stillness were not the keys to unlocking his past but mirrors reflecting the complexity of understanding and interpreting reality. They spoke not with the clarity of revelation but with the subtlety of riddles, each one a piece of a larger puzzle that seemed perpetually incomplete.

As the first light of dawn began to seep through the curtains, casting a pale glow on the chaotic landscape of his investigation, Alex realized the futility of seeking answers in the external chaos mirrored by the articles. The true enigma lay within, in the uncharted territories of his own mind, where the real secrets whispered not in the language of newspapers and maps but in the silent language of memory and self-reflection.

In this vortex of confusion, Alex found himself wrestling with the ephemeral shadows of meaning, each attempt to connect the dots leading him deeper into a quagmire of speculation. The artifacts surrounding him, once beacons of hope in his search for clarity, had morphed into totems of his solitude, silent witnesses to the internal chaos that consumed him. The newspapers, with their frozen snapshots of the world's turmoil, mirrored the turbulence within his own psyche, while the maps, with their sprawling networks of roads and locations, mirrored the convoluted pathways of his thoughts.

Each piece of evidence, each fragment of memory, seemed to drift further away from coherence, like stars receding into the darkness of space, leaving behind a void filled with more questions than answers. The quest for truth, which had once ignited a fire within him, now felt like an exercise in futility, a perpetual chase after a horizon that continually receded with each step forward.

As dawn's first light began to filter through the curtains, casting a soft glow over the chaotic tapestry of his makeshift command center, Alex was struck by a profound sense of alienation. The world outside, with its rhythms and routines, seemed an alien landscape, distant and detached from the existential quagmire in which he found himself ensnared.

The realization that his search for answers had turned inward, becoming a journey not through the external world but through the dark, uncharted territories of his own mind, was both a revelation and a curse. The truth he sought, it seemed, lay not in the tangible artifacts of his investigation but in the elusive, shifting sands of his own consciousness.

In this moment of introspection, Alex understood that the labyrinth he navigated was not one of physical space but of memory and identity, a maze constructed not from the events of the outside world but from the perceptions and distortions of his own mind. The challenge was no longer to map the geography of the Dawson family tragedy but to chart the inner topography of his own psyche, to confront the minotaur of his own fears and uncertainties that lurked in its depths.

With the rising sun illuminating the detritus of his nocturnal odyssey, Alex stood at the threshold of a new understanding, aware that the journey ahead was one that required not just the intellect of a detective but the courage of an explorer, venturing into the unknown regions of the self. The quest for truth, he realized, was ultimately a quest for self-discovery, a journey not to the heart of the mystery but to the heart of his own being.

Caught in this tempest of the mind, Alex grappled with the ephemeral nature of his own memories, each flashback a brushstroke on the canvas of his consciousness, contributing to a portrait that defied comprehension. The images that flickered through his psyche—a child's laughter echoing down an empty hallway, the sharp scent of rain on concrete, a fleeting glimpse of a face half-remembered—merged into a tableau that was both hauntingly familiar and eerily foreign.

The more he attempted to anchor these visions to the reality of his present, the more elusive they became, slipping through his fingers like grains of sand. The temporal dissonance of these flashbacks, oscillating between past and present with no discernible logic or pattern, served to underscore the fragility of his grasp on the continuum of his own life's narrative.

This maelstrom of memory and imagination, where the echoes of what might have been intertwined with the shadows of what was, enveloped Alex in a shroud of introspection. The once-solid ground of his identity now felt like a shifting landscape, every certitude called into question by the phantasmagoria of his inner world.

In this domain where the phantoms of memory held sway, Alex found himself questioning the very essence of his being. Was he merely the sum of these disjointed memories, a puppet danced on the strings of subconscious whims? Or was there a core to his identity, a steadfast anchor amidst the swirling chaos that threatened to consume him?

The relentless onslaught of these visions, each more enigmatic than the last, became a crucible, testing the limits of Alex's endurance and sanity. Yet, within this crucible, within the alchemical fire of his turmoil, lay the potential for transformation. For in confronting the specters of his past, in facing the abyss of his own uncertainties, Alex glimpsed the possibility of rebirth, of forging a self not bound by the chains of fragmented memory but sculpted by the hands of conscious choice and determination.

As the daylight strengthened, casting long shadows across the room that had borne witness to his nocturnal struggle, Alex sensed a shift within himself. The cacophony of his flashbacks, though still present, no longer seemed an implacable foe but a challenge to be met, a puzzle to be solved. In this moment of clarity, Alex realized that the journey through the mire of his past was not a descent into madness but a pilgrimage toward understanding, a path that, though fraught with peril, held the promise of enlightenment and the hope of finding peace amidst the storm.

This realization was both a revelation and a reckoning. The dawn's light, creeping through the gaps in the curtains, cast a gentle but unyielding illumination on the chaos that surrounded him, both physically and mentally. Alex understood that in his fervent desire to find order in the chaos, to draw connections where there might be none, he had inadvertently woven a narrative as convoluted and intricate as the labyrinth of his own thoughts. The maps, with their lines and symbols, had become a metaphor for his attempts to navigate through the murky waters of his consciousness, seeking solid ground where there was only the shifting sands of doubt and speculation.

The newspaper clippings, once believed to hold hidden truths waiting to be unearthed, now seemed to mock his efforts, their headlines blurring into a cacophony of voices that echoed the multifaceted nature of his own psyche. Each article, each snippet of news, had been a stroke on a portrait of a world seen through the lens of his fears and anxieties, a world where shadows loomed larger than life, obscuring the light of clarity and reason.

In this moment of introspection, Alex came to see that the quest for understanding he had embarked upon was less about uncovering an external truth than about confronting the internal maelstrom that had propelled him on this journey. The realization that his search had led him not outward but inward, to the depths of his own mind, was both daunting and liberating. The true labyrinth was not the world with its myriad mysteries and enigmas but the uncharted territories of his own inner landscape, a realm where the most profound discoveries awaited.

The introspective odyssey that Alex had hoped would lead him to a clearer understanding of the events surrounding the Dawson tragedy had instead brought him face to face with the complexities of his own identity and the elusive nature of memory and perception. It was a journey that challenged the very foundations of his understanding of himself and the world around him, revealing the intricate interplay between the mind and the reality it perceives.

As the dawn ushered in a new day, Alex found himself at a crossroads, not of the world's making but of his own. The realization that his efforts to impose order on the chaos had been a reflection of his inner turmoil marked a pivotal moment in his journey. It was a moment of profound introspection, an acknowledgment that the path to understanding lay not in the external trappings of maps and newsprint but in the quiet contemplation of his own thoughts and memories.

This epiphany, born from the depths of his introspective quest, illuminated a new path forward, one that promised not the certainty of answers but the hope of reconciliation with the complexities of his own nature. Alex understood that the true odyssey was not the search for a hidden truth in the world around him but the exploration of the vast, uncharted expanse of his own mind, where the most intricate puzzles of his identity and reality awaited his discovery.

This newfound insight, while daunting in its implications, also offered a sliver of hope. Alex recognized that his path forward necessitated a deep, introspective dive into the recesses of his own mind, a journey that promised to be as perilous as it was essential. The task at hand was no longer one of merely connecting dots on a map or deciphering the hidden messages in newspaper clippings; it was a quest for self-discovery, a pilgrimage into the heart of his own darkness to confront the fears, doubts, and truths that lay buried there.

The realization that the chaos of his external quest mirrored the turmoil within his own mind brought a profound sense of responsibility. Alex understood that to navigate this inner landscape, he would need to confront the shadows of his past, the unresolved conflicts, and the buried traumas that had shaped his perceptions of reality. This introspective journey required a courage of a different kind—the bravery to face the aspects of himself that he had long sought to avoid or deny.

Armed with this insight, Alex prepared to embark on this most intimate of voyages, a journey not through space but through time and memory. He recognized that the answers he sought about the Dawson family and his own enigmatic role in their tragedy would only be found by piecing together the fragmented mosaic of his own psyche. It was a daunting task, for the mind, he knew, could be an obfuscate and treacherous landscape, filled with illusions and traps of its own making.

Yet, in this moment of revelation, Alex felt a resolve steeling within him. The journey ahead would undoubtedly be fraught with challenges, with moments of doubt and revelation in equal measure. But it was a path he knew he must traverse, for only by facing the depths of his own psyche could he hope to find the clarity and peace that had eluded him for so long.

This epiphany marked the beginning of a new chapter in Alex's quest, one that promised a deeper understanding of the intricate weave of fate, memory, and identity. As the first rays of dawn illuminated the room, casting long shadows across the chaos of his makeshift investigation, Alex felt a sense of purpose ignite within him. The journey ahead would be arduous, a voyage across the uncharted waters of the mind, but it was a journey that held the promise of uncovering not just the secrets of a family tragedy but the deeper mysteries of the self.

This inward expedition demanded of Alex not just the tenacity of a seeker but the introspection of a sage, prepared to confront the myriad facets of his own soul. Understanding that the labyrinth of his mind was both the prison and the key to his turmoil, he resolved to face the echoes of his past with a newfound resolve. The specters that had haunted his waking hours and the phantoms that had disrupted his peace were not mere obstacles but guideposts, illuminating the path toward self-revelation and, ultimately, liberation.

The journey Alex envisaged was not merely a quest for the resolution of an external mystery but a pilgrimage towards the heart of his existential enigma. Each memory, each flashback, was a piece of the puzzle that, when assembled, would reveal the mosaic of his identity and the nature of his connection to the Dawson tragedy. He knew that this voyage would require him to peel away the layers of fear, guilt, and denial that had clouded his perception, to confront the raw truths that lay beneath.

With a sense of solemn determination, Alex acknowledged that the road ahead would be fraught with trials that would test the very limits of his courage and conviction. The journey through the shadowed corridors of his mind would be a solitary one, a dialogue between the man he once was and the man he hoped to become. It was a path that promised encounters with the darkest corners of his psyche, places where regret and sorrow had taken root, but also spaces where the light of understanding and forgiveness could flourish.

As he prepared to turn his gaze inward, Alex understood that this exploration of the inner self was as much about reconciliation as it was about discovery. To navigate the complexities of his own psyche, he would need to acknowledge the parts of himself he had long ignored or suppressed, to integrate the lessons of his past into the narrative of his present. This process of internal alignment, though fraught with emotional peril, was essential for breaking the cycle of confusion and despair that had ensnared him.

Embracing this introspective journey, Alex stood ready to traverse the mental and emotional terrain that lay ahead, equipped with the resolve to face whatever truths might emerge. This was a pilgrimage of the soul, a quest not just for the facts surrounding the Dawson family's fate but for the deeper understanding of his own place in the world. As the dawn of this new chapter in his life broke, Alex stepped forward, not with certainty, but with the courage to confront the unknown, to seek the light of truth in the depths of shadow, and to emerge from the odyssey not just with answers, but with a deeper sense of peace and self-awareness.

In this introspective voyage, Alex understood that the minotaur he sought to confront was not a beast of flesh and blood but the manifestation of his own inner demons. These were the fears, the unresolved questions, and the guilt that had shackled him to the past, casting long shadows over his present. The labyrinth was a complex weave of memories and emotions, some corridors illuminated by the clarity of truth, others shrouded in the mist of doubt.

With each step deeper into the maze of his consciousness, Alex felt the weight of uncertainty lifting, replaced by a burgeoning sense of purpose. The journey was fraught with challenges, as paths twisted and turned, leading him at times into the depths of despair, at others towards fleeting glimpses of enlightenment. Yet, with every challenge faced, with every shadow embraced, he found fragments of the self he had lost, pieces of a puzzle that slowly began to form a clearer picture of his identity and his place in the world.

The silence of his solitary quest was punctuated by the echoes of his past, voices and visions that had haunted him, now serving as guides. These echoes spoke not to lead him astray but to challenge him, to force him to question and, through questioning, to seek. In the heart of the labyrinth, in the darkest corners where fear had once reigned supreme, Alex discovered wellsprings of resilience and compassion, qualities he had forgotten he possessed.

This inner odyssey was Alex's to undertake alone, a pilgrimage through the sacred and profane chambers of his psyche. Each memory revisited, each emotion acknowledged, was a step towards the center of the maze, where the minotaur awaited not as a foe but as a reflection of Alex himself. It was here, in the confrontation with the embodiment of his deepest fears, that the true battle for understanding and redemption was fought.

Armed with the hope of discovery and the courage to face whatever truths might emerge, Alex pressed on. The labyrinth, once a prison of his own making, transformed under his steady gaze into a crucible of transformation. The world outside, with its myriad distractions and external mysteries, held no sway over the journey he was now embarked upon. Here, in the solitude and silence of his own mind, lay the keys to the chains that had bound him, the path to liberation not just from the enigma of the Dawson tragedy but from the torment of his own unresolved past.

As the contours of the labyrinth began to shift, revealing new paths and previously unseen connections between the disparate fragments of his life, Alex moved forward with a cautious optimism. The journey was far from over, the minotaur of his fears yet to be fully confronted, but the light of understanding grew brighter with each step, promising not just answers to the mysteries that had plagued him, but a peace and self-awareness that had long eluded him. In the depths of his own psyche, in the heart of the labyrinth, lay not just the darkness of fear but the promise of dawn, a new beginning forged in the crucible of introspection and courage.

Chapter 15: The Descent

In the subdued sanctuary of Dr. Emily Carter's office, with shadows clinging to the corners like spectral spectators, Alex found himself ensnared in the coils of his own fractured psyche. The office, a realm of subdued hues and comforting stillness, had transformed into an arena of confrontation—a crucible where the ghosts of his past and the specters of his doubts emerged from the depths to dance in the half-light. Dr. Carter, a sentinel in this borderland between the known and the nebulous, sat with a presence both calming and commanding, her keen gaze piercing the veil of Alex's defenses.

"I'm standing on the precipice of my own consciousness," Alex whispered, his voice a fragile thread in the thickening silence, "caught between the abyss of madness and the facade of normalcy I've so painstakingly constructed." His hands, restless and betraying the inner turmoil that words could scarcely convey, fidgeted with the frayed edges of reality itself.

Dr. Carter nodded, her demeanor unflappable yet imbued with an empathy that reached across the chasm of patient and therapist. "The journey inward is both treacherous and revealing," she intoned, her voice a beacon in the tempest of Alex's disquiet. "The fabric of reality, as you perceive it, is woven from threads both tangible and ethereal. It's in the unraveling that we find the patterns, the underlying truth that seeks to reveal itself."

As they delved deeper, navigating through the mists of memory and perception, a singularly potent recollection surged forth, breaking the surface of Alex's consciousness with the force of a long-submerged truth gasping for air. He was there again, outside the Dawson's door, the familiar yet alien threshold to a moment that defied comprehension. The door, an unassuming barrier to the domestic scene within, swung open to reveal James Dawson, his features twisted not just in anger but in a kaleidoscope of emotions that mirrored the turmoil roiling within Alex.

The altercation that ensued was not merely a clash of wills but a symphony of chaos, each blow a note in a crescendo of rage that threatened to drown out all reason. Alex, spectator and participant both, watched as his own hands became instruments of a violence that felt both foreign and intimately his own. The aftermath, with James Dawson motionless and the silence screaming, was a tableau that haunted the fringes of his memory, a painting etched in shades of guilt and confusion.

"This memory, real or imagined," Dr. Carter prodded gently, steering Alex through the storm-tossed seas of his psyche, "is a lighthouse in the fog. It signals not just a moment of crisis but a beacon pointing toward the deeper currents that shape your journey."

Alex, caught in the eye of the maelstrom, grappled with the duality of his nature—victim and aggressor, bystander and catalyst. The session, a dance along the razor's edge of sanity, left more questions in its wake than answers, each inquiry a step deeper into the labyrinth of his own making.

Exiting the office, the world Alex stepped into bore the surreal quality of a dream half-remembered. The city around him, with its cacophony of life and light, seemed both achingly real and eerily detached, a stage upon which the drama of his own psyche played out in shadows and whispers. The boundary that had once demarcated the inner from the outer, the self from the other, now lay in tatters at his feet, inviting him to step beyond the threshold and into the unknown.

Thus, Alex found himself at a crossroads, not of streets and signs, but of paths woven from the fabric of his own consciousness. Ahead lay the journey deeper into the heart of his own darkness, where the answers to his torment and the keys to his salvation lay hidden beneath layers of fear, guilt, and revelation. It was a path fraught with peril, a descent into the depths where the monsters of his own creation awaited. Yet, in this descent, there was also the promise of emergence, of a rebirth forged from the crucible of self-discovery and the courage to confront the abyss.

"I'm walking a tightrope over an abyss," Alex murmured, his voice barely breaking the silence of the room. "Below me is either insanity or the revelation that it's been my home this whole time, and everything I've believed... might be nothing but smoke."

Dr. Carter watched him with a steady, unwavering gaze that seemed to anchor him slightly, a lifeline thrown across the chasm widening inside him. "The line between our reality and what we perceive is often thinner than we imagine," she said, her tone even, attempting to draw him back from the edge. "Doubting our senses doesn't necessarily mean losing touch with them. It can be the first step towards truly seeing."

In this session that felt more like a confession, Alex dredged up from the depths of his psyche a memory so vivid it stole his breath. He was there again, outside the Dawson's, the normality of the hallway clashing with the storm brewing in his heart.

The door burst open, and there stood James Dawson, his features contorted not just in anger but something deeper, a reflection of Alex's own inner chaos. A heated exchange ensued, though the words evaporated like mist; only the surge of emotions remained, culminating in a physical altercation that seemed both alien and disturbingly familiar to Alex. His own hands acted with a will of their own, and suddenly Dawson was motionless, a quiet that screamed louder than any words.

As quickly as it had surfaced, the memory — or nightmare — receded, leaving Alex panting, his pulse racing. He sought Dr. Carter's eyes, searching for a shred of clarity, a sign that this violent past was a fabrication of his troubled mind.

"That incident with Mr. Dawson," she started, cautiously navigating through the minefield of his psyche, "do you believe it actually happened, or is it possible your mind is trying to tell you something else?"

Alex's distress was palpable, his face a canvas of fear and confusion. "I don't know. It feels real, as does everything else in these... flashes. But how can I trust my own mind when it shows me such horrors? What if I'm not the bystander I thought I was?"

The weight of his fears seemed to fill the room, a suffocating cloud of doubt and self-recrimination. The therapy session, meant to be a step towards healing, had instead opened a Pandora's box of uncertainties, leaving Alex to wrestle with the possibility that he might have played a far more active role in the Dawson tragedy than he could ever have imagined.

Leaving Dr. Carter's office, the world outside took on an otherworldly sheen, a vivid yet distant reality as if seen through a veil. The certainty of what was real and what was a figment of his imagination had never been more elusive, propelling Alex further into the depths of his own mind, a realm where truth and fantasy intermingled, casting long shadows over his search for peace and clarity.

Dr. Carter's calm was the anchor in the storm of Alex's turmoil. "Our grasp on what we call reality is not as firm as we imagine," she suggested, her voice a beacon in his fog of confusion. "Doubting what we see, feel, or remember doesn't necessarily push us towards madness. Rather, it's a step on the path to deeper insight, a crucial phase in the journey towards healing ourselves."

Her words hung in the air between them, a lifeline thrown to a man drowning in his own psyche. "Consider," she continued, "that every person's reality is a unique tapestry woven from their experiences, beliefs, and perceptions. Yours is no different. What you're experiencing, these fractures in your perception, they're not signs of a mind breaking apart but of one asking to be understood, to be made whole."

She leaned forward slightly, bridging the physical gap on the couch with a gesture of empathy. "It's as if your mind is a puzzle, and you're holding pieces that don't seem to fit. But the picture they form is not wrong, just incomplete. Our work, your journey, is about finding where those pieces belong, to see the fuller image they're trying to show you."

Alex listened, the tumult within him quieting just a fraction. Dr. Carter's steadfastness, her refusal to see his fractured reality as a symptom of failure or insanity, offered a glimmer of hope in the darkness. "So, you're saying this... conflict within me, it's not a descent into chaos but a struggle to emerge on the other side, stronger and more whole?"

"Exactly," Dr. Carter affirmed, her voice firm yet gentle. "This turmoil, the questions you're grappling with, they're not just obstacles. They're opportunities for growth, for healing. Your reality, as fluid as it seems, is yours to shape. And questioning it, far from being a sign of losing your way, is actually the first step towards finding it."

In Dr. Carter's office, amidst the turmoil of his unraveling, Alex found an unexpected sanctuary. Here, in the presence of his therapist's unwavering calm, the idea that his splintering reality might not be an end but a beginning took root. The notion that his doubts could be the very thing to guide him through the darkness offered a slender thread of hope to cling to, a possibility that perhaps, in the very questioning of his reality, lay the path to his healing.

As Dr. Carter guided Alex through the labyrinthine corridors of his subconscious, they stumbled upon a memory so vivid, it was as if a veil had been lifted, revealing a scene etched in stark relief against the backdrop of his mind's shadowy realms. There he was, rooted to the spot in the poorly lit corridor of the Dawson residence, where the muffled cacophony of an ordinary family evening trickled through the cracks beneath their door—a deceptive serenade to the storm brewing within him.

The light in the hallway flickered, casting eerie shadows that danced along the walls, mirroring the tumult in Alex's heart. He could hear laughter, the clinking of dinner plates, the everyday symphony of a family unaware of the dark undercurrent pulling at the edges of their domestic bliss. And there, poised on the precipice of action and indecision, Alex felt an alien surge of emotion overwhelming his senses.

The door, a barrier between two worlds, suddenly swung open, revealing James Dawson, his features contorted in anger or perhaps fear—a reflection of the emotional tempest Alex himself was caught in. Words were exchanged, their exact nature lost to the depths of Alex's memory, yet the emotion behind them was as palpable as the tension that filled the air. Words like barbs, they pricked at Alex's composure, each syllable a spark in the powder keg of his restraint.

Without warning, the dam broke. The hallway, once just a passageway, became an arena for a clash of wills, of words turned to action, a violent ballet choreographed by primal instincts long buried. Alex, witnessing the memory as if from outside his body, watched in horror as his hands, seemingly of their own volition, struck out. The sound of flesh meeting flesh was grotesquely clear, a punctuation mark in the sentence of their confrontation.

James Dawson fell, a puppet with its strings cut, and silence thundered in Alex's ears, a deafening void where the cacophony of conflict had just been. The memory receded as swiftly as it had appeared, leaving Alex gasping, his present reality crashing back with the weight of a thousand doubts.

"What if that wasn't just a memory?" The question tore from Alex's lips, a whisper of dread. "What if I...?"

The weight of implication hung between them, an unspoken horror at the possibility that Alex might not just be an observer in his own story, but a participant in ways he dared not fully comprehend. The revelation of this memory, with its visceral clarity and emotional weight, was a Pandora's box, unleashing questions that Alex feared, yet knew, he must confront if he was ever to find his way out of the darkness that enveloped him.

The silence of the hallway was abruptly shattered as the door burst open, revealing James Dawson, his features contorted by a fury as palpable as the tension that now crackled in the air between them. Words flew like daggers, their sharp edges lost to Alex's memory, yet the emotional charge behind each syllable was unmistakable, igniting a firestorm of anger within him that he struggled to contain.

In that charged moment, the world narrowed to the space between them, every detail etched with a clarity born of the adrenaline surging through Alex's veins. The faded wallpaper, the flickering light that struggled against the encroaching shadows, even the distant sound of a television somewhere in the building—all receded into the background, leaving only the immediacy of confrontation.

As if propelled by a force outside his control, Alex felt his body react, muscle and sinew coiled and then released in a flurry of motion that was both foreign and frightening in its intensity. His hands, acting as if divorced from his will, struck out with a violence that echoed the turmoil churning inside him. The sound of his fist meeting flesh was grotesquely clear, a harsh punctuation to the rush of blood in his ears and the roar of his own heartbeat.

The altercation, swift and brutal, reached its climax as James Dawson stumbled and then fell, his body hitting the ground with a finality that echoed ominously in the narrow hallway. The aftermath was a tableau of shock and disbelief, the silence that followed as thick and suffocating as the darkness that seemed to press in from all sides.

Alex stood frozen, the reverberations of what he had done—a violence born of an anger he hadn't known he possessed—ringing in his ears. The reality of James Dawson, unmoving at his feet, was a chasm opening beneath him, threatening to swallow him whole into a void of guilt and remorse.

The memory, vivid and visceral, receded as quickly as it had surged, leaving Alex adrift in the aftermath of its revelation. The echo of those moments, of actions and reactions that seemed both alien and intimately his own, was a haunting melody that played over and over in his mind, each note a question mark that loomed larger and more insistent in the dim light of Dr. Carter's office.

The vivid recollection, or perhaps the cruel trick of Alex's mind, melted away into the shadows of the room, its departure as sudden and disorienting as its arrival. Alex found himself thrust back into the stark reality of Dr. Carter's office, his breathing heavy, chest heaving as if he'd just run a marathon. His pulse hammered against his temples, a frantic rhythm that seemed to underscore the intensity of the experience he'd just endured.

He turned towards Dr. Carter, seeking in her calm, composed presence some anchor to the reality he hoped he hadn't lost. His eyes, wide and imploring, searched her face for any flicker of disbelief, any hint that she too sensed the tangible quality of the memory that had so violently intruded upon their session. The air between them was charged with Alex's desperate need for validation, for some assurance that the dark narrative that had unfolded in his mind's eye was nothing more than a figment of his troubled psyche.

Dr. Carter met his gaze, her expression a carefully maintained mask of professional concern that offered no immediate judgment. In the silence that stretched between them, filled only by the sound of Alex's labored breathing slowly returning to normal, a multitude of unspoken questions hung heavy. Her eyes, steady and unflinching, seemed to probe the depths of Alex's turmoil, searching for the threads that might lead them out of the tangled web in which they found themselves.

The room, with its subdued lighting and the faint ticking of the clock on the wall, became a sanctuary of sorts, a temporary respite from the storm of confusion and fear that raged within Alex. Dr. Carter's presence, both reassuring and enigmatic, promised a semblance of stability in the chaos, a guiding hand through the fog of doubt that now clouded Alex's mind.

As the moments passed, the intensity of the memory began to fade, its edges blurring as reality reasserted itself with the solidity of the chair beneath Alex, the soft hum of the air conditioning, and the reassuring normalcy of Dr. Carter's office. Yet, the echo of the confrontation with James Dawson, real or imagined, lingered, a shadow that clung to the edges of Alex's consciousness, a reminder of the fragile barrier that separated his inner world from the world outside.

"This... altercation with Mr. Dawson," Dr. Carter began carefully, "do you believe it happened? Or does it feel more like something your mind might have created?"

Dr. Carter's inquiry, tender yet probing, served as a beacon in the murky waters of Alex's psyche. Her words, poised between the realms of professional detachment and genuine concern, seemed to reach across the chasm of Alex's turmoil, offering a lifeline back to a semblance of stability.

Alex wrestled with the question, the gravity of its implications anchoring him momentarily in the present. The memory of the altercation, with its vivid fury and visceral fear, had surged through him with the force of a tempest, leaving no corner of his consciousness untouched. Yet, the suggestion that it might be a figment of his imagination, a dark blossom of his inner chaos, introduced a fissure of doubt that was both terrifying and oddly comforting.

He found himself teetering on the precipice of belief and skepticism, his trust in his own perceptions eroding under the relentless assault of uncertainties. The prospect that his mind could conjure such a detailed and disturbing scenario was a testament to its troubled depths, a reflection of the turmoil that churned beneath his calm exterior.

"I... It felt real," Alex replied, his voice a thread of sound in the vast silence of the room. "But now, questioning it... I'm not sure. It's like trying to grasp smoke."

Dr. Carter nodded, her expression a mask of professional neutrality, yet her eyes conveyed a depth of understanding that transcended mere clinical interest. "Our minds are powerful entities," she offered, "capable of creating realities as a means to process or escape from our fears and traumas. Recognizing this doesn't diminish your experiences; it offers a path to understanding them."

Alex absorbed her words, the concept of reality as something malleable and subjective, a fluid tapestry woven from the threads of perception and memory. The notion that his confrontation with Dawson could be both a memory and a construct of his troubled mind was a paradox that left him adrift, yet it was also a lifeline, offering the possibility of navigating through the storm towards a clearer understanding of himself and the events that haunted him.

Alex shook his head, frustration and fear etching lines into his face. "I don't know. It felt real, but so does everything else in these... episodes. I can't tell the difference anymore. What if I'm not just a witness? What if I...?"

Alex's admission hung in the air, a confession shrouded in the shadows of what might be, a question too harrowing to voice in its entirety. His gaze dropped to his hands, as if they might hold the answer, or perhaps, reveal the stain of guilt he feared. The silence that followed was a palpable entity, thick with the weight of unspoken possibilities and dark conjectures.

"I understand," Dr. Carter responded, her voice a soft counterpoint to the storm of emotions raging within Alex. "The line between reality and what our mind conjures can become blurred, especially under stress or trauma. It's natural to question, to doubt, especially when the mind presents us with such vivid scenarios."

Her words were meant to console, to offer solace in the face of the abyss Alex found himself peering into. Yet, the comfort they were supposed to bring felt distant, like a beacon lost in fog. Alex's mind raced, a whirlwind of thoughts and fears, each more daunting than the last. The possibility that he might have played an active role in the tragedy that had unfolded just a floor above his own, that he might be more than a mere bystander caught in the wake of disaster, was a notion that chilled him to his core.

"What if my hands are not clean? What if I..." Alex's voice trailed off, unable to complete the thought, yet the implication hung between them, heavy and ominous.

Dr. Carter leaned forward, bridging the distance with a gesture that spoke of empathy and understanding. "Alex, it's crucial we explore these thoughts, no matter how dark or unsettling. Facing them, understanding their origin, is the first step towards healing. Remember, fear of a thing often gives it more power than the thing itself deserves."

Her attempt to guide him back from the edge was a lifeline thrown across the chasm of his turmoil. Yet, for Alex, the struggle was far from over. Each revelation, each moment of clarity, seemed only to deepen the mystery of his own psyche, leading him further into a web of doubt and self-recrimination.

As the therapy session with Dr. Carter drew to a close, Alex was left to shoulder the weight of uncertainty alone, feeling the fabric of the known world transform into an alien landscape, impenetrable and distant. The unanswered questions that loomed in his mind cast long shadows, blurring the line between memory and madness, leaving him adrift in the murky depths of his own psyche. This swift descent into doubt and despair caused the ground of his reality to shift unsettlingly beneath him, challenging the very essence of his existence and the truths he had always held. With more questions than answers, Alex found himself navigating a labyrinth of confusion, isolated in his quest for clarity, as the session's end marked the beginning of a solitary journey through the tumultuous waters of his mind.

Stepping out from Dr. Carter's office, the world that greeted Alex was at once sharper in its clarity and yet oddly detached, as if he viewed it through a veil of glass, distorting and refracting the reality beyond. The contrast between the internal tempest of his thoughts and the external calm of the streets laid bare the profound dissonance within him. The concrete beneath his feet felt both solid and insubstantial, the bustling noise of the city a distant echo rather than a vibrant symphony of life.

This duality of perception ensnared Alex in a limbo of his own making, where the familiar landmarks of his life transformed into unfamiliar signposts, guiding him further into uncharted territories of his psyche. Memory and imagination intertwined indistinguishably, weaving a dense fog that obscured the path to understanding his own truth. Guilt, a specter that loomed large, cast long shadows over the innocence he sought to claim, each step forward a plunge into deeper ambiguity.

As Alex navigated this altered reality, the once-clear demarcations of his identity blurred, merging into the gray areas that his mind struggled to compartmentalize. The echoes of his session with Dr. Carter reverberated through the caverns of his thoughts, a haunting reminder of the questions unanswered and the fears unaddressed.

With each footstep, the labyrinth within Alex spiraled tighter, its corridors lined with the phantoms of doubt and the specters of guilt, leading him on a ceaseless quest for a truth that danced just beyond his grasp, shrouded in the penumbra of his own conflicted emotions. This journey, embarked upon in the aftermath of revelation and confusion, promised no easy resolutions but held the potential for transformative understanding, should he find the courage to confront the darkness at its heart.

Chapter 16: Echoes of the Past

Navigating the dimly lit pathways of his mind, Alex embarked on a relentless quest, each memory unraveling before him like a scene from a forgotten play, stark and unyielding in its clarity. These were not mere shadows of the past, but vivid reenactments of moments filled with tension and discord, each one etching deeper lines into the canvas of his psyche.

The memories came unbidden, sweeping across the landscape of his consciousness with the ferocity of a storm, leaving him breathless and disoriented in their wake. In one moment, he was standing in the midst of a bustling bazaar, the air thick with the scents of exotic spices and the clamor of voices haggling over prices. The next, he found himself on a rain-slicked street, the neon glow of signs reflecting in puddles underfoot, as an undercurrent of animosity pulsed through the night.

Each scene unfolded with agonizing detail, immersing Alex in the reality of those fleeting snapshots in time. The faces of those he encountered were blurred, their features indistinct, yet their emotions—anger, fear, desperation—were as tangible as if they stood before him in the flesh. Alex watched, a spectator within his own mind, as his hands acted of their own accord, pushing, striking, defending, each movement a testament to a survival instinct he didn't know he possessed.

These flashes of violence, disconnected from any narrative he could comprehend, left him reeling, questioning not only the nature of these memories but his very identity. Was he merely reliving the actions of another, or were these experiences a window into a darker aspect of his own soul?

As he journeyed deeper into the recesses of his memory, the line between observer and participant blurred, the distinction between past and present growing increasingly tenuous. With each step forward, the corridors of his mind seemed to twist and turn, leading him not toward enlightenment, but further into a web of confusion and doubt.

The memories, for all their vividness, offered no solace, only more questions. They were fragments of a larger story, pieces of a puzzle that Alex struggled to piece together. The more he uncovered, the more he realized the complexity of the labyrinth he navigated, a labyrinth constructed not of stone and mortar, but of fear, guilt, and the elusive shadow of truth.

In this odyssey through the depths of his own psyche, Alex was both hunter and hunted, seeking answers in a landscape where certainty was as fleeting as the shadows that danced at the edge of his vision. With each memory explored, the hope of finding a way out of the darkness dimmed, replaced by the growing realization that the key to his salvation—or his damnation—lay within the very memories he sought to understand.

This journey through the corridors of memory was Alex's alone to make, a solitary voyage across the tempestuous sea of his past. Here, in the silence of his own mind, he faced the echoes of his actions, the specter of violence that haunted each recollection. The journey was a crucible, testing the limits of his courage and his will to uncover the truth buried beneath layers of mystery and fear.

As Alex's mind grappled with the relentless surge of memories, the very essence of time and space seemed to warp around him. The solitude of his introspective quest shattered abruptly, thrusting him into the heart of a city whose history was as layered and complex as his own psyche. No longer was he enveloped in the quietude of introspection; instead, he stood beneath the imposing expanse of the Parisian sky, where the transition from the internal storm of his thoughts to the looming tempest above was as sudden as it was stark. This abrupt shift, a harsh reminder of the tumultuous journey he was on, left him reeling, caught in the liminal space between the darkness of his internal world and the shadowy reality of a city at dusk.

Under the brooding Parisian sky, as twilight bled into the fabric of the evening, Alex found himself adrift on the ancient cobblestones that had borne witness to countless stories, none perhaps as cryptic as his own. The city, usually alight with an effervescent glow, lay subdued beneath the weight of storm clouds, casting long shadows that stretched across the narrow street, merging with the darkness growing within him.

He was not alone. Ahead, a silhouette emerged from the gloom, a figure that seemed both part of the city's endless tales and eerily detached from them. The air between them crackled, charged with an unspoken tension that drowned out the distant sounds of the city—the soft clatter of a café closing up, the distant laughter of lovers lost in their private universe. Here, in this secluded alley, there was only the impending storm, both above and within.

As the first drops of rain began to fall, hesitant at first then gaining confidence, the figure moved, a specter gliding on the wet stones, its movements deliberate, a counterpoint to the chaotic beating of Alex's heart. Words were exchanged, their content lost to the growling of the heavens above, yet their intent pierced the veil of misunderstanding, striking at the core of Alex's tumultuous soul.

The response from within him was visceral, a raw pulse of energy that surged through his veins, igniting a fire that had long lain dormant. Muscle and instinct took over where reason and restraint faltered, propelling him into the heart of the confrontation. They clashed amidst the shadows and rain, figures entwined in a ballet as old as time, a struggle for dominance, for survival.

The confrontation, swift as a summer storm, left its mark upon both the victor and the vanquished. As quickly as it had escalated, it ended, the figure retreating into the mist that now enveloped the city like a cloak. Alex stood alone, the taste of adrenaline bitter on his tongue, the echoes of the encounter reverberating through the empty streets.

The city around him, once a backdrop to his solitary conflict, slowly came back to life, indifferent to the drama that had unfolded in its midst. The rain, now a steady downpour, washed away the remnants of the altercation, leaving behind a sheen on the cobblestones that reflected the myriad lights of Paris, each one a beacon in the darkness.

As the storm above began to wane, giving way to the quiet calm that often follows, Alex found himself at a crossroads, both literally and metaphorically. The violence of the encounter, though fleeting, had peeled back the layers of his own façade, revealing a glimpse of the depth of his own despair, his capacity for both violence and remorse.

In the aftermath of the storm, both within and without, Alex was left to ponder the enigma of his own nature, the duality of his existence—a man caught between the light of understanding and the darkness of his own doubts. The streets of Paris, with their timeless charm and hidden stories, offered no answers, only a reflection of the tumult that raged within his soul.

As Alex wandered the rain-soaked streets of Paris, lost in the tumult of his own conflicted thoughts, the world around him seemed to shift abruptly, as if reality itself had twisted under the weight of his inner turmoil. Without warning, the cool dampness of the French capital evaporated, replaced by the stifling heat of a distant land. The suddenness of the transition was disorienting, a jolt to his senses, catapulting him from the introspective quiet of a city nursing the bruises of a recent storm to the overwhelming sensory assault of a bustling marketplace under a relentless desert sun. It was as though he had stepped through a portal, leaving behind the introspective shadows of one city to confront the glaring light of another, each step forward a leap into uncertainty, each breath a gasp amidst the swirling sands of memory and reality.

Beneath the unforgiving gaze of the Egyptian sun, its rays a merciless beacon over the bustling heart of Cairo, Alex found himself ensnared in the vibrant chaos that was the city's lifeblood. The air was thick, charged with the scent of spices, the din of haggling voices, and the vibrant tapestry of humanity that wove itself through the narrow alleyways and expansive squares. Amidst this whirlwind of activity, a sense of foreboding took root deep within him, a discordant note in the symphony of the day.

Without warning, the tide of the crowd parted to reveal a figure, as indistinct as a mirage and yet unmistakably ominous. The confrontation that ensued was a storm brewing amidst the calm, a clash of wills as sudden as it was inexplicable. Words were exchanged, their meanings obscured by the roar of the city and the pounding of Alex's heart, yet their intent was as sharp as the sunlight that split the sky.

The escalation was rapid, a blur of motion and emotion that swept Alex along in its current. There was a push, a moment of weightlessness, and then the undeniable reality of resistance overcome. A figure stumbled back, their form a silhouette against the backdrop of the city's eternal dance, and then collapsed, the impact resonating through the stone and sand, a punctuation to the altercation that had shattered the day's illusion of peace.

As quickly as it had begun, the conflict evaporated, the crowd closing back in like water filling the space left by a stone. The figure, once a direct antagonist in Alex's immediate world, became nothing more than another layer in the city's deep, complex history, a story ending as abruptly as it had commenced.

Alex stood, the afterimage of the confrontation burning behind his eyelids, the echo of the fall ringing in his ears. The memory, however, was as elusive as the desert wind, slipping through his grasp, leaving behind a residue of questions unanswered, emotions unexplored. The marketplace around him continued its relentless pace, indifferent to the drama that had unfolded within its embrace.

As the sun continued its relentless march across the sky, Alex was left to ponder the shadows it cast, both around him and within his own soul. The altercation in the heart of Cairo, with its swift descent from mundane to monumental, mirrored the internal battles he fought, a reflection of the turmoil that plagued him. The streets of Cairo, with their ancient wisdom and timeless stories, offered no solace, only a mirror to the conflict that raged within, a battle between the man he was and the man he feared he might become.

From the sun-scorched tumult of Cairo's streets, where every shadow seemed to dance with the echoes of his own internal discord, to the silent, snow-blanketed avenues of New York, Alex's journey was one of stark contrasts. The abrupt shift from the vibrant chaos of an ancient city, alive with the pulse of centuries, to the serene stillness of a modern metropolis under winter's gentle shroud was jarring. As if stepping through a portal from one world to another, Alex transitioned from the heat of conflict under an unforgiving sun to the cold solitude of an urban snowscape. This sudden change, as harsh and unsettling as the flashbacks that tormented him, underscored the relentless unpredictability of his quest for understanding—a quest that carried him across the varied landscapes of his memories, each more disorienting than the last.

In the hushed silence of a New York evening, cloaked under a pristine layer of snow, Alex found himself a solitary figure amidst the city's slumbering giants. The skyscrapers loomed above, indifferent sentinels to the human drama unfolding on the streets they overshadowed. The usual cacophony of the city—the blaring horns, the rhythm of countless footsteps, the constant murmur of life—was subdued, replaced by a stillness that seemed almost otherworldly. In this frozen tableau, the turmoil raging within Alex felt all the more incongruous, a storm raging against the calm.

As he navigated the snow-laden paths, his footsteps the only blemish on the otherwise unblemished white, a sense of unease settled over him, a prelude to the encounter that awaited. From the shadows cast by an overhanging awning, a figure emerged, their presence a disruption to the tranquility of the night. Their breath, visible in the frigid air, mingled with Alex's, creating ephemeral clouds that marked the rhythm of their silent standoff.

The confrontation that ensued was a stark deviation from the peace of the winter night, a testament to the contrasts that defined Alex's life. Movements sharp and deliberate cut through the chill air, each gesture a testament to the tension that crackled between them. Words were unnecessary, the language of their bodies speaking volumes in the silence, communicating in the shorthand of adversaries long acquainted with each other's methods.

The struggle, intense and fleeting, was a dance of shadows against the snow, a delicate play of light and dark that mirrored the conflict within Alex's own heart. It ended not with a crescendo but with a quietude that matched the surroundings, the finality of the encounter marked by a stillness so profound it seemed as if the very air held its breath.

The aftermath left no trace on the pristine snow, the scene as untouched and serene as before their paths had crossed. The adversary, like the confrontation itself, faded into the night, leaving Alex alone with the echoes of the struggle. The city, so often a witness to the stories of its inhabitants, kept its counsel, the secrets of the night swallowed by the vast, indifferent expanse of white.

In the wake of the encounter, Alex stood amidst the silent sentinels of the city, the snow beneath him untarnished by the violence of moments before. The dissonance between the peace of his surroundings and the violence he had engaged in struck him with a chilling clarity. This New York evening, with its blanket of snow and whispered secrets, reflected the duality of his existence—a life marked by fleeting connections and unresolved conflicts, played out on a stage indifferent to its players.

The stillness of the scene belied the turmoil that churned within, a turmoil that the serene façade of the snow-covered city could not soothe. Alex's journey through the night was a metaphor for his larger quest—a search for meaning in a world that seemed as mutable and elusive as the snowflakes that danced in the cold air, each one a fleeting moment of beauty in a world fraught with unseen battles.

The sky above Sydney Harbor was an ominous palette of grays, the brooding clouds rolling in from the sea a visual echo of the unrest that plagued Alex's mind. The atmosphere was charged, electric with the anticipation of the storm's fury, a natural tumult that mirrored the internal chaos Alex felt swirling within him. The air was thick with the scent of rain, a precursor to the deluge that would soon unleash upon the city, washing its streets in a torrent of nature's own reckoning.

On the pier, where the wooden planks bore the slick sheen of the first hesitant raindrops, Alex stood face to face with a figure that seemed almost a manifestation of the storm itself—dark, unpredictable, and charged with a palpable intensity. The backdrop of the harbor, with its boats bobbing gently in the increasingly agitated waters, offered a stark contrast to the scene of confrontation that unfolded between them.

The dialogue between Alex and his opponent was lost to the roar of the wind and the distant rumble of thunder, their words carried away as quickly as they were spoken, leaving only the raw emotion of their exchange hanging in the air like the charged particles before a lightning strike. The encounter, though devoid of sound, was a cacophony of movement and expression, a silent ballet performed on the cusp of the storm's arrival.

As the first true bolts of lightning rent the sky, illuminating the scene in stark flashes of white light, Alex and his adversary seemed to draw energy from the tempest itself. Their movements, shadowed against the dramatic tableau of the storm-lit harbor, were a dance of figures poised on the edge of violence, each step, each gesture a testament to the tension that crackled between them with the electricity of the impending storm.

The climax of their encounter, much like the storm overhead, was both explosive and ephemeral. A clash of wills, a flurry of motion that ended as suddenly as it began, dissolving into the rain-soaked air with a finality that left Alex gasping for breath, his heart pounding in time with the thunderous applause of the heavens.

As quickly as it had materialized, the memory faded, slipping through Alex's grasp like water, leaving behind only the lingering sensation of adrenaline and the unresolved echo of conflict. The harbor, once a stage for this dramatic encounter, returned to its role as a mere backdrop to the city's daily life, indifferent to the human drama that had played out upon its pier.

In the aftermath, Alex was left to ponder the significance of the confrontation, a puzzle piece in the vast mosaic of his fractured memories. The stormy afternoon at Sydney Harbor, with its elemental fury and unresolved tensions, was a metaphor for the turmoil that raged within him—a storm of questions with no clear answers, a journey through the heart of darkness in search of a light he was not sure existed.

As Alex navigated the stormy seas of his mind, each recollection served as a beacon, momentarily illuminating the murky depths of his psyche before plunging him back into shadow. These memories, fragmented and disjointed, were like shards of glass from a shattered mirror, each reflecting a moment of conflict and violence that painted a chilling portrait of a man at war with himself.

This thread of aggression that wove its way through his memories was unnerving, a dark undercurrent that flowed beneath the surface of his consciousness, suggesting a depth to his character that Alex was loath to explore. With every scene that unfolded before his mind's eye, he was forced to confront the possibility that the violence he witnessed—and perhaps perpetrated—was not an anomaly but a fundamental aspect of his being.

Each flashback, from the shadowed alleyways of Venice to the neon-lit streets of Tokyo, from the rain-drenched pier in Sydney to the snow-silenced avenues of New York, presented a tableau of confrontation and conflict that Alex found increasingly difficult to dismiss as mere coincidence. The consistency of these encounters, the recurrence of this theme of violence, suggested a pattern that was too pronounced to ignore, a signature of sorts that spoke of impulses and actions that defied his self-image as a man of peace and reason.

The realization that these memories, these glimpses of other selves in other places, might collectively hint at a darker truth about his nature was a pill bitter with implications. With each memory that surfaced, Alex was forced to question not just the events they depicted but the very essence of who he was. The specter of violence that haunted these recollections was a specter of himself, a shadowy figure that moved through the scenes of his past with a disturbing familiarity.

This realization was a vortex, pulling him deeper into introspection, into the heart of a mystery that seemed as boundless as his own soul. The more he sought to piece together the puzzle of his existence, the more elusive the picture became, a mosaic of moments that refused to coalesce into a coherent whole. The violence that linked these memories was a chain that bound him to a past he could neither fully recall nor completely understand, a reminder of the man he feared he might discover in the depths of his own mind.

In this journey through the corridors of his memories, Alex was both the hunter and the haunted, pursuing the truth of his past while evading the implications of what he might find. The violence that underscored each memory was a clue to a puzzle he was unsure he wanted to solve, a riddle that spoke of a darkness within that threatened to overshadow the light of his search for understanding. With each step deeper into the mystery of his own psyche, Alex was forced to confront not just the specter of the man he might be but the reality of the man he was, a duality that was as compelling as it was terrifying.

Alex's journey into the recesses of his memory was a precarious dance on the knife-edge of his own duality, a constant battle between the darkness that seemed to stalk him through his recollections and the tranquility for which his soul yearned. Each flashback unfolded before him with the clarity and immediacy of a scene observed through crystal-clear water, yet they slipped away before he could grasp their meaning, leaving him gasping for comprehension in their wake.

This dissonance, the stark contrast between the violence that erupted with alarming frequency in his memories and the serene life he believed himself to lead, was a riddle wrapped in the enigma of his own psyche. The scenes that played out in his mind's eye were rich with detail—the sharp tang of fear in the air, the adrenaline-fueled clarity of the confrontations, the haunting aftermath of silence that followed—but they were frustratingly devoid of context, fragments of a puzzle that refused to fit together.

Alex found himself caught in a whirlwind of past and present, each flashback a tempest that threatened to uproot the foundations of his identity. The more he attempted to stitch these fragments into a coherent narrative, the more elusive the truth became, a horizon that retreated with every step he took toward it. The dichotomy of his existence, of a man who craved peace yet was haunted by violence, was a labyrinth with no discernible exit, a maze that seemed to fold back upon itself with each attempt to navigate its complexities.

The urgency of his quest, the need to reconcile these disparate aspects of his being, drove Alex forward even as doubt clouded his path. The flashbacks, with all their vivid brutality, were a call to arms, a challenge to delve deeper into the morass of his memories in search of the key that would unlock the secrets of his past. Yet, they were also a warning, a harbinger of the darkness that might lie at the heart of his journey, a darkness that could either consume or enlighten.

In this odyssey of self-discovery, Alex was both the explorer and the terrain, the seeker of truth and the repository of mysteries. The violence he witnessed in his flashbacks was a thread that connected him to a past he could not remember, a signal that there was more to his story than the peace he sought to embody. Each snippet of memory, each burst of violence, was a piece of a larger story, a narrative that Alex was compelled to uncover, not just to understand his role in the events that haunted him but to come to terms with the man he was—and the man he might become.

In the quiet of his apartment, surrounded by the ghosts of memories that refused to be silenced, Alex found himself wrestling with the implications of the violent echoes that haunted his every moment of solitude. Each memory, each flash of violence that painted his recollections with strokes of darkness, was a whisper from a past he couldn't fully grasp, a puzzle that begged to be solved yet defied every attempt at understanding.

Was he simply a witness to these tumultuous events, his consciousness adrift on the currents of time, passively observing the unfolding of scenes that bore no direct relation to him? Or were these fragmented glimpses into chaos and conflict more than mere specters of a forgotten past? Could they be signposts, guiding him toward an unsettling revelation about the very essence of his being?

These questions hung in the air, tangible in the stillness that enveloped him, a mist that clouded his vision and muffled the sound of his own thoughts. The thread of violence that ran like a scarlet ribbon through each memory was too pronounced to ignore, too visceral to dismiss as the mere imaginings of a troubled mind. Yet, the lack of context, the absence of a clear beginning or end to each scene, left him grasping at shadows, seeking solidity in a world made of mist.

Alex pondered the possibility that these memories, far from being disjointed nightmares or the detached observations of a wandering soul, might be pieces of a mosaic that, when assembled, would reveal a portrait of himself in stark relief—a portrait that might hold the key to understanding the violence that seemed to shadow him, an indelible mark on the canvas of his psyche.

The notion that he might be more than a passive observer in these scenarios, that he might have played an active role in the violence that threaded through his memories, was a chalice brimming with a bitter draught. It was a possibility that chilled him to his core, yet it was one he could not afford to ignore. For if these memories were indeed reflections of his own actions, then the path to understanding them—and, by extension, himself—was fraught with implications that could unravel the very fabric of his identity.

In the solitude of his apartment, with the night pressing against the windows like an inquisitive specter, Alex realized that the journey ahead was not just about piecing together the fragments of his past. It was about confronting the possibility that the darkness he had witnessed was not just around him but within him, a part of his own nature that he must come to terms with if he was ever to find peace in the labyrinth of his own making.

The silence that followed this realization was not empty but charged with the potential for discovery, for in the heart of this darkness might lie the light of understanding, a beacon to guide him through the storm of his own memories toward the harbor of truth.

Alone in his quest for clarity, Alex encountered the dual challenge of unraveling the tangled threads of his history while grappling with the deeper enigma of his very self. Each flashback served as both a beacon and a riddle, guiding him deeper into the recesses of his psyche, toward the core of his personal enigma. This journey was not merely a trek through the forgotten or repressed corners of his mind; it was an odyssey of self-discovery, fraught with apprehension and shadowed by the specters of his own making.

With every step taken on this inward trek, Alex moved through a landscape of his own memories, each more shadowed and uncertain than the last. The path was littered with questions that seemed to multiply the further he ventured; each answer unearthed only leading to further mysteries. This voyage through the mists of his past was a solitary endeavor, a confrontation with the darkest aspects of his identity that many would shun.

Yet, there was a promise in this journey, a potential for illumination beyond the darkness. The very act of facing these shades of memory, of daring to sift through the debris of past deeds and thoughts, was in itself a quest for a light of understanding that might illuminate not just the mysteries of his past actions but the very essence of who Alex was.

This expedition into the depths of his own soul was marked by moments of stark clarity as well as stretches of bewildering obscurity, mirroring the unpredictable nature of memory itself. Each recollection, each moment relived in the silent theater of his mind, was a piece of the puzzle that was Alex, a clue to the nature of the man who navigated through these internal landscapes.

The realization that the journey to understand his past was intrinsically linked to the discovery of his true self was both a burden and a revelation. The shadows that danced at the edges of his consciousness were not just obstacles to be overcome but signposts, guiding him toward a deeper, perhaps more unsettling, understanding of his identity.

In the quiet of his solitary search, amidst the ghosts of memories long buried, Alex found himself standing at the crossroads of fear and enlightenment. The road to uncovering the truths of his past was paved with the stones of introspection and self-examination, a path that wound through the darkest recesses of his mind to the possibility of a dawning understanding. Whether such enlightenment could ever truly be attained remained to be seen, but the very act of embarking on this journey was a testament to Alex's courage to confront the unknown territories of his own psyche, in the hope of finding not just answers but peace.

Chapter 17: The Confession

In the austere confines of the interrogation room, Alex found himself alone, enveloped by the harsh and unrelenting glare of fluorescent lights. These lights threw long, dark shadows across the faded linoleum, enhancing the room's oppressive ambiance. Across from him, Detective Laura Henderson sat, her expression betraying a flicker of surprise despite her years of navigating the unpredictable waters of criminal confessions. She maintained a professional posture, yet the tension in her shoulders spoke volumes. The room was otherwise enveloped in silence, punctuated only by the monotonous drone of the air conditioning and the muffled bustle of the police station beyond the door, sounds that seemed to belong to another world entirely.

Detective Henderson's eyes, sharp and calculating, remained fixed on Alex, attempting to read the subtleties of his demeanor. The cold, sterile light bathed Alex in an almost spectral glow, accentuating the gaunt features of his face and casting deep hollows under his eyes, as if he were a ghost haunted by his own secrets. The silence hung heavy between them, laden with expectation, as the detective prepared herself to navigate the complexities of the confession that was about to unfold.

"I did it," Alex stated, his voice carrying a resonance that belied its detachment, as if it reverberated from some obscure depth within him. "I'm responsible for the tragedy that befell the Dawson family." His declaration filled the room, the words heavy with the gravity of his admission yet veiled in ambiguity that had characterized his exchanges with law enforcement from the outset.

Detective Henderson, maintaining her composure, observed Alex carefully. The confession, stark and unembellished, floated in the air between them, fraught with implications yet obscured by the layers of uncertainty that enveloped Alex's psyche. Her expression remained unreadable, schooled in neutrality, but her eyes narrowed slightly—a silent acknowledgment of the complexity of the situation unfolding before her.

The fluorescent lights overhead flickered momentarily, casting a brief shadow across Alex's face, as if to underscore the darkness of the revelation. The detective leaned slightly forward, her hands clasped together on the table, bridging the physical space between them as she prepared to delve deeper into the heart of Alex's confession. The room, already charged with the tension of disclosed secrets, seemed to contract, drawing the walls closer around them as they ventured further into the murky waters of truth and accountability.

Detective Henderson's features were an exercise in restraint, her expression carefully neutral as she absorbed Alex's statement. Her experience had schooled her in maintaining composure in the face of unexpected revelations, yet the undercurrent of her surprise and skepticism flickered briefly in her eyes before being swiftly masked. "Can you elaborate on what happened, Alex? Please, detail the events as you recall them," she urged, her voice steady and professional.

Her pen hovered above the notepad, a silent sentinel ready to capture his words, to dissect them for truth or fabrication. Alex's hands were clasped tightly in front of him, his knuckles whitening as he prepared to revisit the shadows of his past. The air between them felt charged, heavy with the gravity of his impending words.

As Alex inhaled deeply, the room seemed to hold its breath with him. He began to speak, his voice a low cascade that filled the sparse room with the echo of memories. "It was late; the streetlights cast long shadows on the road, the kind that twist and turn with your mind," he started, his words painting a vivid picture of the night in question.

"The Dawsons were arguing—I could hear them as I approached their apartment. The walls were thin, the conflict within them palpable and piercing. I stood there, outside, frozen by indecision," Alex continued, his gaze distant as if he were witnessing the scene anew. Detective Henderson wrote swiftly, her pen scratching across the paper in sharp, deliberate strokes.

"I remember feeling overwhelmed, drawn into the heart of their turmoil as if it mirrored my own internal storms. It was then, in that moment of shared strife, that I acted," Alex's voice broke, a crack in the veneer of his detached recounting. His fingers trembled visibly, the memory stirring the depths of his troubled psyche.

Detective Henderson leaned closer; her earlier skepticism tempered by the rawness of his confession. "What did you do, Alex?" she asked, her tone softer, yet insistent, pushing him to reveal the extent of his involvement.

Alex's next words came as a whisper, strained with the weight of his guilt. "I pushed open the door, the noise of their anger drowning out my hesitation. I... I intervened, but not as a peacemaker. There was a struggle, confusion, fear—it all melded into one. And then, silence. A dreadful, echoing silence that I've not since escaped."

As he recounted the events, Detective Henderson noted each detail, her notepad a growing testament to the tragedy of that night. Alex's account, while coherent in some respects, was punctuated by lapses into a narrative that suggested more than just physical involvement; it hinted at a psychological entanglement with the events that unfolded.

Her task was to untangle the story, to sift through his words for evidence that could either condemn or exonerate him. But as Alex's story spilled out, it became increasingly clear that this was no simple confession; it was a glimpse into the convoluted interplay between a troubled mind and a possibly tragic reality.

As Alex delved into the depths of his memory, the chronology of his account twisted like the back alleys of a forgotten city. He recounted the events leading up to the murders with an eerie detachment, as if he were merely an observer of his own actions, narrating a script written in the fog of a distant nightmare. The scenes spilled from his lips disjointed and surreal, scattered fragments of time and space that defied the linear progression of events.

"The evening began as any other, or so it seemed," Alex's voice floated across the interrogation room, his eyes reflecting a haunted uncertainty. "I walked the familiar path to their home, each step heavy with a foreboding I couldn't quite place. It was as though I was following the echoes of a story already written, already played out beneath the dim streetlights."

His words painted a picture of a man walking through a world both sharp and indistinct, the edges of reality blurred by the darkness that crept around him. "I heard their voices before I saw them, a cacophony of anguish that cut through the quiet of the night. They were arguing, their words laden with a desperation that mirrored the chaos brewing within me."

As he approached the crux of his narrative, the actual moment of violence, Alex's voice faltered, his narrative fracturing under the weight of the memory. "Then, there was a moment—a fragment of time where everything seemed to stand still. I was inside, standing there amidst the storm of their lives. There was shouting, a flash of movement, and then... silence."

He struggled to piece together the sequence of events, his recollections swirling in a tempest of emotion and fragmented images. "It's like trying to remember a dream upon waking—the harder you try to grasp the details, the more they slip away. I saw flashes of anger, fear, and then... nothing but shadows."

Detective Henderson listened intently, her pen barely keeping pace with the disjointed flow of Alex's confession. The narrative was elusive, a puzzle where the pieces didn't quite fit, each detail clouded by the ambiguity of Alex's perception.

"The aftermath was just as broken," Alex continued, his gaze lost somewhere in the flickering light above. "I remember the cold, the overwhelming silence, and the feeling that what had happened was both inevitable and impossible."

His account left more questions than answers, a labyrinthine narrative woven through with the threads of psychological disarray and unresolved guilt. The events as described by Alex were not laid out with the clarity of confession but rather suggested through the haze of a deeply troubled mind, challenging Detective Henderson to untangle truth from the intricate web of his fractured recollections.

"I saw them... the Dawsons... through the glass," Alex murmured, his voice drifting as if carried on a distant wind, eyes glossing over with a film of detachment. The ambiguity of 'the glass' he referenced loomed in the interrogation room, casting doubt whether he meant a physical barrier or an ethereal divide that separated his perceived self from the stark reality of his actions.

"Time seemed to warp around me," Alex described, his hands moving as if to shape the air, illustrating the surreal bending of moments he experienced. "I was both there and merely a witness to my own existence. I saw the anger and the fear ripple through the room like a tangible force, and I... I reacted instinctively." His voice trailed off, lost in the echoes of memories he struggled to piece together.

He paused, collecting his thoughts—or perhaps, attempting to corral the shadows of that night back into the recesses of his mind. "It's as if I'm caught in a loop, perpetually returning to that instant, unable to alter or escape it. This aggression, this violence... it haunts me, not just as a memory but as a premonition of what I am, or what I'm doomed to repeat."

Alex's description of the event painted a picture of a man ensnared by his own history, doomed to witness and re-witness the horrors of a path seemingly preordained. "It wasn't just then; it's as if it's always been, an endless cycle of aggression that I'm trapped within, unable to break free from."

Detective Henderson, absorbing each word, noted the blend of resignation and confusion in Alex's tone. The narrative he spun was fractured, like light through cracked glass, each shard reflecting a different, distorted version of the truth. Her task was to navigate these reflections, to find the reality obscured by the fractured psyche of the man before her.

Detective Henderson shot a brief, inscrutable look towards her partner, whose expression mirrored her own mix of skepticism and concern. They were both deeply familiar with Alex's psychiatric history, detailed in the thick file that lay between them on the table. Yet, the convoluted nature of his confession, weaving between stark reality and troubling illusion, presented a new and daunting puzzle.

Her partner's eyes flicked back to Alex, watching him with a blend of wariness and intense focus. The layers of Alex's narrative, tangled with psychological threads and enigmatic self-reflection, demanded a delicate approach to untangling truth from fiction—a task both detectives knew would test the limits of their investigative experience.

With a measured breath, Henderson leaned slightly forward, her elbows resting on the cold metal table, her fingers tented in contemplation. "Alex," she began, her voice steady, attempting to steer the conversation towards more concrete ground, "you mention cycles of aggression and a feeling of being trapped in a loop. Can you clarify—are these feelings you're experiencing now, or are they part of what you saw that night at the Dawson's?"

The question hung in the air, dense with implication. Henderson and her partner remained silent, giving Alex the space to navigate his thoughts, aware that each response might peel back another layer of the complex psychological landscape he inhabited. The challenge was not merely to discern the truth of the Dawson family tragedy, but to understand the depths of disturbance that might distort Alex's own perception of reality.

Detective Henderson's tone was firm yet measured, designed to pierce through the fog of Alex's convoluted testimony without adding pressure that might fracture his fragile state. "Alex, when you mention being 'there,' I need to understand clearly — are you saying you were physically inside the Dawson's apartment when the incident occurred?" She kept her eyes fixed on him, her gaze sharp and assessing, yet not unkind.

The room felt charged with a palpable tension as she posed the question, the stark fluorescent lighting casting deep shadows that seemed to accentuate the gravity of the moment. Her words, carefully chosen, hung between them, awaiting Alex's interpretation, which would either anchor his claims to a tangible reality or drift further into the abstract realm of his troubled perceptions.

Alex's response was slow, hesitant, as if extracting each word from a deep and dark place within himself. His eyes, previously darting around the room, now settled on some unseen middle distance, focusing on a point beyond the walls of the sterile interrogation room.

Alex's hands clenched, then unclenched, his knuckles white, reflecting the internal struggle as he grappled with the articulation of his experiences. "It's not as straightforward as simply being 'present,'" he began, his voice threaded with a blend of exasperation and surrender. "I feel caught in an incessant loop, where my actions echo across different times and places, unbound by the usual constraints of time and space. It's as if I'm destined to replay these moments of violence, each scenario a variation of a theme I can't escape."

His gaze drifted away from Detective Henderson, focusing instead on a point somewhere beyond the immediate confines of the room. "This murder, the tragedy of the Dawson family, it haunts me like a pervasive shadow, one that stretched back even before the events themselves unfolded. It's as if I had always been a part of it, inevitably drawn to that moment."

The room fell silent, the hum of the fluorescent lights overhead now seeming overly loud in the charged atmosphere. Alex's description suggested a depth of confusion and torment about his own sense of reality, painting his confession not as a straightforward admission of guilt but as an expression of being ensnared in a cyclical pattern of foreboding and regret.

Detective Henderson, maintaining her composure, noted the complexity of Alex's psychological state. It was clear that his perception of his involvement was entangled in a broader, more abstract struggle with his identity and his past—a past that seemed to bleed into his present, clouding his understanding of both.

Detectives Henderson and her partner sat back, exchanging glances that communicated their shared perplexity. The task before them was daunting: deciphering a confession that wove through the tangled corridors of Alex's mind like a thread through a dark maze. Alex's narrative, rife with mentions of "cycles of violence" and ominous "shadows" that pursued him across the boundaries of time, painted not the clear picture of a man confessing to crimes in a traditional sense, but rather revealed the profound disturbances that lurked in the depths of his psyche.

The implications of his words transcended the standard parameters of criminal guilt, plunging into the murky waters of mental illness where past, present, and future collided in unsettling echoes. His assertion that the murder was both a part of him and yet apart from him, a shadow foretold, challenged not only the detectives' understanding of his mental state but also strained the very boundaries of how guilt is traditionally ascertained and adjudicated.

Detective Henderson, her experience as a seasoned investigator clashing with the unnerving nature of this case, leaned forward, her voice steady but her mind racing to map out the implications of Alex's words. "So, you're suggesting that these acts, these...

repetitions of violence, they feel predestined? Like you're reliving them rather than committing them in real-time?" she asked, seeking clarity yet dreading the complexity of the answer she might receive.

The room, charged with the weight of Alex's revelations, seemed to close in around them, the fluorescent lights flickering slightly as if reacting to the tension. Each word Alex had spoken added another layer to the enigmatic puzzle that now lay between them, a puzzle that was less about solving a crime and more about understanding the cries of a tormented soul trapped in a relentless cycle of psychological torment.

As the interrogation drew to a close, a palpable tension settled over the room, the atmosphere thick with the unresolved complexities of Alex's testimony. Detective Henderson and her team, seasoned yet visibly unsettled, faced the formidable task of disentangling the strands of truth woven into the fabric of Alex's distorted perceptions. His confession, far from shedding light on the grisly events that had unfolded, had instead broadened the scope of their inquiry, plunging them into the depths of his troubled psyche.

The air was thick, almost suffocating, as the detectives gathered their notes, the pages filled with Alex's disjointed memories and elusive admissions. The challenge before them was daunting: they had to navigate not only the legal implications of his statements but also the intricate maze of his mental condition. Far from reaching a conclusion, Alex's narrative had opened a Pandora's box of psychological inquiries that demanded a delicate and thorough exploration.

Detective Henderson, her expression one of grim determination, paused at the doorway, her mind racing with the implications of what they had heard. "This is just the beginning," she murmured to her partner, her voice low, carrying a weight that was felt more than heard. The investigation, already complex, had taken a turn into uncharted territories of the human mind, where guilt intersected with mental illness in a shadowy dance of cause and consequence.

The room emptied slowly, the echo of Alex's words lingering like a specter. The detectives' steps were heavy, burdened by the knowledge that ahead lay a path riddled with more questions than answers. The session had concluded, but the journey into the labyrinthine nature of Alex's truth was just beginning, its corridors extending far beyond the stark walls of the interrogation room into the dimly lit halls of human consciousness.

Outside, the city continued its ceaseless hum, oblivious to the profound complexities unraveled within the confines of that small, fluorescent-lit room. Yet, for Henderson and her team, the world seemed slightly altered—a landscape where the line between reality and illusion was as thin and fragile as the whisper of sanity in Alex's troubled confession. They left the room not with a sense of closure, but with a renewed commitment to uncover the reality buried beneath layers of psychological turmoil, a reality as elusive and fraught as the mind that had disclosed it.

Chapter 18: A Trial of Shadows

The trial of Alex swiftly morphed into a magnet for public fascination, weaving a complex tapestry of mystery, personal tragedy, and the perplexing depths of the human psyche. The courtroom, a grand stage set against a backdrop of towering columns and sweeping arches, became the arena for a gripping legal and psychological drama. Every hushed whisper, every rustle of paper in this solemn expanse, amplified the tension, casting a palpable sense of urgency and significance over the assembled crowd. As the trial unfolded, the air thickened with anticipation, every observer leaning forward, caught in the spell of unfolding drama, where every statement and pause crackled with potential revelations.

Right from the start, the trial teetered on the edge of coherence, straddling the lines between clarity and chaos. The prosecution strove to assemble a convincing case from the tenuous threads of circumstantial evidence intertwined with Alex's fragmented and often perplexing confessions. Witnesses paraded before the jury, each one adding layers to the conflicting images of Alex. Some portrayed him as a benevolent soul, seemingly devoid of any capacity for violence, painting pictures of his gentle demeanor and acts of kindness. In stark contrast, others presented tales of a man shadowed by turbulence, prone to sudden, inexplicable outbursts that hinted at a deeper, darker volatility.

The courtroom buzzed with tension as each new witness took the stand, their stories weaving a complex narrative that left jurors and spectators alike grappling with the dichotomy of Alex's character. The air was electric, each testimony adding fuel to the flickering flame of intrigue and speculation that filled the room. The prosecution and defense clashed fiercely, a dynamic duel of words and wits, each trying to sway the jury to their side of this enigmatic puzzle. The pace of the trial accelerated with each passing moment, building a crescendo of suspense that held the courtroom in its grip.

Eric Nolan, the proprietor of a nearby store, was called early in the trial, his testimony anticipated with keen interest. He claimed to have encountered Alex on the evening in question, presenting an account that was both vivid and unsettling. Initially, Nolan painted a picture of Alex as deeply agitated, his movements erratic and his demeanor suspicious, stirring murmurs of intrigue across the courtroom.

However, as the defense took to the rigorous cross-examination, cracks began to appear in Nolan's narrative. Under the relentless questioning, his testimony began to waver. The precision of his earlier statements gave way to uncertainty, revealing a landscape of doubt and confusion. Pressed further, Nolan admitted that the shock of the events — witnessing the immediate aftermath of the murder — might have distorted his perceptions, casting shadows of doubt over the reliability of his observations.

This concession shifted the atmosphere in the courtroom dramatically. What had seemed like a straightforward testimony morphed into a complex, multi-layered revelation that challenged the jury's understanding of the facts. The defense capitalized on these inconsistencies, weaving them into their broader portrayal of a case built on unstable foundations. The pace of the proceedings quickened, each new question adding a pulse of tension to the air, as the narrative of Alex's guilt became ever more blurred and contested.

The defense, in a calculated move, shifted the trial's focus from the specifics of the night in question to the labyrinthine depths of Alex's psyche. They lined up a series of expert witnesses, each one poised to unravel the complexities of dissociative disorders and the profound impact of trauma on memory and perception. This approach not only challenged the reliability of Alex's confession but also painted a broader picture of a man ensnared by his own mind's betrayals.

Dr. Emily Carter, a renowned psychologist with an authoritative presence, became a pivotal figure in this narrative. As she took the stand, the courtroom's atmosphere tensed, reflecting the gravity of her testimony. Dr. Carter spoke with precision, her words meticulously chosen to convey the chaos of Alex's psychological state. She described his dissociative experiences as episodes where time itself seemed to fold, blurring the lines between past, present, and future, thus casting doubt on his ability to distinguish reality from his distorted perceptions.

Her testimony dove deep into the essence of temporal confusion—how Alex's moments of clarity were interspersed with long stretches where time appeared to loop back on itself, creating a perpetual cycle of confusion and re-experience. This, Dr. Carter argued, was not merely a psychiatric symptom but a fundamental barrier to forming coherent memories or engaging with reality in a linear fashion.

As she detailed the clinical aspects of such conditions, the courtroom's energy shifted. The jurors leaned forward, captivated yet confounded, as they tried to reconcile the clinical explanations with the human story unfolding before them. The defense's strategy was clear: to sow enough doubt about Alex's mental state that the jurors would question whether his actions were the product of a deliberate intent or a tragic consequence of his psychological disarray.

The pace of the trial accelerated with each expert's testimony, each contributing a new layer of complexity to Alex's profile. The sharp, rapid-fire exchange between the defense attorneys and the witnesses contrasted starkly with the prosecution's earlier narrative, adding a dynamic and compelling twist to the proceedings. This strategic pivot not only enlivened the trial but also refocused the debate on the broader implications of mental health in the realm of criminal responsibility.

The courtroom hushed to a palpable silence as Alex stepped up to the witness stand, the air thick with anticipation. The trial had already been a rollercoaster of emotional and psychological explorations, but nothing had prepared the spectators and jury for the spectacle of Alex's own words. His testimony unfolded like a storm, chaotic and unpredictable.

With every eye fixed upon him, Alex began to speak, his voice initially steady but gradually fracturing as his account progressed. He spoke of distant places and violent encounters, each detail surfacing with a vividness that seemed to pull the courtroom into the depths of his haunted memories. "I've seen violence erupt like a sudden storm," he explained, "in places you've only read about in headlines. And each time, it felt like a prelude to... to that night."

As he delved into his premonitions of future tragedies, the line between reality and hallucination blurred. Alex described his overwhelming sense of dread, a foreboding that he was destined to play a role in some horrific event. "It was as if I were being pulled along by the tide, unable to resist the current," he said, his voice trembling with the weight of his admission.

The courtroom listened, riveted and unsettled, as Alex recounted the night of the Dawson family's tragedy. "There was this force, an oppressive shadow that seemed to cloud my thoughts, dictate my actions," he confessed, his hands clenched in his lap as if to anchor himself to the present. "I remember feeling as if I were both there and not there, as if someone or something else was guiding me."

His testimony oscillated wildly, a meandering narrative that captured his inner turmoil and the spectral forces he believed were at play. At times, his words were lucid and poignant, offering a glimpse into the terror of feeling one's actions being controlled by an unseen force. At other times, his words spiraled into confusion, leaving the jury grappling with the reality of his experiences.

In the solemn silence of the courtroom, Alex's words resonated with a chilling depth, his tone laced with a quiet desperation that gripped every listener. "I felt as though I was under the sway of shadows cast from another era," he began, his voice barely more than a whisper yet carrying an eerie power that drew the room into his haunted reality.

"Driven by an unseen hand, compelled by forces beyond my comprehension," Alex continued, his eyes scanning the crowd, seeking an understanding that seemed just beyond his grasp. His hands trembled slightly, visible to all present as he clutched the stand, his knuckles whitening with the effort. "Whether these forces were borne of reality or the constructs of my fractured mind, I remain uncertain."

The courtroom hung on every word, the air thick with anticipation and dread. Alex's testimony wove a narrative that was as compelling as it was horrifying, blurring the lines between historical hauntings and the all-too-real specter of his actions. His confession painted a picture of a man not only battling with his inner demons but also grappling with the possibility that his darkest moments might be influenced by external, possibly supernatural, forces.

His voice grew stronger, more urgent, as he delved deeper into his perceived reality. "It's like being caught in a relentless storm, where past sins and future fears converge in a maelstrom of confusion and compulsion," he explained, his gaze distant, as if reliving every moment. "Each act, each decision seemed preordained, scripted by a history I was part of yet apart from."

As Alex's description spiraled into the realm of the metaphysical, the courtroom shifted uncomfortably, the spectral nature of his claims sending shivers down spines. The notion that he could be an actor in a drama not entirely of his own making challenged not only the legal framework but also the philosophical boundaries of culpability and free will.

The intensity of his narrative reached a peak, leaving the audience and the jury caught between skepticism and an unnerving consideration of the unthinkable. "Am I merely a vessel for these shadows, an echo of atrocities from another time?" Alex posed the question to the room, his voice cracking under the strain of his haunted musings.

As he concluded, the echoes of his words lingered in the air, a haunting refrain that left the courtroom in a state of eerie contemplation. The impact of his testimony was profound, casting a long shadow over the proceedings and leaving the jurors with a complex puzzle: was Alex a man driven to violence by the unseen forces he described, or was he a deeply troubled individual lost in his delusions?

The tension in the room built as Alex's voice grew more desperate, his story more convoluted. "It's always there, this cycle of violence that follows me, haunts me... Did I act alone that night? Was I merely an instrument of something far greater, far darker than myself?" he questioned aloud, his gaze drifting over the faces of the jury, seeking not just their judgment but their understanding.

As Alex's testimony reached its peak, the courtroom was enveloped in a thick silence, broken only by the soft clicks of reporters' keyboards and the distant hum of the city outside. His final words hung heavily in the air, a stark reminder of the enigmatic and deeply troubled nature of his psyche.

The impact of his testimony was immediate and profound. The jurors, previously mere observers, now found themselves thrust into the heart of a psychological labyrinth, tasked with deciphering whether Alex was truly responsible for his actions or merely a pawn in a much larger, darker game that played out in the shadows of his mind. The atmosphere was charged with a mix of empathy and horror, each person in the room wrestling with the implications of Alex's haunting narrative.

As Alex was led away, the weight of his words lingered, casting long shadows of doubt across the trial. The climax of his testimony did not simplify the task before the court; rather, it compounded the mystery, leaving all who were present to wonder about the nature of free will, the power of unseen forces, and the deep, often unseen currents that steer the human psyche.

The tension that Alex's words had woven into the fabric of the trial was palpable, and as the jury retreated to deliberate, the sense of unease was palpable. His narrative had not only outlined the events but had also invited a deeper exploration into the darker, uncharted territories of the human psyche, where the lines between reality and madness, guilt and innocence, were irrevocably blurred.

The deliberations of the jury transformed into a grueling marathon, each member wrestling with the tangled web of Alex's testimony, their faces etched with the weight of their responsibility. In the confines of the deliberation room, a palpable tension throbbed like a pulse, as the jurors found themselves deadlocked, caught between the sharp edges of the law and the murky depths of psychological complexity.

Arguments flared and waned as they dissected each piece of evidence, the scale of justice oscillating wildly. On one hand, the facts laid bare a path towards guilt, punctuated by Alex's own erratic confessions and the circumstantial evidence that painted a chilling portrait of potential violence. Yet, each of these seemingly solid points was undermined by the profound insights provided by psychiatric experts, who painted a picture of a man ensnared in the throes of mental illness, his perception of reality distorted beyond ordinary understanding.

"The question isn't just whether he did it," one juror argued, their voice slicing through the heated discussions, "but whether he was in control of his actions, whether he understood the nature of what he was doing." This sentiment echoed around the room, a reminder of the profound legal and moral complexities at play.

Another juror countered, leaning forward with a furrowed brow, "But where do we draw the line? At what point does personal responsibility take hold, and to what extent do we consider mental illness an absolution of guilt?"

These questions reverberated through the room, colliding with the stark reality of the crime and the shadowy nuances of Alex's mental state. The reliability of his memory, so crucial to the heart of the case, was now a specter of doubt casting long shadows across their decision-making process.

As hours turned into days, the jury's deadlock reflected the broader societal debate on the intersections of law, mental health, and morality. Each juror felt the gravity of the decision they were to make, aware that their verdict would extend far beyond the confines of the courtroom, touching upon the very essence of justice and human empathy.

The atmosphere grew thick with frustration and the burden of unanswered questions, as they continued to circle back to the haunting complexity of Alex's case. Was it just to convict a man who may not have been aware of the reality of his actions? How could they be certain beyond a reasonable doubt when the very fabric of the defendant's perception was so irrevocably frayed?

Finally, they returned to the courtroom, a collective air of unresolved tension surrounding them. Faces drawn and weary, they filed in, their steps heavy with the burden of their unresolved consensus, ready to deliver a verdict that no longer seemed as definitive as the law demanded. The trial, so filled with twists and psychological turns, had brought them to a precipice of legal and moral ambiguity that offered no easy answers.

As the weeks unfurled, the trial of Alex morphed into something far greater than a mere adjudication of guilt or innocence; it became a deep dive into the enigmatic realms of human consciousness. The courtroom, with its austere benches and stoic columns, transformed into an unlikely arena for a philosophical debate that captivated not just the jury but anyone who bore witness.

Legal proceedings intertwined with probing inquiries into the nature of free will and the essence of reality. Expert witnesses from the fields of psychology and neurology took the stand, their testimonies interspersed with dense jargon, attempting to map out the labyrinthine workings of the human mind as it related to criminal actions.

Philosophical arguments about determinism and responsibility were bandied about, each point and counterpoint reverberating under the high vaulted ceilings, turning the courtroom into a pulsating hub of intellectual and ethical conflict. The spectators and media lapped up every word, the air thick with anticipation and the weight of existential deliberation.

Legal experts dissected precedents, while laypersons grappled with the unsettling notion that the mind could be both jailor and prisoner. The debate seeped out from the confines of the courtroom, igniting discussions in coffee shops, online forums, and evening news segments, each venue rehashing the day's proceedings and speculating on the broader implications for justice and mental health awareness.

Inside the courtroom, the pace accelerated as the trial neared its conclusion. Arguments became more pointed, the stakes visibly higher. Lawyers on both sides sharpened their strategies, presenting their closing arguments with a mixture of legal acumen and philosophical insight, striving to sway the jury not just on the facts but on the deeper, more troubling questions of ethical responsibility and human understanding.

The judge presided over this spectacle with a somber realization of the case's complexity, guiding the proceedings with a steady hand and a keen awareness of the legal and moral minefields being navigated. As the final arguments were made, the courtroom held its breath, awaiting a verdict that would inevitably be seen as a landmark decision, a verdict that would resonate far beyond the life of Alex and the tragedy of the Dawson family, touching upon the very core of what it means to be human.

Ultimately, the trial of Alex transcended the simple examination of a solitary violent act, expanding into a profound exploration of perception and mental reality. It plunged jurors and spectators alike into a whirlwind of philosophical dilemmas, challenging them to untangle the intricate threads that link truth to perception, guilt to innocence, and reality to illusion.

This intricate tapestry of concepts swirled throughout the courtroom, turning each session into a heated debate that questioned not only Alex's culpability but also the very essence of justice and consciousness. Lawyers articulated their points with a fervor that resonated beyond the cold facts of the case, reaching into the realm of metaphysical speculation, where every statement about mental health could be interpreted as a comment on the human condition itself.

The jurors, encircled by arguments rich with legal and psychological implications, found themselves at the heart of a vortex, where traditional views on accountability were buffeted by modern understandings of psychological disorders. They wrestled with questions that seemed to shift shape with each new piece of testimony, each expert opinion adding layers of complexity to their task, making the boundary between verdict and philosophical judgment increasingly porous.

As the trial wound to its climax, the atmosphere in the courtroom thickened with anticipation and the heavy responsibility felt by all involved. The public, captivated by the unfolding drama, was left to ponder the shadowy junctures between mind, morality, and law, each revelation from the trial sparking wide-ranging debates that extended into the fabric of societal norms.

When the final arguments were delivered, they reverberated like a thunderclap, echoing the tumultuous journey through human psyche and legal theory that had captivated the nation. The jury, burdened with a decision that now seemed to bear the weight of profound ethical considerations, retreated to deliberate, leaving a courtroom—and a public—suspended in a state of eager uncertainty, awaiting a verdict that would inevitably resonate as a profound commentary on the interplay between law, psychology, and the elusive nature of truth.

Chapter 19: The Verdict of the Mind

As the trial approached its climactic finale, the courtroom was suffused with an almost tangible tension, each participant collectively holding their breath in suspenseful anticipation of the verdict. But for Alex, the external drama of the courtroom slowly diminished, overshadowed by the far more intense tempest swirling inside his own mind. With every minute drawing nearer to the jury's decision, Alex's grip on reality grew increasingly tenuous. He found himself ensnared in a relentless torrent of hallucinations, each more disorienting than the last, obscuring the boundaries between the tangible world and the phantasms of his mind, between stark truths and the deceitful shadows of deception. As the real world and its judgments faded into the periphery, Alex spiraled deeper into this internal abyss, confronting specters that questioned not just his innocence but the very essence of his perception and sanity.

In an instant, the judge's familiar countenance warped into that of an imposing, faceless specter cloaked in the murk of shadows. The jurors, once mere men and women, twisted into ethereal forms, their faces blurring into obscurity, their whispers coalescing into a sinister symphony of discordant tones. This jury of specters did not deliberate over the facts of a mundane murder; their eerie murmuring seemed to penetrate deeper, judging

Alex on a cosmic scale—his very soul on trial. The air in the courtroom thickened, crackling with the electric charge of an otherworldly tribunal, setting the stage for judgments not bound by human laws but dictated by the arcane laws governing the recesses of the mind.

Perched uneasily at the defense table, Alex's blink acted as a catalyst, transforming the mundane courtroom into a portal of otherworldly judgment. Walls stretched endlessly, drawing upwards as the ceiling dissolved into an abyss of surreal hues—a sky bleeding colors unseen on any earthly palette. This spectral transformation enveloped the room in a sinister, other-dimensional beauty that chilled the spine.

In this eerie realm, the judge transfigured into a colossus draped in obsidian veils, his face a void where features should reside, commanding the courtroom with an unworldly presence that defied the laws of nature. Shadows swirled around him like dark fire, his silhouette a blur of power and terror.

The jury, too, transformed from a group of peers to a council of ghosts, their faces shimmering into non-existence, then back to haunting, distorted visages. They huddled together, a gathering of ethereal beings, their whispers cascading over one another in a haunting cacophony that seemed to resonate from another dimension. The words they spoke were not just foreign; they were otherworldly, discussing fates not just tied to life and death but to the very fabric of reality itself.

Their ghostly deliberation transcended the mundane world, pondering not merely the fate of a man accused of murder but the essence of his soul's journey through darkness and light. Each murmur reverberated through the transformed space, echoing off the twisted architecture that no longer resembled any courthouse known to man.

In this hall of twisted reality, Alex watched as the boundaries of existence blurred, the surreal proceedings painting a stark portrait of a cosmic trial where the stakes were eternal, and the jurors' verdict might well determine more than his guilt—they might dictate his very place in the universe.

As the spectral courtroom scene shattered like glass under the force of reality's hammer, Alex's senses reeled, hurling him from the abyss of the infinite back to the sharply defined edges of the Dawson's living room. This abrupt transition felt like being yanked awake from a nightmare, only to find oneself in another dream layer, equally vivid and disturbing. The harsh light of the setting sun threw grotesque shadows that danced on the walls, blurring the line between the dead and the living, between Alex's haunted memories and the chillingly tangible figures before him. This disorienting shift, from the cosmic judgment to a ghostly family reunion, seemed orchestrated by some cruel puppeteer, keen on tormenting him with alternate realities where the past remained unmarred by violence.

With another involuntary blink, the grim courtroom dissolved, replaced instantly by the familiar, yet uncanny, surroundings of the Dawson family's living room. The setting sun cast long shadows across the floor, bathing the room in an eerie, golden light that seemed both welcoming and foreboding. There, gathered around, were the Dawsons—alive, breathing, their faces a mix of disbelief and dread.

James Dawson, the patriarch, stepped forward, his features twisted in a grimace of confusion and suspicion. His voice, heavy with an emotion that tugged at the very air, broke the tense silence. "Why are you doing this, Alex?" he implored, his words hanging between them like a blade poised to strike.

Alex, mouth agape, struggled to formulate a reply, but the words clung to his tongue, unspoken. The intensity of James's stare bore into him, searching, accusing, demanding an explanation that Alex could not deliver.

Just as the tension reached its peak, the scene fractured violently. The air seemed to crackle and hiss, and then, like a mirror struck by an unseen force, the world around Alex splintered. The shards of reality flew towards him, each piece a twisted reflection of might-have-beens: laughter never shared, tears never shed, and countless moments stolen by fate's cruel hand.

Each fragment of glass was a window into a different reality, where the Dawsons celebrated birthdays, enjoyed quiet evenings, and lived the mundane, beautiful life that was ripped away from them. Alex reached out, desperate to touch these fragments of lost time, but as his fingers brushed against the cold, sharp edges, the visions dissolved into mists of what could never now be.

Reeling from the intensity of the vision, Alex found himself back in the shifting, morphing courtroom, the ghostly echoes of the Dawsons' voices haunting the corners of his mind, leaving him to grapple with the harrowing thought of his involvement in their undoing and the stark reality of their absence.

No sooner had the spectral whispers of the Dawson family faded than Alex's reality fractured anew. The courtroom, a once-sturdy bastion of order, splintered into countless reflections as he stumbled forward into an expansive hall of mirrors. Each step echoed ominously in the suddenly cold air, transitioning him from one haunting encounter to another. In this new, bewildering realm, the very fabric of his identity was thrown into question, mirrored endlessly in a kaleidoscope of realities that distorted and magnified every thought and fear. The labyrinthine gallery, with its relentless reflections, thrust Alex into a relentless pursuit of his fragmented self, each mirrored surface revealing and yet obscuring the truth of who he might truly be.

Without warning, the disorienting whirl of colors and sound coalesced into a stark, chilling clarity as Alex stepped into a labyrinth of towering mirrors. Each surface shimmered with the light of an undefined source, reflecting not just his physical form but the myriad possibilities of his existence. The air was thick with the metallic scent of old glass and the sharp tang of his own rising fear.

As he wandered deeper into the maze, the mirrors mutated the reflections: one frame cast him as a savior, cloaked in valor, his features set in a grim determination; another twisted his visage into that of a malefactor, his eyes dark pools of remorse and anger; yet another painted him as an onlooker, passive and distant, a ghost within his own story.

With each tentative step, the reflections fractured, a kaleidoscope of identities splintering and recombining. The crisp snap of his footsteps echoed off the glass, a staccato beat that seemed to mock his faltering resolve. Here, in this mirrored world, each version of himself confronted him with accusations and accolades alike, a chorus of what-ifs that pierced his conscience with needle-like precision.

The labyrinth seemed to pulse with a life of its own, its corridors narrowing and then expanding, as if breathing around him. Shadows flickered at the edge of his vision, elusive and teasing, beckoning him further into the depths of his own psyche. Each mirrored surface not only challenged his perception of who he was but also stripped away the layers of self-deception and denial that had cocooned him from reality.

As Alex reached the heart of the labyrinth, he stood surrounded by an amphitheater of mirrors, each one reflecting back at him a moment of his life — moments of joy, of despair, of triumph, and of defeat. The cacophony of reflected emotions was overwhelming, and Alex felt the sharp sting of tears in his eyes as he realized that each mirror held not just a reflection but a judgment.

In this hall of mirrors, the most haunting image was that of his own eyes staring back at him — a reminder that no matter how far he journeyed into the maze, the truest reflection was the one that revealed the depths of his soul. Here, in this surreal tribunal of glass, Alex faced the ultimate verdict on his character, delivered not by a jury of his peers but by the unyielding gaze of his own multiplied eyes.

As the endless reflections diminished into nothingness, Alex was thrust back into the harrowing confines of the courtroom. This sudden shift from the infinite regress of his mirrored selves to the stark, darkened court was jarring. Silence enveloped him, thick and oppressive, punctuated only by the soft, menacing murmurs of the shadows that now populated the jury box. Each shadow seemed to pulsate with a life of its own, their whispers weaving a tapestry of judgment that resonated with a cold, otherworldly authority. Here, in this desolate version of the courtroom, Alex faced not a panel of his peers, but an assembly of spectral entities, their presence both undefined and unnerving.

Suddenly, the labyrinthine corridors of mirrors dissolved into the stark, imposing structure of the courtroom. Alex found himself standing alone, the familiar benches and gallery shrouded in an impenetrable darkness that seemed to swallow the light. The judge's bench loomed ominously empty, and the jury box was a cavernous void, filled with the shifting, whispering forms of shadows that defied form or feature.

From the depths of this shadowed assembly, a voice emerged—a resonant, omnipresent tone that echoed off the marble and wood with a supernatural clarity. It was neither male nor female but carried the weight of absolute authority, its timbre vibrating through the air and into Alex's very bones.

"Guilty," the voice intoned, its declaration resonating through the now cavernous courtroom like a gavel's final, damning blow. "Guilty of wandering too far into the labyrinths of your own psyche, of losing yourself in a maze without end."

The shadows in the jury box stirred, their forms coalescing into a spectral jury, their verdict not concerning the mortal laws of man but the deeper, more esoteric laws of the mind. "You stand condemned," the voice continued, each word a hammer strike, "not by society, nor by the law, but by the very essence of your own consciousness. Guilty of allowing the darker corridors of your psyche to overshadow the light."

The air around Alex grew colder, the shadows darker, as if the very atmosphere sought to isolate him further from the world he once knew. The walls of the courtroom seemed to pulse and breathe, contracting like the chamber of a vast, dark heart.

"You have been judged," the voice pronounced, as a chill wind swept through the courtroom, the spectral jury's whispers growing louder, a dissonant chorus that filled the room with the chilling sound of verdicts passed in the recesses of nightmares.

Alex, standing alone at the center of this spectral court, felt the weight of each word like a shroud, wrapping him in the cold realization of his solitude. His own fears and doubts, the monsters of his mind, had tried and convicted him, sentencing him to a reality fragmented by his fractured perceptions.

As the last vestiges of the hallucination dissolved, Alex remained haunted by the spectral clatter of a gavel—a sound that seemed to echo from the depths of his own mind. The courtroom's stark reality gradually reclaimed its form around him, each element sharpening into focus as if seeping through the fractures of his distorted perceptions. There, amidst the solid lines of wooden benches and the steady gaze of an all-too-real judge, the weight of the forthcoming verdict pressed heavily upon him. The boundary between his inner chaos and the external order of the court became painfully distinct, emphasizing the stark contrast between the judgments rendered in the recesses of his mind and those pending in the tangible, unforgiving world of law and order. The air was thick with anticipation, every breath a reminder of the crucial decision looming— a decision that would seal not just his fate, but perhaps the understanding of his very reality.

In the heavy stillness that enveloped the courtroom, as the jury deliberated behind closed doors, Alex grappled with a profound revelation. The true verdict, the one that resonated deepest, had not been declared by any external authority but had unfolded within the dark recesses of his own mind. This internal judgment, wrought from the tangled skeins of memory, perception, and self-identity, had ensnared him in a twilight zone—a nebulous realm where the stark, linear truths sought by law and the therapeutic resolutions offered by medicine failed to penetrate.

Caught in this interstitial void, Alex felt the boundaries of reality and illusion, sanity and madness, blur with an intensity that was both terrifying and enlightening. Each hallucinatory episode had chipped away at the façades of his understanding, revealing layers of deeper, more complex truths about his existence. The courtroom, with its rigid structures and solemn rituals, seemed increasingly like a distant echo, irrelevant to the internal court where his fate was truly being decided. Here, in this indeterminate space, Alex faced the monumental task of reconciling the disparate parts of himself, understanding that the jury's impending decision was but a superficial closure to the profound odyssey of self-discovery he had unwittingly embarked upon.

As the proceedings lurched forward, reclaiming the solemn rhythm of the courtroom, Alex remained seated, a solitary figure amidst the swirling tempest of his own unraveling psyche. The real-world verdict still hung in the balance, its announcement pending like a distant storm cloud, yet Alex was adrift in the more tumultuous and expansive sea of his own mind. Here, the stark binary of guilt and innocence melded into broader, more profound queries—those that probed the very essence of human nature and the shadows it harbors.

Around him, the courtroom buzzed—a stark contrast to the introspective silence he experienced. Lawyers shuffled papers, the judge surveyed the room with a measured gaze, and the jury returned, their faces inscrutable, bearing the weight of their imminent decision. Yet, these external motions felt like mere echoes to Alex, distant and somewhat disconnected from the internal dialogue that commanded his full attention.

In this psychological hinterland, Alex grappled with the elemental forces of truth and deception, morality and sin. Each thought, each memory that surfaced, seemed to challenge the very notions upon which the law attempted to anchor its judgments. Here, in the vast, uncharted depths of his consciousness, Alex encountered not just reflections of the man he was accused of being, but glimpses of countless potential selves, each shaped by choices and circumstances as fluid and volatile as the sea itself. This internal maelstrom, far removed from the structured deliberations of the courtroom, was where his true trial was being conducted—a trial without judge or jury, yet with the highest stakes imaginable.

Chapter 20: Disjointed Echoes

As Alex perched on the edge of the courtroom bench, time stretched into an agonizing tangle of moments, each second dilating into an eternity of suspense. His heart thrummed a frantic rhythm, oscillating between terror and anticipation, awaiting the words that would seal his fate. The courtroom lay submerged in an unnatural stillness, as if the world beyond Alex had slipped into a soundless vacuum. The only sensation penetrating this bubble of isolation was the persistent ring in his ears and the biting chill of the marble floor against his bare feet.

The air around him seemed to thicken, time inching forward at a grudging pace. Faint murmurs seeped through the walls from the bustling corridor outside, a ghostly reminder of the life continuing just beyond his reach. As he waited, suspended in this purgatory of uncertainty, Alex's mind embarked on a turbulent journey through his past.

Visions of arid deserts with sand that filled his mouth with a dry, gritty taste flooded his senses, juxtaposed against memories of standing in the pouring rain in Paris, the droplets weaving through his hair, warm and relentless. His life had been a mosaic of experiences, each memory a vibrant tile in the vast tapestry of his worldly explorations. He recalled the spice-laden air of Middle Eastern markets, the icy sting of the Siberian winds, and the lush greenery of the Amazon that clung to his skin with humid fingers.

Yet, amidst this wealth of worldly memories, this moment felt starkly alien. A profound disorientation took hold as he pondered his own identity amidst the tumult of his recollections. "Who am I?" the question echoed silently through the caverns of his unsettled mind. As the seconds ticked by, every whispered conjecture from the hallway, every shadow that danced along the courtroom walls seemed to mock his predicament with a spectral indifference.

This was uncharted territory, a chapter of his existence that no amount of global wanderings or cultural immersions could have prepared him for. Here, in the sterile air of the courtroom, waiting for a verdict that might just as much condemn his spirit as absolve it, Alex faced not just a legal judgment but an existential reckoning that challenged the very essence of his being.

The name "Alex" pierced the thick silence of the courtroom, reverberating off the high ceilings with a clarity that startled him. Dr. Emily Carter was leaning forward, her expression etched with a professional concern that seemed to slice through the muffled atmosphere. As Alex's gaze shifted to meet hers, he found a semblance of the present moment.

"Alex, are you okay? Just relax, you're doing fine," she soothed, her voice a low, melodic balm crafted from years of calming the stormy seas within her patients' minds. Her presence was a brief anchor in the tempest of his thoughts.

However, this fleeting moment of solace was abruptly shattered by the rising voices outside the courtroom. Detective Henderson's distinct timbre, sharp and commanding, cut through the other muffled sounds, pulling Dr. Carter's attention away from Alex. With a swift, apologetic glance, she stood and moved towards the courtroom door, her demeanor shifting from therapeutic calm to professional urgency in an instant.

As Alex watched her rush toward the disturbance, something peculiar caught his eye. Dr. Carter's identification badge, swinging from a lanyard around her neck, bore an uncanny resemblance to the badges worn by the police officers who had first escorted him into the station. The glint of the badge in the fluorescent light of the courtroom seemed to blur the lines between ally and authority, between protector and captor.

For a moment, Alex felt the walls of the courtroom extend beyond their physical boundaries, encapsulating a world where roles were ambiguous and allegiances unclear. The badge—a symbol of authority and aid—now hung in his mind as a token of an ever-deepening mystery. As Dr. Carter disappeared through the doorway, the echo of her footsteps a fading promise, Alex was left to ponder the dual nature of those sworn to protect and to probe, their roles as fluid as the hallucinations that had so recently plagued his mind.

The voices outside grew louder, a cacophony of urgency that hinted at revelations just beyond his reach. Each word from the corridor seemed to weave into the fabric of the ongoing drama, a narrative thread pulling tighter, promising that the resolution of his story was imminent yet obscured by the veil of unfolding events. Alex sat back, his heart racing with anticipation, as the courtroom awaited the return of its temporary deserters, the next act of the trial ready to commence in this theater of justice and judgement.

The oppressive silence returned to envelope Alex, suffocating in its completeness until it was abruptly shattered by the firm tap of a police officer on his shoulder. "Come on, Alex, it's time to go. Dr. Clark said she'll talk to you again later this week," the officer's voice broke through the stillness, its tone signaling an end to the immediate proceedings.

Alex turned to face the officer, recognizing him instantly as the same individual who had been a silent sentinel outside the Dawsons' door on that fateful night. His presence brought a surge of memories, and with them, a cascade of urgent questions. "But what about the verdict? What has the jury decided? Am I free?" Alex's voice climbed with each word, the confusion and fear that had been momentarily dammed breaking free.

The officer met Alex's gaze with a steadiness that seemed out of place in the charged atmosphere. "Don't worry," he said in a voice designed to calm, "as soon as we get a verdict, I'll come get you." His words were meant to reassure, but they hung in the air like a promise too fragile to trust.

Guiding Alex gently by the elbow, the officer led him out of the courtroom. The hallway outside was stark in contrast; cold and brightly lit, its sterile scent of cleaning solvents and disinfectants a sharp assault on the senses. As they walked, a mundane question from the officer punctured the surreal bubble that seemed to encase the moment. "Where are your shoes?" he asked, a note of practical concern threading through his tone.

Alex looked down at his bare feet, the cold of the tiled floor seeping into his skin, adding a physical chill to his internal turmoil. "I'm not sure," he replied, his voice a mix of bewilderment and resignation. The question, so ordinary yet so absurd in his current state, underscored the disarray of his life. It was a stark reminder of how far he had drifted from normalcy, how fragmented his existence had become.

As they continued down the corridor, the echo of their footsteps a rhythmic reminder of the journey's inevitability, Alex was left to grapple with the duality of his situation. Each step took him further from the unresolved tensions of the courtroom and deeper into a labyrinth of personal uncertainty. The officer's presence, both guardian and guide, offered little in the way of comfort, serving instead as a marker of the boundaries within which Alex's fate was still being negotiated. In this interstitial space, every sensation and half-heard conversation seemed to be a coded message regarding his future, each one more enigmatic than the last.

Navigating the labyrinthine corridors of the facility, Alex felt each turn—left, then right—deepen the disorientation swirling within him. The hallways stretched interminably, lined with countless doors, each identical and foreboding, suggesting secrets behind every secured entry. The officer leading him moved with mechanical precision, his badge card swiping through security locks with a beep that punctuated the silence between them, segmenting the eerie quiet with each authorized passage.

As they passed yet another secured door, Alex caught a fleeting glimpse of Detective Jamison stepping out of a room. The detective's eyes briefly met his, a flicker of recognition crossing his features before he hurried on. Behind Jamison, framed by the stark institutional backdrop, stood a woman dressed in white. Her posture rigid, she stared out a window obscured by a metal grate, her gaze fixed on whatever scant view the barred outlook offered. Her presence, a stark contrast to the drab surroundings, piqued Alex's curiosity but offered no answers.

Continuing their journey, they approached a large open area that broke the monotony of the enclosed hallways. Here, amidst rows of desks, sat Eric, positioned at what appeared to be his preferred workstation. His familiar face, usually a comfort, now seemed to hold a weight of knowledge. As Alex passed, Eric's hand lifted in a wave, his expression enigmatic, tinged with a knowing gravity that suggested an unshared understanding. The gesture, simple yet laden with implication, left Alex with a prickle of foreboding.

What secret did Eric know that he did not? The question hung heavily in Alex's mind as they moved beyond the room, each step taking him further from the possibility of an immediate answer. The corridors seemed to tighten around him, the air growing thicker with the scent of antiseptic and the undercurrent of secrets just beyond his grasp. The rhythmic echo of their footsteps became a metronome to his rising anxiety, each tap a reminder of the unknowns multiplying around him.

Alex's mind raced, trying to piece together the fragmented clues, the half-glimpses of faces and snippets of overheard conversations that floated back to him through the corridors of his memory and the halls of this enigmatic facility. Each new turn in the hallway felt like a twist in the narrative of his life, leading him deeper into a plot he could neither predict nor understand, driven by characters who knew more of the script than he did.

As the officer guided him towards an unmarked door at the end of the hallway, the sense of impending revelation grew. What lay beyond that door? Freedom, confinement, or some truth even more profound? Alex could only follow, his fate in the hands of others, his story yet to find its ending.

As Alex rounded the corner, his heart skipped a beat at the sight of the man who had loomed like an omnipresent specter over the entirety of his trial. There he stood, the judge who had presided with a stony demeanor, now stepping down from his elevated judicial pedestal to the stark reality of the hallway. His robe was gone, replaced by a stark white suit that seemed to vanish with the light around him. As the gap between them narrowed, Alex felt the officer's grip on his arm constrict, a silent but firm declaration that there was no turning back.

The judge's eyes, once distant and impartial behind the bench, now bore into Alex with an intensity that was almost palpable. Without a word, he reached for the handle of a door that Alex had not noticed before—a nondescript portal that seemed incongruous with the rest of the sterile hallway. As it swung open, a wave of familiarity washed over Alex. Beyond that threshold lay his own apartment, or an uncanny recreation of it. Every detail was meticulously replicated, from the worn-out sofa with its sagging cushions to the small stack of books on the coffee table, each spine creased from repeated readings.

As Alex crossed the threshold of his apartment, the door closed behind him with a soft, definitive click. Freed from the grip of his escort, he stood alone in the silence of his living space. The familiarity of his surroundings—once a comforting sanctuary—now took on a surreal quality under the weight of recent events. The air hung heavy with a peculiar scent, an unplaceable undercurrent that seemed to hint at concealed truths and staged realities.

Turning slowly, Alex's gaze swept over his modest living area. The bookshelf caught his attention, its volumes lined up like silent witnesses to his inner turmoil. He approached and pulled one down, a well-worn paperback he'd read countless times before. As he flipped it open, a slip of paper fluttered to the floor. Bending to pick it up, Alex unfolded the note to find a message scrawled in a hurried but familiar hand:

"Proceed to Antarctica. Await further instructions upon arrival."

The room felt both smaller and infinitely expansive as Alex processed the directive. The absence of both the judge and the officer, the inexplicable instructions—everything compounded the surreal sensation enveloping him. The books around him, once escapes into imagined worlds, now felt like portals to yet another layer of reality he was compelled to navigate.

Standing in the quiet aftermath of his trial, with the door to his past firmly shut and the window to another obscure mission intriguingly open, Alex was left to ponder the layers of his existence. The note in his hand was the only tangible link to what might lie ahead, casting his future into a realm of ice and isolation—a stark contrast to the warm, familiar confines of his current enclosure.

www.ingramcontent.com/pod-product-compliance
Lightning Source LLC
Chambersburg PA
CBHW051303130726
47987CB00004B/1647